HARDBALL

A RINEHART SUSPENSE NOVEL

NOVELS BY JIMMY SANGSTER

Private I
Foreign Exchange
Touchfeather
Touchfeather Too
Your Friendly Neighborhood Death Pedlar
Snowball
Blackball

A RINEHART SUSPENSE NOVEL

HARDBALL

JIMMY SANGSTER

HENRY HOLT AND COMPANY / NEW YORK

Copyright © 1988 by Jimmy Sangster
All rights reserved, including the right to reproduce this
book or portions thereof in any form.
Published by Henry Holt and Company, Inc.,
115 West 18th Street, New York, New York 10011.
Published in Canada by Fitzhenry & Whiteside Limited,
195 Allstate Parkway, Markham, Ontario L3R 4T8.

Library of Congress Cataloging-in-Publication Data
Sangster, Jimmy.
Hardball.
(A Rinehart suspense novel)
I. Title.
PR6069.A53H37 1988   823'.914   88-9219
ISBN 0-8050-0890-X

Henry Holt books are available at special discounts
for bulk purchases for sales promotions, premiums,
fund-raising, or educational use. Special editions
or book excerpts can also be created to specification.

  For details, contact:

  Special Sales Director
  Henry Holt and Company, Inc.
  115 West 18th Street
  New York, New York 10011

First Edition

Designed by Paula R. Szafranski
Printed in the United States of America
10 9 8 7 6 5 4 3 2 1

*For
Andrew
and
Joanna*

HARDBALL

A RINEHART SUSPENSE NOVEL

1

"We don't call them bodyguards in England," James said to Stephen Wise. "We call them minders."

"Minders, bodyguards, what's the difference! Just so you know what's involved."

"You tell me," said James.

"I thought you were the expert."

"That was a long time ago."

"I shouldn't have thought it was something you'd forget."

"It's not like riding a bicycle," said James. "Minding comes in all shapes and sizes. Someone like . . . Yasir Arafat, for example, is different than minding a celebrity who's received a couple of kinky phone calls. With Arafat, you've got half the Jews in the world wanting your client dead. With the celebrity there's just one sick psychopath. That's assuming you're minding somebody who some other body wants dead. On the other hand, you could be minding an alcoholic, or an addict to make sure he doesn't get to the stuff that's killing him. You could also be a minder in a nightclub, otherwise known as a bouncer, or a minder for a thoroughbred racehorse or for a parcel of money. There's a lot of things need minding these days."

"That's how you started, isn't it? Minding your ex-wife."

Okay, so now James knew how Wise had got on to him. "Is this her idea?"

"She just happened to say that was how she first met you. She sends you her best, incidentally."

"Bully for her," said James. "Can I have another Scotch?" Without waiting for an answer, he walked over to the bar and helped himself.

Stephen Wise tilted back in his executive-type chair behind his reproduction Louis Quinze desk. "Maybe I made a mistake," he said.

"Maybe you did," said James.

"Maybe you just came for the Scotch."

"I've got better at home. Which is where I'd rather be right now." Only half was true; the Scotch he had at home didn't compare to Wise's.

"Then I take it you're not interested."

"I'm here, aren't I?" James walked back to the chair on the opposite side of the desk. "Suppose you tell me what it's all about, then I'll tell you whether or not I'm interested."

James had long ago learned that if something sounded too good to be true, it invariably was. Driving back to the beach, he searched for a catch. He couldn't find one. Wise's proposition had been simple and straightforward. He had a client who needed to rent a house for three months. This client was extremely wealthy. He traveled extensively accompanied by a personal valet, a cook, a secretary and a great deal of loose cash. It seemed the client had recently been ill and now needed a quiet retreat, preferably on the beach where he could take long walks and where nobody would bug him.

"He requires one-hundred-percent anonymity," Wise had said. "That's where you come in. You screen all the visitors. Anybody asks, you have some old friends from England staying with you. My client *is* English, as a matter of fact. So are his staff. So in the unlikely event any stranger gets to talk to any of them, their accents will only go toward confirming your story. I have been authorized to offer you three months' rent at fifteen thousand dollars per month."

That was exactly double the amount his last tenant had paid, and that had been for a summer rental. "He'll pay that for a place he's never seen!" said James.

"As a matter of fact, he *has* seen the property. Apparently he was a guest of your ex-wife there once. Before your time, I believe."

"Dinner guest or sleep-over guest?"

"I have no idea. Does it matter?"

James told him it didn't.

"I am also authorized to pay you an additional five thousand dollars per month for the other services I mentioned. The minding. You own a gun, I assume."

"I don't shoot people," said James. For the kind of money Wise was talking about, he was prepared to consider it. He'd just been offered sixty thousand dollars. He could pay off his overdraft, replenish his savings account, buy a new dishwasher for his own kitchen in the guest house and have an extremely merry Christmas to boot. That reminded him of something.

"Will he be here over the holidays?"

"He wants to move in as soon as possible, but no later than December fourteenth."

"The fourteenth will be fine," said James. That was in four days' time. "What's his name?" It could be Attila the Hun for all he cared.

"Smith," said Wise, without change of expression.

"We've got a lot of them in England," said James.

He stopped at the market on the way home. There he bought something extravagant for his supper and some cleaning supplies. If a guy was going to pay fifteen grand a month he was entitled to have the place look respectable when he checked in. He put his car in the garage and, after dropping off the food in the guest house, he took the cleaning materials across to the main house and started work. Two hours later, he locked the place up and returned to the guest house where he started to pour himself a large Scotch. Abruptly, he changed his mind. Instead, he climbed into a track suit and went for a run on the beach. By the time he got back he'd decided to hell with eating in. He'd spoil himself by going out to dinner.

While he was dressing he debated whether or not to try to rustle up a date. He decided against it. There was nobody current in his life right now. There hadn't been for some time. He'd never really been into one-night stands, although, AIDS notwithstanding, they were still readily available. He drank a large Scotch while he was dressing, then another. He decided that perhaps a date might not be such a bad idea after all . . . even if it was just to have somebody to talk to. A celebration was in order and one couldn't really celebrate solo. He dug out his address book and poured himself another Scotch.

Three answering machines, two busy signals and one "Sorry, busy tonight" later, he gave up on the idea of going out. He unwrapped the smoked salmon (guaranteed Scottish) and seasoned the steak. After a small internal debate, during which he drank another Scotch, he opened his last good bottle of red wine. The smoked salmon had obviously never been anywhere nearer to Scotland than Nova Scotia, but it was okay. He nearly burned his steak while he was eating the salmon, rescuing it just this side of ashes.

There was an old movie of Katherine's on the TV, which he watched while he ate. Halfway through the movie, the shadow figure of his ex-wife started to push long-forgotten buttons. He changed channels and caught the tail end of a sitcom which was remarkable only for its complete lack of humor. He switched the TV off altogether. In the silence that followed the canned laughter, he heard a noise from outside. Someone was approaching his front door. Maybe the "Sorry, busy tonight" lady had changed her mind; maybe one of the answering machines had been picked up; maybe he might get laid tonight after all. Then the footsteps, accompanied by a small tapping sound, passed by his front door. Whoever it was out there was obviously heading for the main house. He opened the door and started outside.

"Hey!" he called.

The man walking toward the main house stopped and turned toward James. He didn't say anything.

"Can I help you?" asked James.

The man looked toward him for a moment longer, then turned and continued toward the main house.

"Hey! Fella! Just hold it a goddamn minute."

Again the man turned toward James. The only light was that leaking from the open door of the guest house. At this distance it was insufficient for James to make out his features. He was tall, slim and walked with a slight limp. He was carrying a walking stick. When he spoke, it was in a soft voice with the faintest trace of an accent that James couldn't place.

"This is not your concern," he said.

"Maybe not. But it's my house."

There was sufficient light for James to see that the man didn't believe him. It had happened before. Middle-aged beach bums didn't own three-million-dollar houses. If they did, they didn't live in the guest house.

"This is not your concern," said the man again.

"It will be if you don't get your ass off my property."

"Michael," said the man.

"I don't care what your name is. Just get—" James started to say. He didn't finish. He was suddenly enveloped from behind and lifted clear off the ground by what felt like a forklift truck. At the same time he was blasted with a smell of garlic which didn't quite disguise the underlying halitosis of the goliath called Michael. "Don't upset Mr. Langer," croaked a voice close to his ear.

Sober, James would probably have let things slide. But he had consumed four or five Scotches and a bottle of red wine. There was nothing like an excess of booze to sharpen the reactions and blunt the judgment. He drove his elbow back hard, aiming for where he thought he could do the most damage. The only harm he did was to break his arm. At least, he felt like he'd broken it. It was like hitting a steel plate. There wasn't even a grunt of protest. Shit! Michael, whatever he was, must be wearing a suit of armor. There was something else he could try. He recalled vaguely the words of an old ex–Royal Marine who had taught unarmed combat to junior policemen in London a hundred years ago. "Go limp . . . let the bugger think he's gotcher 'elpless. When he relaxes reach back between your legs and grab him by the goolies. Tear 'em orf if you gotta." It was worth a try. He went limp. He needn't have bothered. He still felt he was being gripped by a couple of articulated tree trunks. There was one way out remaining. Do as the man had asked.

"Okay, okay. I won't upset Mr. Langer. Now put me down before you break something."

The tall, thin man nodded at Michael, who immediately lowered James back onto his feet and released his grip. James turned to see what kind of a dinosaur he was dealing with. He wanted to get the full measure of his adversary before resorting to his ace in the hole. Once more, the booze clouded his judgment. He should have bowed politely, apologized for the inconvenience he'd caused and backed off a couple of miles. The man confronting him was the largest person he'd ever seen outside a natural history museum. He looked like a fugitive from a prehistoric movie, dressed in a dark suit instead of animal skins. But James was really pissed off by now. After all, this was his own front yard, his own home. Wasn't an Englishman's home supposed to be his castle, to be defended against the barbarian? He made his next move. This was the one designed to end all arguments. It never failed. He lashed out with his foot, kicking the gargantuan very hard right in the crotch. At least, that was his intention. He'd always considered himself a fast mover when the adrenaline was pumping, but obviously it wasn't pumping fast enough, or Michael's was pumping a lot faster. Before James's foot connected, it was grabbed by a giant hand, and James found himself standing one-legged while the man responsible for this indignity began to squeeze the foot he was holding. At the same time he grinned down at James, exposing a mouthful of doubtful teeth in a face that resembled a Halloween pumpkin in texture, shape and color. James had read somewhere that there were 176 separate bones in the average foot. His sneakers didn't provide much protection. He figured around 115 had been crushed before he finally felt honor had been satisfied.

"Okay, okay. I'm sorry." He half turned. "Tell him I'm sorry for Christ's sake."

Again Langer nodded at Michael, who immediately released his grip.

James fell over. The two men looked down at him.

"Please get up," said Langer.

"I think something's broken." He couldn't decide which hurt the most, his shattered elbow, his broken foot or his wounded pride.

"Nothing is broken, I assure you. Michael is very careful." He nodded at Michael who reached down toward James with a hand like a side of beef. James brushed aside the proffered assistance and climbed to his feet unaided. He ignored the man named Michael and took a good look at Langer for the first time. He was a shade over six feet tall and not as slim as James had first imagined. It was the suit that did it. James wasn't an expert on clothes, but even he knew that the suit Langer was wearing had to have cost in the region of a thousand dollars. The body that it draped was well built, probably muscular. The face was tidily arranged, all the features the right size and in proportion. Eyes blue; ears small; mouth straight and rather thin-lipped; hair light brown, combed back without a parting; clean-shaven jaw; tanned complexion; age difficult to tell but probably around sixty-five. There was a thin scar running from just beneath the hairline on the left, losing itself in his right eyebrow. It was an old scar.

"This is twenty-two seventy-five Old Beach Road, is it not?" he said.

James agreed that it was.

"The home of Jonathan Bradley?"

"The home of James Reed," said James.

Langer thought about this for a moment. "Mr. Reed?" he asked, finally.

"One and the same," said James. He wanted to rub his elbow and put his foot up on something soft.

Langer looked back toward the darkened main house, then toward James again. "Jonathan Bradley does not live here?"

"James Reed lives here."

"It seems I've been misinformed."

"Tell it to the cops," said James.

Langer ignored the implied threat. He ignored James too. "We'll go now," he said to Michael, who was standing behind James. He started toward the gate, his walking stick tapping lightly on the flagstones. The behemoth named Michael moved ahead of him and opened the gate. A moment later they'd both disappeared.

James limped toward the front gate. He was in time to see Michael holding open the rear door of a stretch limousine. Langer got in. A moment later, Michael was behind the wheel. The car started up. As it pulled away, James made a mental note of the number before closing the front gate and snapping on the padlock he rarely used. He hobbled back to the guest house, poured himself a stiff Scotch and went to bed.

He had just dropped off to sleep when the phone rang. He struggled up through half a dozen layers of oblivion, instinctively reaching for the bedside phone.

"What?"

"This is Gloria," said a voice on the other end of the line.

"Gloria who?" James was having trouble remembering his own name right now.

"Same old James," she said, helping him out.

Memory started to trickle back to him. "Hey, Gloria. I called you earlier."

"I just picked up the message. Long time no hear, lover."

"That's why I called." Which one was Gloria? Gloria! Right! The Malibu real-estate broker.

"Why?"

"Why what?"

"Why did you call?"

"I was feeling nostalgic?"

"Admit it. You were feeling horny."

"That too."

"And you thought you'd call good old Gloria. She's always grateful for a one-night stand."

"Don't put yourself down, Gloria."

"I'm not. You are."

He was still too drunk to argue with her. "I'm sorry," he said.

"Don't be. I'll be there in twenty minutes."

Before he could tell her not to bother, the line went dead.

Shit! He climbed out of bed and went into the living room where he looked up her number. He punched it out, mis-hitting the buttons three times in a row. Finally he heard it ringing. A moment later her answering machine came on to the line. Like it or not, she was on her way. He cleaned his teeth, something he'd forgotten to do before he sacked out. He went back into the bedroom and started to straighten up the bed.

The headache that had been lurking just behind his eyes started to assert more authority. It had been a rough evening. His elbow still hurt. So did his foot. His self-respect had taken a beating too. It was a long time since anyone had manhandled him the way Langer's gorilla had. Right now, sex was the last thing he felt like. Maybe he'd lie down for a moment, just until Gloria arrived. Reflect on the pleasures to come and try to build up a little enthusiasm. He stretched out on the bed and closed his eyes.

The next thing he was aware of was a ringing sound. She'd arrived. He rolled over and put his feet to the floor. He was surprised to realize that he felt much better. Amazing, the recuperative powers of a ten-minute snooze. Then he saw that it was broad daylight outside. He looked at his bedside clock. It was eight thirty-five. And it wasn't the front door bell, it was the telephone. He picked it up.

"Bastard!" said Gloria.

"What happened to you?"

"What happened to *me!* What happened to you?"

"Nothing happened to me. I was waiting for you."

"So how come the front gate was locked?"

He'd forgotten about that. "It was?"

"I banged on the fucking thing for twenty-five minutes."

"I must have dropped off," said James.

"Do everybody a big favor and drop off again. From a high place."

The phone went dead.

Okay. So he'd send her some flowers. Maybe a bottle of champagne. He might even ask her for a date. He felt very horny. A hangover sometimes affected him that way. But first things first. He pulled on a robe and went to unlock the front gate and take in his L.A. *Times*. He was just closing the gate again when he saw what was painted on it. She must have broken into the garage somehow and found an old can of paint.

JAMES REED IS A SHIT!

It was the paint he used to touch up the terrace that overlooked the beach, a particularly glaring white, designed to withstand sun and seawater. It would take a sandblaster to clean it off.

The paint can was standing outside the garage door, which was still open. He picked it up and went into the garage to put it back where it belonged. She'd been at work on his car too. One side carried the information that JAMES REED IS A ROTTEN LAY, the other announced that JAMES REED IS A PUTZ. He'd forgotten that Gloria was Jewish. It wasn't much as cars go, but it was the only one he had. Maybe he wouldn't call her after all. Anybody this vindictive was capable of causing serious damage to life and limb.

Back indoors, he squeezed some juice and put on the coffee. While he was waiting, he looked up the number of his local garage. When he got through he asked to speak to Roger.

"James Reed," he said, when Roger came on the line.

"I won't fix it," said Roger.

"You don't even know what it is yet."

"I don't care what it is. I told you last time you brought that heap in here it was past fixing."

"It needs a paint job."

"Listen . . . having that wreck of yours anywhere near my

place, I lose half my customers. Do me a favor, Mr. Reed, take it someplace else."

"You owe me, Roger." He'd once done the man a small favor . . . so small, he'd forgotten what it was.

"Wrong. You owe me. One hundred and sixty-three dollars and twenty-seven cents. You've owed it to me so long if I charged interest it'd be close to a grand by now."

"I'll bring you a check when I drop the car off. I'll need a loaner too."

There was an audible sigh on the other end of the line. "What time?"

"I've got a meeting in Beverly Hills at noon. See you at eleven."

He hung up the phone before Roger could come up with any more objections. He poured himself a cup of coffee, strong and black; then, because he felt he owed it to his body after the abuse he'd put it through last night, he went for a run on the beach. It was a short run. By the time he'd covered a quarter of a mile he was puffing like a two-pack-a-day man. He'd given up smoking five years ago. He staggered back to the house, had another cup of coffee, took a shower, dressed and drove to the garage.

Fortunately, Roger's Engine and Body Shop was at the far end of Old Beach Road, just behind the market, so he didn't have to drive along Pacific Coast Highway in his traveling billboard. He pulled into the front of the garage and started to get out. A long, lean figure with a shock of sandy-colored hair and filthy oil-splattered jeans and a workshirt came running from the service area.

"For Christ's sake, Mr. Reed! Take it around back before anybody sees it," said Roger. Then he saw the artwork. "Hey! What you been up to, man?"

"Nothing," said James.

"A rotten lay and a putz. The chick must know you real well."

"You can take it around back yourself," said James. "Where's my loaner?"

"I didn't want to put your system into shock," said Roger. "So I looked for some wheels to match your own near as I could. Not easy outside a wrecker's yard. But I found just the thing."

James looked around. Apart from a beat-up panel truck, there was nothing else in sight. "So where is it?"

"You're looking at it."

Before he handed over the keys to the truck, Roger reminded James of the check he'd been promised.

"One sixty-three . . . right?"

"And twenty-seven cents."

James wrote out the check and handed it to Roger, who looked at it for a moment. "Is it good?"

"What do you care? You've got my car as security."

"Your car isn't worth a hundred and sixty-three bucks. Do all of us a favor, Mr. Reed. A paint job's gonna cost you three fifty at least. Let me call the scrap yard and have them pick it up."

"I'd like it the same color," said James.

"Sure . . . rust. When do you need it?"

"No hurry. Call me when it's ready."

He took the keys to the truck from Roger and climbed in behind the wheel. The cab smelled like it had last been used for transporting fish. As he drove from the garage, he saw that Roger had called a couple of his guys from the body shop to look at James's car. They were standing around it, shaking their heads.

"How did you know his name was Bradley?" asked Wise.

James was in his office, glancing over the lease that had been drawn up. It was made out in the name of Smith.

"He had visitors last night. What's this clause mean . . . the lessee shall have the right to terminate the agreement without prior notice?"

"Don't worry about it. Read the next paragraph. What kind of visitors?"

"A guy named Langer and his minder. It says here if he decides to quit, he doesn't get any of his rent money back."

"Seeing as he's paying the whole three months in advance, you should be so lucky. What did he want?"

"Who?" James took a pen from Wise's desk and prepared to sign the lease.

"Langer. What did he want?"

"Jonathan Bradley."

"What did you tell him?"

"That he'd got the wrong address. Where do I sign this?"

"There . . . and there on the bottom of the page. How do you know it was his minder?"

"Take my word for it," said James. He signed his name where Wise had told him. "So . . . while I'm prepared to abide by the spirit of this agreement and respect my tenant's anonymity, it seems he doesn't have it anymore. At least, not as far as Langer is concerned. Who is he, anyway?"

"Langer? I haven't the faintest idea."

"Bradley?"

"I told you. He's very rich. He's English. And he's looking for some peace and quiet."

"Come on, Mr. Wise. You're about to give me a check for sixty grand on his behalf. You can tell me more than that."

"It's all you need to know right now."

"Okay . . . just tell me one thing. Is he on the run from anything?"

Wise looked genuinely shocked. "Good heavens, no. Why do you ask?"

"If Langer was looking for me, I'd run."

"He could be a friend . . . a business associate."

"I think I'd prefer him as an enemy," said James. "But whatever, he's close to Bradley. He knew where to look for him. We only agreed to this yesterday afternoon." He put the pen back on the desk and started to fold his copy of the lease. "Okay . . . when's he going to pitch up?"

"I'll call him and tell him the lease has been signed and he's free to move in any time. I'll let you know." He pressed a button on his desk and asked his secretary to bring in James's check.

"Better tell him about Langer too," said James.

Wise made a note on a pad in front of him. "I'll do that."

The secretary came in with a check which she handed to Wise. He glanced at it and passed it over to James. It was for sixty thousand dollars, drawn on a Beverly Hills bank and signed by Wise. James filled out a deposit slip from the back of his checkbook, addressed an envelope to his bank and asked Wise's secretary to mail it for him.

Back home, the front gate still announced JAMES REED IS A SHIT. He fetched the can of white paint from the garage and painted out Gloria's opinion. Then, because a white gate set into a dark brown frame looked strange, he painted the frame too. That looked weird, so he painted the fence on either side of the gate. He'd almost finished when he ran out of paint. He debated for a moment whether it was worth driving to the hardware store to pick up another can, then he decided the hell with it. He had sixty thousand dollars in the bank, let somebody else paint the fucking fence. He went indoors to have a drink.

There were two calls on his answering machine. One was a hangup, a pet peeve of his. The other was from Wise's office, would he please call back.

"Mr. Smith will be arriving tomorrow," said Wise. "Around noon."

"Did you tell Mr. Smith a man named Langer is looking for Mr. Bradley?"

"I called his secretary. They'd already left."

"If you do get in touch, you might mention the extra five grand a month he's paying me doesn't cover minding him against the likes of somebody like Langer."

"Why didn't you tell me that this morning?"

"You might not have given me my money."

"You're right. I probably wouldn't. Anyway, I can't get in touch with them. They're in transit. You'll have to tell him yourself when you see him. Better still, talk to Jane. That's Jane Reynolds, his secretary. In fact, any business you have to discuss with Mr. Smith, do it through her."

"What about the cook and the valet?"

"What about them?"

"Names?"

"I've no idea. Is there anything else?"

James told him there wasn't and hung up. He poured himself a Scotch and started to make a shopping list.

When he got back from the market, he drove the panel truck straight into the garage. He unloaded the supplies and carried them to the front gate. With his arms loaded, as they were, he leaned against the gate with his shoulder to open it. The paint was still wet. For a moment he was stuck to the gate like a fly to flypaper. He pulled his windbreaker free and kicked the gate hard with his foot. It flew open and he heard a yell of pain and surprise. Normally he would have walked straight through and apologized to whoever it was, but his visitors last night had sharpened his suspicions of everything and everybody. He dropped his packages. There was the sound of breaking glass . . . champagne or Scotch, he didn't know which. Then he kicked the gate once more, harder this time, and went through fast, ready for anything. There was a girl standing just inside, nursing her elbow where the gate had hit it. She looked as if she was trying to make up her mind whether or not to cry. As James came in, she made her decision. Crying was out.

"You clumsy bastard," she said. She was around thirty. Five feet six inches tall, about 120 pounds. Perfect, decided James.

"Sorry," he said.

"I should bloody well think so." Her accent pegged her as English. "Why didn't you ring the bell or knock on the gate, or just leave the deliveries in the garage."

"Because I live here."

"Oh!" She gave the matter some thought. "You're still a clumsy bastard," she said, finally.

"Did I do any permanent damage?"

"I think you broke my arm."

James's elbow still hurt from last night. He knew how she felt.

"Let me look at it."

She backed away from him quickly. "Don't you dare. You'll get paint all over me."

She was very pretty, with a roundish face framed by dark red hair, cut quite short. A line of freckles marched in a determined line across the bridge of her nose. Her eyes were green and she had a mouth that looked like it would be better employed laughing than scowling. She was wearing a skirt, a silk blouse, with a cashmere sweater thrown over her shoulders. Her shoes were sensible, and, like her clothes, neat, tidy and rather boring. Even if she hadn't spoken, James would have guessed she was English.

"How can I help you?" he asked.

"I understand Mr. Smith is living here."

For somebody who hadn't even put in an appearance, his tenant was sure getting a lot of visitors. "Not until tomorrow," said James. He went back out of the gate and started to sort out the bag of groceries he'd dropped. It was a bottle of Scotch that had broken. The champagne was still intact. She followed him out and watched him for a moment. "Are you the caretaker?" she asked.

"More or less."

He fetched a carton from the garage and transferred the contents of the dropped bag. She continued to watch him. There was no unrecognized car parked in the street. James wondered briefly how she had got here.

"Are you sure it's tomorrow?" she asked him finally.

"So I've been led to understand."

Another pause. "I wonder if I might make a telephone call?"

"Be my guest," he said. He picked up the box of groceries, kicked the remnants of the broken Scotch bottle closer to the fence—he'd sweep up the glass later—and led the way toward the guest house.

"Phone's over there," said James, heading toward the kitchen area. He dumped the box on the counter and started to unpack it, separating his stuff from what was to go over to the main house. After a quick, incurious look around, his visitor had walked over to the phone on the bar and punched out a number. James watched her surreptitiously. If you liked your women slightly heavier than current fashion decreed, she was a very good-looking lady. The California women he knew were invariably bone-thin and went into a decline if they put on an extra ounce. She'd make a sensational lay. He could drown himself in her breasts and thighs. He started to feel horny again. Obviously there was no answer from the number she was calling, because after a minute she hung up.

"Shit!" she said.

"Problems?"

She ignored the question. "Do you have the number of a taxi service?"

"Where do you want to go?"

"Back to Beverly Hills."

"How did you get here?"

"By taxi. I paid it off when I arrived."

"I'd lend you my car, if I had one."

"I can't drive."

The only reason a person couldn't drive a car in California was because they'd had their license taken away. Children were weaned from their mother's breast straight onto a steering wheel. He looked up a cab company in the Yellow Pages and gave her the number. She called and was told there'd be somebody to pick her up inside half an hour.

"Would you like a cup of coffee while you're waiting?" asked James.

She declined and said she'd not bother him anymore. She'd wait outside.

"No need," said James. She thanked him and went outside anyway. James heard the front gate being closed. He sorted his marketing and carried the stuff he'd bought for his tenant across to the main house. As he walked back to the guest house, he remembered the broken glass. He collected a broom and went outside to clear it up. The girl was still waiting for her taxi.

"Half an hour could be an hour and a half," said James. "The offer's still open."

"Perhaps I'll accept after all," she said. There was a slight edge of condescension in the way she said it, rather as if the lady of the manor were accepting an invitation from one of her tenants to step inside his cottage. In spite of it, James still fancied her. This time, when she came in, she sat down. She looked around the place as if seeing it for the first time.

"I'm going to have a drink," said James. "You sure you don't want anything?"

"Thank you, no." Again the chatelaine edge to her voice. James went behind the bar and poured himself a short Scotch, adding plenty of water.

"Have you lived here long?" she asked. She didn't sound particularly interested.

"Four or five years," said James.

"I imagine the main house is rented most of the time."

"Not as often as I'd like." He moved to a chair across from where she was sitting. She had very sexy legs.

"Do the owners ever use it?" She was just making small talk.

"I can't afford to."

She thought about this for a moment. "You're the owner?" she asked, finally.

"Lock, stock and barrel."

"You told me you were the caretaker." There was accusation in her voice. She didn't like the idea that she might have committed a social gaffe.

"Caretaker, maintenance man and landlord," said James.

"Perhaps I will have a small drink after all," she said. James went back behind the bar and poured the white wine she asked for. After a couple of sips, she started to relax a little. Obviously credentials had been upgraded.

"My name's Carmichael. Betsy Carmichael," she said.

"James Reed."

"You must forgive me. When I saw you arriving in that broken-down old van, I thought . . ."

"It happens all the time," said James. There was a long silence, during which James continued to admire her legs. She glanced at her watch.

"What can be keeping that taxi!"

"If you're going to stay in Los Angeles, you ought to do something about getting another driver's license."

"I told you. I can't drive."

"Really can't drive?"

"I never learned how," she said. "That's not strictly true. I took some lessons once."

"And . . . ?"

"Hopeless. I'm dyslexic behind the wheel of a car. I read the signs backward, I forget which is left and right, I'm always in the wrong gear, and usually on the wrong side of the road. Complete disaster. I gave my driving teacher ulcers."

"If you're going to be around for a time, maybe I could teach you."

"I don't think so, Mr. Reed," she said.

"Meaning you're not going to be around or you don't want me to give you driving lessons?"

"Both," she said. Then she changed the subject. "Have you any idea what time Mr. Bra— . . . Smith will be arriving tomorrow?"

"I was told to expect him around noon."

"Could I leave a message?"

James fetched her a pad and a pencil. She thought about what she wanted to say, then she started writing.

"Do you have an envelope?" she asked him when she had finished.

He fetched her an envelope and she sealed the note inside, pressing the flap down firmly. "I think I'll wait for my taxi outside. I'd hate for him to arrive and not find me," she said.

"Whatever," said James. He promised to give Mr. Smith her note the moment he showed up, and walked her to the gate.

"You should put up a Wet Paint sign," she said.

"Time I do that it'll be dry. If your taxi doesn't come soon, you're welcome to come back inside."

"You've been very kind." She didn't sound like she meant it.

He opened the gate for her and she walked through. Just before he closed it he saw Langer's limousine parked fifty yards up the street, facing this way.

"Do you know a Mr. Langer?" he asked.

He might have asked her if she knew Adolf Hitler. The color

drained from her face, leaving her freckles even more pronounced.

"What do you know about Langer?" she asked.

"That's his car up the street."

She showed admirable restraint not turning in the direction of his nod. "Are you sure?"

"Certain," said James.

"Perhaps I will wait inside," she said.

She came back onto the property. "Can you lock the gate?" she asked.

James put on the padlock that had so infuriated Gloria last night. Betsy had a thought. "What about my taxi?"

"He can ring the bell. If he doesn't, we'll find some other way to get you back into town."

They went back into the guest house. "May I have another drink?" she asked.

James poured her another glass of wine. He was about to top off his Scotch, then he changed his mind. If he hadn't been drunk last night he'd not have made an idiot of himself. In the event that Langer and his minder decided to pay another visit, he didn't intend to make the same mistake again.

"Would you excuse me a minute?" he said.

"Where are you going?" She really was frightened.

"To the bathroom."

Color came back to her cheeks. "I'm sorry," she said. "It's just that . . ." She left it unfinished.

In fact, James only went as far as the bedroom. There, he dug into the back of his closet and produced an old tennis bag. From it he took something wrapped in an oil-stained cloth. He had never liked guns. He had only bought this one because when he had been married to Katherine, she had insisted. Everybody who was anybody in Beverly Hills had at least one gun in their house. They were just another appliance, like the cooker or the freezer. His was a pump-action twelve-bore shotgun. It had been advertised and sold as a sporting weapon. Like its manufacturer, James knew it was useless for shooting anything other than people, and then only if they weren't more than fifteen feet away. He unwrapped it. The sea air hadn't done too much damage that he could see. He located a box of shells in the section of the tennis bag reserved for cans of balls. He loaded five of them into the gun. If big Michael came at him again, he was going to get a nasty surprise. He left the gun propped just inside the bedroom door before going back into the living room. Betsy Carmichael was at the bar helping herself to another drink. This time it was from his best bottle of Cognac. She had the good manners to look slightly embarrassed.

"I hope you don't mind," she said.

"Go right ahead."

"Can I pour you one?"

"Not right now, thank you." He moved to the window and took a look toward the front gate. The padlock looked solid and secure. Not that it would deter anyone who really wanted to get onto the property. One good kick from the other side and the gate would lose its hinges. And if they didn't want to make a noise they only had to walk a hundred yards along the road to where there was a public access to the beach and then a hundred yards back along the sand to the rear of the house. There, a disinterested boy scout could have found half a dozen different ways to get in. Security wasn't too high on the priority list down here. He felt Betsy Carmichael move in close behind him.

"What can you see?" she asked. For the first time she was close enough for him to smell her perfume. It was very light, unlike what he'd grown used to in a town where you could often smell your date before she opened the front door. As she leaned closer, trying to see what he was looking at, he felt the pressure of her breast on his arm. An irreverent thought crossed his mind. Keep her frightened enough with threats of Langer lurking in the vicinity and he could get her into the sack inside half an hour. He'd had experience with frightened women before. Fear started their hormones pumping like crazy. Trouble was, right now, he was almost as nervous as she was.

"Don't worry," he said. "Nobody's going to break in in broad daylight." She didn't move away from him. If anything, she pressed even closer. "Who is he, anyway?" he asked.

"I thought you knew," she said. "You recognized his car."

"He was here last night."

"What did he want?"

"Bradley."

If she noticed the correct use of the name she didn't question it. "What did you tell him?"

"I told him he'd got the wrong address."

"He believed you?"

"Last night, he believed me. He's probably checked up since then. Who is he?"

She moved away from him now. "I don't know."

James decided to approach it from another direction. "What does he want?"

"I've no idea."

"Maybe I should go outside and ask him."

"No! Don't do that. Please."

James had no intention of going anywhere near Langer. At least, not until he knew a hell of a lot more than he did right now. He asked her if she wanted another brandy. She told him she had to go to the bathroom. He told her to go right ahead, and that's how she spotted the gun propped just inside the bedroom door. She came back into the living room carrying it in both hands.

"It's loaded," said James. He didn't trust women around guns.

"What's it for?"

"Rats," he said.

"You don't shoot rats with a shotgun."

"We do in Malibu." He took it from her and put it on a shelf under the bar.

"It's because of Langer, isn't it?"

The sound of the buzzer from the front gate saved him having to come up with an answer. "That'll be your cab."

"It might be Langer."

"There's only one way we're going to find out."

"Be careful," she said.

He walked out to the front gate. "Who's there?" he called.

"Cab for Carmichael," came a voice.

"Be right with you," said James. He turned back toward the guest house. Betsy was standing half in and half out of the front door, holding the shotgun.

"It's your taxi," he said.

She shook her head vigorously and beckoned for him to join her.

"Hang on," called James to the invisible cabdriver. He walked back to Betsy. Again, he took the gun from her. "I'll walk you out," he said.

"I'm not going."

"Listen . . . even if Langer is still waiting, he's not going to try anything."

"How do you know? He might follow me back to Beverly Hills."

"You just told me you don't know who he is and you don't know what he wants. Why should you think he'd follow you?"

"I was lying."

"Meaning you *do* know who he is."

"Kind of."

"Do you want to stay here?"

"May I? At least until he's gone."

"I'll get rid of the cab." He went back to the gate. Before unlocking it he leaned the shotgun against the fence. He opened the gate and told the cabdriver he wouldn't be needed after all. He gave him five dollars for his trouble. A quick look up and down the street showed him Langer's car had gone. God knows how long ago it had left. He relocked the gate, collected the gun and walked back to the guest house. Betsy was waiting just inside the front door.

"Is he still there?" she asked.

"Sure is," said James. He closed the front door, went behind the bar and poured himself a drink. It was going to be an interesting evening.

Betsy told him she wasn't hungry, but he should go right ahead and make himself something to eat if that's what he wanted.

Better still, as long as she was hanging around, she'd throw a meal together for him. It would help take her mind off what was waiting outside.

"What exactly *is* waiting outside?" asked James.

She started rummaging around in the fridge. "Typical bachelor's fridge," she said. "Eggs, bacon and booze. Where do you keep the vegetables?"

James showed her. "Tell me about Langer," he said as she tipped everything out onto the countertop.

"He's a business associate of Jonathan's."

"What business?"

She discarded a couple of potatoes which had started to go moldy. "Just business," she said.

There was more than one way to skin a cat. James fetched her another brandy.

"Perhaps he's gone," she said.

"Drink your brandy. I'll check it out."

James went to the front gate and peered out into the empty street.

"He's still there," he told Betsy when he came back.

She'd helped herself to another brandy while he'd been outside. She didn't seem as concerned as she had earlier.

"So tell me about him," said James.

"He frightens me." She was in the kitchen chopping those vegetables she considered fit for consumption.

"Why does he frighten you?"

"He's a scary man. So's that monster who works for him."

"You're not telling me anything," said James.

"What do you want to eat with these vegetables?"

James told her there was a steak in the freezer which would go down very well right now. She said she was a vegetarian, and while she didn't actively disapprove of other people eating red meat, she sure as hell wasn't going to cook it for them. Using whatever herbs she could find, she did something miraculous with the vegetables before dumping them into an omelette light enough to float off the plate. James had drunk his last bottle of decent red wine last night so he had to content himself with a bottle of California plonk. Betsy stuck to the brandy.

She sat across from him while he was eating. James had a lot of questions lined up in his head, but he was enjoying himself too much to push the matter. Besides, he knew she'd get around to it eventually. She did, two brandies later.

"What do you know about Jonathan Bradley?" she asked.

"He's English. He's been sick. He wants someplace quiet to stay for a few months while he recuperates."

"His name isn't really Bradley," she said.

"It's not Smith either."

"At least, it is Bradley, but it's not, if you see what I mean."

"No," said James.

"He changed it. Actually, his father changed it."

"From what?"

"Perhaps I shouldn't tell you."

"Nobody's twisting your arm," said James. He was content to wait.

She peered at him across the top of her brandy glass. "You're studied indifference is totally unbelievable," she said. She had a slight problem with "totally unbelievable." It came out more like "tolatty unblievibible."

Another pause during which she drained her already empty glass.

"It's Glessen," she said.

"What is?"

"Jonathan's name. At least, it was Glessen, now it's Bradley."

"The German bankers?"

"English now. That's why they changed the family name to Bradley."

"I'm impressed," said James.

"I thought you might be."

The Glessen family. European merchant bankers for generations, second only to the Rothschilds in wealth and power.

"Where does Jonathan fit into the family tree?"

"He doesn't fit at all, poor darling. That's his main problem.

In fact, he's spent most of his life trying to forget the family even exists. His uncle was Fritz Glessen, the one who went to prison after the war."

"Hitler's banker," said James. Glessen had been sentenced to fifteen years and confiscation of all his assets by the War Crimes Commission. He had died in prison.

"Jonathan's father was Fritz's younger brother. He came to England after the war and started up the bank again. That's when he changed his name. Jonathan was born in England."

"Where does Langer fit in?"

"I don't know." She was lying again, but he let it pass.

"And where do *you* fit in, Betsy Carmichael?"

"I'm a friend of Jonathan's."

"How good a friend?"

She started to tell a story about how the two families were very close and how she and Jonathan had been like brother and sister. She got herself sidetracked somewhere during the narrative and James found himself listening to how it was growing up in a large country house in the Cotswolds where her parents did a great deal of hunting and shooting and the children were confined to the nursery and only let out to be shown off to the weekend houseguests. He allowed her to ramble on, only half listening. Finally, she ran out of steam. "Am I boring you?" she asked.

"Not at all," lied James.

"I think I'm drunk. I've been told I'm boring when I'm drunk."

"You're not boring. Go on."

"I don't think I want to. In fact, I know I don't. I want to go to bed."

"Any particular bed?"

"My own. Will you drive me back to town?"

"Certainly," said James. "Just let me check if Langer's still hanging around outside."

"On the other hand," she said quickly, "perhaps I could sleep on your sofa."

"I'll sleep on the couch," said James. "You can take the bed."

"You're very gallant. I'm completely at your mercy."
Ain't that the truth, thought James.

He found a new toothbrush for her and left her in the bathroom while he started to stack the supper dishes. A couple of minutes later she called to him from the bedroom. "My zip's stuck." It wasn't, but James didn't argue. He helped her undress, a highly erotic experience which took longer than it should have due to the fact she kept throwing her arms around his neck and mashing her ample bosom up against his chest. Finally she was down to her bra and panties. "Well, go on," she murmured.

James went on. She was clinging to him hard now. He was forced to unfasten her bra by reaching around from the front. "Don't stop now," she said. He disentangled himself from her embrace and peeled off her panties. She was a natural redhead. Shades of his ex-wife, thought James.

She refused to get under the bedclothes, instead she lay spread-eagled on top of the bed looking like an exotic starfish waiting for the tide to come in. When he said he needed to brush his teeth, she told him please to hurry. As he went into the bathroom, her hand was already working away between her legs. He didn't want her to finish without him, so he was very quick with his toilette. He needn't have bothered. By the time he came out, she was sound asleep. He thought seriously for a moment about waking her. He decided against it. She was too drunk to enjoy herself, and he was probably far enough in the same direction to ruin his performance anyway. Booze had been doing that to him lately, sharpening the urge, dulling the ability. Instead, he pulled on a robe and went back into the kitchen to finish the dishes.

Ten minutes later he set out to patrol his domain. He didn't think Langer would have come back, but he took the shotgun with him anyway. The night was as quiet as a seaside graveyard, just the lapping of the water and the distant barking of a dog. He walked out onto the beach and looked back along the row of houses on either side of his own. Most of them were dark. Beach people went to bed early unless they were partying.

He wondered briefly if Bradley/Glessen was going to be a party man. Glessen . . . one of the richest families in Europe. He should have asked for more rent.

After a few minutes he started to feel the cold. The nights were chilly at this time of the year. He walked back through to the front of the house. There, he checked the padlock on the gate and confirmed that Langer's car hadn't put in a reappearance. He put the chain on the front door and turned out the lights in the living room.

Betsy hadn't moved. She still lay flat on her back, her legs apart, breathing noisily. Without waking her he pulled the bedclothes from under her and covered her up. Then he rolled her to one side of the bed and got in beside her. She still smelled good. Better in fact. Now her light perfume was overlaid with the faint odor of her body. He started to feel horny again. He turned away from her and went to sleep before he did something he knew he'd regret in the morning.

2

Betsy was still sleeping when he crept out of bed at seven thirty. He put on some coffee, then went back into the bedroom to fetch his track suit. Barefooted, he went for a run on the beach. All the regulars were out, walking their dogs, jogging, or just enjoying a sparkling new day where the air was as clean as the shore, unsullied at this time of the year by visitors' garbage.

As soon as he got back he looked in on Betsy. She hadn't moved. All that was visible was an untidy mop of red hair. He squeezed a couple of oranges into a glass and took the juice in to her. He sat on the edge of the bed and gently prodded her awake. For a brief moment there was panic in her eyes. Where the hell was she? Then she remembered.

"Oh my God!" she said. She struggled to a sitting position, exposing her breasts. She grabbed the covers quickly, clutching them to herself in a panic of embarrassment that, after last night, James found faintly ludicrous.

"Good morning," he said.

She saw her panties on the back of a chair where James had thrown them. He hadn't seen anyone blush for longer than he could remember. Among the people he knew, it had gone out of fashion, like modesty and good manners.

She took the orange juice from him and drank it without

coming up for air. She studiously avoided looking him in the eye. She was obviously working out the best way to approach the situation she had awakened to. Outrage. Gratitude. Indignation. Apology. The whole catalogue was sorted quickly. She made her decision. She smiled at James, allowing her eyes to grow misty.

"It was wonderful," she said.

"What was?"

"Last night." An edge of doubt crept in. "Wasn't it?"

"Sensational," said James. "How do you like your coffee?"

"Black, please. And . . . do you have any aspirin?"

James fetched her coffee and aspirin, then left her alone while she showered and dressed. She came into the living room half an hour later. She had pulled herself together remarkably well. She looked as neat and tidy as when James had first seen her yesterday.

"Please, can you call me a taxi?" she said.

"Wouldn't you like to wait?"

"What for?"

"Your childhood chum arrives around noon."

She looked nervous. "Listen . . . I was a little . . . indiscreet last night. I don't mean physically. I was that too, even if it was marvelous. I shouldn't have told you about Jonathan. I *did* tell you about Jonathan, didn't I? I mean, about who he is."

James confirmed her indiscretion.

"I'd be extremely grateful if you didn't mention it," she said.

"Not a word," said James.

"I really would like to go home now please. Tell Jonathan I'll call him this afternoon."

James phoned for a cab. While they were waiting, she tried to make small talk, without much success. She kept forgetting to finish her sentences, her mind wandering off someplace else. There was obviously something she wanted to ask him and she didn't know how to go about it. Eventually the cab arrived and he walked her out to the front gate. A moment before he opened it, she grabbed his arm.

"He's not still there, is he?"

James told her that when he got up this morning Langer's car had been gone. He helped her into the cab and closed the door. She wound down the window. "Will you be around this evening?" she asked. "I mean, if I visit Jonathan, will I see you?"

"Just knock on the door."

She looked as if she was trying to say something else. She didn't make it. "Beverly Wilshire Hotel," she said to the cabdriver.

As he started the engine, she changed her mind. "Please wait a minute," she said. She leaned half out of the window toward James. "I know it's terrible of me . . . incredibly bad manners . . . nothing like this has ever happened before . . ."

James felt sorry for her. He was about to tell her that her virtue was intact, that nothing had happened last night, but she didn't let him speak. "The fact is . . . I'm sorry . . . but I can't remember your name."

James told her his name. By the time the cab pulled away he'd already gone back inside, slamming the gate far harder than was necessary.

Jonathan Bradley and his entourage arrived at twelve fifteen. James was watering the small patch of grass between the guest house and the main house when the front gate opened and a man came in. He was over six feet tall, wearing a turtleneck sweater and tan slacks. He exuded an almost indecent impression of good health and vitality.

"Hey, you!" he called in James's direction. "Find Reed and tell him Mr. Smith's here."

James resisted the urge to turn the hose on him. "I'm Reed."

The man looked at James as though he seriously doubted it. "You're the landlord?"

"That's me."

The man looked past him toward the main house. Then back to James. "You own this joint?" James confirmed that the house was, in fact, his.

" 'Strewth," said the man. "I should've emigrated here m'self." He stuck out his hand. "Fairman. Bruce Fairman. Australian, in case you hadn't guessed." James had guessed. The accent was thick enough to sell Foster's lager. "You wanna give me a hand in with the boss man," said Fairman. "I can manage him on m'own, but it's easier when there's two 'n I don't trust that nigger Cooper not to drop the poor bugger on his arse just for laughs." James turned off the water and followed Fairman out to the street.

There were two cars parked out front. One was a stretch limousine which took up enough space for two ordinary vehicles. The other was a station wagon. A large, overweight black guy who James assumed was Cooper was removing a collapsible wheelchair from the trunk of the limo. He was wearing a hideously patterned Hawaiian shirt and ill-fitting pants that looked as if they were made out of burlap. "This here is the landlord," said Fairman, by way of introduction. Cooper flashed some enormous teeth in James's direction as he set the wheelchair down and opened it up.

Fairman went straight to the rear door of the limo and opened it. "Let's go, boss," he said to someone inside. The first person to emerge was a woman. James's first impression was that she was nothing special to look at. Average height, average build, fairly long brown hair fastened in a ponytail, very little makeup, good skin, grayish wide-set eyes, clothes undistinguished. If she'd sat next to him at a bar, he wouldn't have walked away but neither would he have bothered striking up a conversation. He assumed this was the secretary, Jane Reynolds. She smiled vaguely in his direction before moving away from the car to give Fairman room to climb in.

"Come on, sport," he said to James. "Give me a hand."

James walked to the limo and looked in. Fairman was just helping the occupant to slide over toward the open door. Jonathan Bradley was around thirty-four years old and looked sixty. He was painfully thin and had lost a good deal of his pale blond hair. He was wearing a large pair of dark glasses that hid his eyes completely. James just knew they had to be sunken, it went with the rest of the image, sallow skin and a two- or three-day growth of beard. He was wearing a lightweight suit that looked as if it might have been slept in and his feet were encased in carpet slippers. He didn't smell too good either. James figured the late Howard Hughes probably looked something like this during his last few weeks.

"Mr. Reed," he said, when he saw James. "I'm Mr. Smith." His voice was soft and well modulated. He held out a hand and James shook it carefully. He didn't want to break anything. It was like shaking hands with a corpse.

"May I call you Bradley?" said James. Because of the glasses, he was unable to read Bradley's reaction.

"Providing you don't do it in public," said Bradley, finally. He didn't ask how James had found out.

"You want to grab him on your side," said Fairman.

James reached into the car and hooked a hand under Bradley's armpit. Fairman did the same on the other side and together they lifted him out of the limo and deposited him in the wheelchair. A bag of groceries weighed more.

"You show Cooper the way, sport. I'll start unloading our stuff," said Fairman. He turned to Cooper. "Soon as you get the boss settled you get your black ass back here 'n give me a hand. Right?"

If Cooper was offended, he gave no sign. "Right," he said. Then to James. "Lead on Mr. Reed."

As James led the way toward the gate, Jane Reynolds joined him. She smiled at him without any warmth. "I'm Jonathan's secretary."

"Miss Reynolds," said James. She had a pretty smile. Pity the rest of her didn't match. He held the gate open and allowed Cooper to wheel Bradley through ahead of him. Fairman was already taking cases from the station wagon and stacking them on the roadside. James fell into step beside the wheelchair.

"Wise didn't tell me about the wheelchair," he said. "We might have to shift the accommodations around some."

"No need," said Bradley. "I get around perfectly well most of the time. It's just that we've been traveling for three days now and I'm rather tired."

I bet you are, thought James. You look rather dead. He wondered briefly if Bradley were suffering from AIDS. He certainly showed all the visible symptoms. He opened the front door of the main house, then helped Cooper lift the wheelchair up the couple of steps so that Bradley could be pushed indoors.

"It's larger than I remember," said Bradley, looking around.

"You're smaller is what it is," said Cooper.

"You're probably right, Jeff," said Bradley. He turned to Jane. "Well?"

"It's very nice. Exactly as you described."

"I've been here before," he said to James. "When your ex-wife lived here."

"So I was told," said James.

"They were good days," said Bradley reflectively. He seemed to be trying to remind himself how good they had been. "Wheel me out on the terrace, Jeff. Then go give Bruce a hand." He turned to James. "Perhaps you'd be kind enough to give Jane a quick tour of the house. Show her where everything is." Cooper started to wheel him out. "Come back later," he called to James. "We'll talk about the old days."

James gave Jane a tour of the house finishing in the master bedroom. It was one of the largest rooms in the house, with floor-to-ceiling windows overlooking the sea. His-and-hers bath and dressing rooms led off. On the infrequent occasions James had stayed here with Katherine, it had been his favorite room.

"Very nice," said Jane. She pulled a small notebook from her purse and started to go through a checklist.

"Is there a safe?"

There was. James showed her where it was, let into the floor at the back of the main closet.

"Tell me about the security system."

James showed her the intricacies of the alarm system. How to switch it on; how to switch it off; when it was triggered and what happened as a result. He didn't bother explaining that the police had become so tired of rushing out to false alarms, that the whole system had become an expensive liability rather than an asset.

"Do you have a cleaner?"

James gave her the name and the number of his contract cleaners. He explained how to get to the local market. He promised to take his own vehicle out of the garage to make room for the limo and the station wagon, though he doubted the garage was deep enough to accommodate the limo. The telephone was connected; the number was unlisted; there was an internal line to the guest house in case anyone needed James in a hurry; the inventory was in the drawer of the writing desk . . . and if there was anything else she needed, he'd be watering the garden.

As he came downstairs, Fairman and Cooper came in carrying the last of the baggage.

"Everything cool, sport?" said Fairman.

"I've shown Miss Reynolds around."

"Good on you. Where's the boss?"

"On the terrace."

Cooper dumped the bags he was carrying. He produced a large handkerchief and mopped his ample brow.

"Where's the kitchen, Mr. Reed? I gotta start thinking 'bout food for this lot."

"Don't you go servin' up no grits," said Fairman.

"I'm from Jamaica, man. Not Louisiana."

"You're the cook?" said James.

"I'm the cook, the chauffeur, the gofer, you name it, Mr. Reed, if it's nigger's work, I'm it."

James looked toward Fairman, who was arranging the baggage into separate piles. "I guess that makes you the valet."

"You want your pants sponged and pressed, just bring 'em over," said Fairman. "Also if you want a massage, or you need lifting in or out of the bathtub, or you feel like losing a few dollars at backgammon, or you just need somebody to yell at because you're feeling low . . . I'm your man." The phraseology was lighthearted, but James detected a hard edge in the delivery. He was about to leave when Jane Reynolds came downstairs.

"A couple of things I forgot to mention," said James. "Betsy Carmichael will be calling this evening."

"Good old Betsy," said Fairman. If anything, the edge in his voice had grown even sharper.

"Quit worrying about Betsy," said Cooper. "She don' mean no harm."

"She don' mean no good neither," said Fairman, mimicking Cooper's accent.

"And a guy named Langer is looking for Mr. Bradley," said James.

"Shit!" said Cooper.

"Son of a bitch!" said Fairman.

Jane Reynolds didn't say anything for a moment. "He's been here?" she asked finally.

"Day before yesterday."

"What did you tell him?"

"He'd got the wrong address."

"Did he believe you?"

"I guess not. He was back again last night."

She turned toward Cooper and Fairman. "Do we tell him?"

"Yes," said Cooper.

"No," said Fairman, simultaneously.

It was none of his business, so James left them to argue it out between themselves.

Half an hour later Cooper knocked on the guest-house door and asked if James would mind telling him how to get to the market. James started to give him directions, then he changed his mind and said he'd come along. He told Cooper there were a couple of things he needed to buy, which there weren't. Normally he liked to stay well clear of his tenants and their domestic arrangements. Providing they paid their rent on time and didn't upset the neighbors, he let them get on with it. But this time it was different. For some reason, Bradley had decided to pay him five grand a month. He wasn't too sure what he was supposed to do, but he figured the more he could find out about Bradley and his entourage, the better he'd be able to earn his money.

They took the station wagon to the market. Cooper wasn't a very good driver. But he was good talker, even if he didn't say much. Sure he liked working for Bradley; the pay was good and he got to travel all over. He got on fine with Bruce. The Australian's "nigger" talk didn't bother him, it was just his way of being matey. "If he called me an abo, it'd be different. The Aussies hate the aborigines. Treat 'em worse than the blacks in South Africa," Jane could be a bit of a drag, with her prissy manner, but she meant well and she was a good nurse.

"I thought she was his secretary," said James.

"She is, man. But she's a trained nurse too. Real handy lady to have around. She gives the boss his shots, takes his blood pressure, sees he eats right."

"What's the matter with him?"

"I'm a cook, man, not a doctor."

"Come on! You must have some idea."

"If I did, I wouldn't tell you. It's none of my business and the way I see it, it ain't none of yours neither."

"You're right," said James. "It's none of my business. Hang a left at the next intersection."

Cooper hung a suicidal left that had James braking so hard on the passenger side that his foot practically went through the floor.

"You all right, man?" asked Cooper.

"I'm fine," said James. "You wanna steer over to the right side of the street."

Cooper swung the wheel. "Where I come from the left side is the right side."

"Maybe we should paint a Union Jack on the car," said James. "Just so's other drivers will know to look out."

"I'm a shitty driver wherever," said Cooper.

James wandered around the market with Cooper, watching him buy enough food and top-price wine to stock a small and very expensive restaurant. As they loaded the car, James offered to drive home, but Cooper said he was a nervous passenger. James knew just how he felt. He strapped himself in firmly, then changed his mind and unclipped the seat belt in case he needed to bail out of the station wagon in a hurry.

"You're not from round these parts, are you?" said Cooper, as they drove out of the parking lot.

"I'm from London originally. I've been here . . . seven years now." Shit, was it that long!

"I miss it," said Cooper. "Working for the boss, we don't get to go back very often." He drove through a stop sign without slowing.

"That was a stop sign back there," said James.

"Yeah. I saw it. How about you, friend? You ever get homesick?"

"No," said James. It was the truth. "Hang a left at the signal."

Cooper turned left where he was told and narrowly missed a limousine that was pulling out onto the main highway. "Who's Langer?" he asked.

"He's one mean motherfucker," said Cooper.

"I figured that much. What does he want?"

"Shit, man. I don't know." He was lying. "What's it to you, anyway?"

"I'm supposed to be minding your boss while he's here. It'd be a help if I knew what I might come up against. Like that pet rhino of Langer's, for example."

"Hey! He's something else, isn't he? Remember that James Bond film . . . oriental guy . . . Oddjob, I think that was his name . . . that's who he reminds me of."

"You've met him, then."

"I got the scars to prove it." He changed the subject. "What does a guy do nights round here?"

"What did you have in mind?"

"Someplace I can hang out with the brothers and sisters—down a couple of beers—maybe get laid."

"The brothers don't hang out much in Malibu," said James.

"That figures. Honkyville."

"We've arrived," said James.

Cooper hit the brakes. James hit the windshield.

James helped Cooper carry the stuff up to the main house. He was just leaving when Bradley called his name from the living room. He was still in his wheelchair, sitting in front of the open doors leading out to the terrace. He looked better than he had earlier. There was a patch of high color on his cheeks. Either he's been at the booze or nurse Jane Reynolds had given him a shot. James had a pretty good idea what kind of shot it was. "You've met Karl Langer, I hear," he said.

"Night before last."

"What did you tell him?"

"I didn't know anyone named Bradley. I was expecting a man named Smith."

"Did he say how he got this address?"

"No."

"Somebody must have told him."

James assumed he was supposed to consider the remark as a question. He answered with a question of his own. "One of your people?"

Bradley shook his head. "No way."

"Is it important?" James asked.

"I suppose not. He'd have found out one way or another. He always does."

"Should I know anything about him? Like, if he pitches up again do you want me to see him off?"

"Could you do that?"

"Sure I could," said James with far more confidence than he felt. "If he isn't invited onto the property and he still insists on coming in I can call the police and have him arrested."

"Nobody takes the laws of trespass seriously?"

"I wouldn't report a trespasser. I'd report an intruder."

"I see." Bradley was silent for a moment. He was still wearing his sunglasses. It was impossible to read his expression. He changed the subject abruptly. "You've met Betsy, I hear."

James admitted to having met Betsy Carmichael.

"I'm very fond of Betsy," said Bradley. "We grew up together."

"So she told me."

"What else did she tell you?"

"That she's as scared of Langer as everyone else seems to be."

"Poor Betsy." He didn't enlarge on it. "Perhaps you'll have dinner with us this evening."

James accepted the invitation. He hoped they might uncork a couple of the bottles of wine Cooper had just bought. "You still haven't told me what you want me to do about Langer," he said.

"Let's play it by ear," said Bradley.

On his way out, James went into the kitchen. Cooper was unpacking the groceries. Fairman was sitting at the kitchen table drinking from a can of beer.

"Hi, sport!" he said when he saw James.

"I'm going out for an hour," said James.

"So?"

"You're on your own till I get back."

"We'll survive," said Fairman.

James backed the panel truck out of the garage and drove to the public library. There he found a European copy of *Who's Who*. He looked up Glessen. There were still branches of the family who'd not changed their name. One in Germany and one in France. He looked up Bradley. Jonathan's father was listed in a short entry.

> BRADLEY, William. Chairman, Glessen Bank (UK). Born 1912. Married Gertrude Carlton, London 1952. Two children. Elena b. 1953 and Jonathan b. 1955.

On an impulse, he looked up the name Langer. There were two entries. Both for men in their mid-sixties, neither of them with the Christian name Karl. Not quite sure what he had been expecting to find, he returned the book and drove home. Betsy Carmichael was just paying off a cab. James waited for her and then held the front gate open.

"Thank you, James," she said.

"You remembered my name. I'm flattered."

"Don't rub it in," she said. "I was drunk."

"We'll talk about it later," said James.

"Oh, I don't think so," she said, primly. "I'm here to visit Jonathan."

"Then we can talk about it over dinner. He's democratic, Jonathan is, he doesn't mind eating with the help."

"I'd appreciate if you didn't mention last night," she said.

"Which particular part of last night don't you want me to mention?"

"You know what I'm talking about," she said. She had started to blush.

"Tell me," said James.

"You really are a shit," she said.

"You're right," said James, beginning to feel sorry for her. "I won't say a word."

Before he went over to the main house for dinner, James checked that the lock was on the front gate. He walked out to the beach and checked that the gate to the outside steps leading up to the terrace was also secure. Then he walked back around to the front door and rang the bell. The door was opened by Cooper, now dressed in dark pants, white shirt and bow tie topped by a starched white jacket. If he hadn't been so fat he'd have looked elegant. "Good evening, sir," he said. He stepped aside for James to come in. "Mr. Bradley is expecting you."

"Bit upmarket, aren't we?" said James.

"I buttle as well as cook," said Cooper. "Now get your honky ass in here, I've got too much work to stand gossiping on the doorstep."

James came in. "Where's everyone at?" he asked.

"In the living room. You want me to announce you?"

"I think I can manage on my own."

"Have fun," said Cooper. He disappeared back toward the kitchen.

James walked through to the living room. They were all there. Bradley was without wheelchair. He was sitting in one of the armchairs in front of the fireplace. The fire was burning brightly, reminding James to order more logs tomorrow. Bradley had changed into a tuxedo. There were a couple of stout walking sticks resting against the arm of the chair. Betsy Carmichael was seated on a footstool in front of him. Jane Reynolds and Bruce Fairman were sitting on the sofa on the opposite side of the fireplace. It could have been a cozy little domestic scene except for the tail end of a remark James caught just as he came in.

". . . such a dumb cunt, you know I can't do that," Bradley said to Betsy. Then he saw James. He smiled with his mouth. His dark glasses prevented James from seeing if he was smiling with his eyes too, but he doubted it. He could see the man was quite drunk. "Ah, the landlord's here. Come and join us. Get him a drink, Betsy."

"I can get it," said James, heading for the bar.

"Betsy," said Bradley. There was a thin edge in his voice. Betsy stood up quickly. She was blushing again.

"What would you like, Mr. Reed?"

"A Scotch and water would be fine. Light on the Scotch, heavy on the water."

"I heard you were a heavy drinker, sport," said Fairman.

"Shut up, Bruce," said Bradley.

"Not when I'm working," said James.

"Sorry, sport. I forgot. You're our first line of defense, aren't you."

Betsy handed him his drink without meeting his eye. Being English, she'd forgotten the ice. James helped himself.

"Did you bring your gun with you?" asked Bruce. "Or are you going to take on the ox bare-handed?"

"Shut up, Bruce," said Bradley again.

"Come on, boss. What's this guy gonna do that I can't?"

"Stay sober," said Bradley. Something in the tone of his voice did more than the two "shut up"s. Fairman subsided into a sulk. "Sit down, Mr. Reed. Make yourself comfortable."

James took the spare armchair across from Bradley. Betsy had returned to the stool at Bradley's feet. There was a short silence, broken finally as Jane Reynolds stood up and announced she was going to the kitchen to see if she could give Cooper a hand.

"Go with her, Betsy," said Bradley. For a moment it looked as if Betsy might give him an argument. Then she stood up and followed Jane out of the room without a word.

"Bruce. Take a walk around the property."

"Uh!" Bruce Fairman had been miles away. "What for?"

"Because I ask you to," said Bradley.

Fairman stood up. James noticed for the first time the bulge of what had to be a handgun beneath his loose-fitting jacket. He walked out without a word.

"I'd like another drink," said Bradley. "How about you?"

"No thanks," said James. He hadn't touched the one that Betsy had given him.

Bradley started to struggle to his feet. "Let me get it," said James, starting up.

"I can manage, thank you."

James watched Bradley stand up. He took a walking stick in each hand and moved slowly over to the bar. He didn't actually limp, it was more of a shuffle, dragging his feet like a very old, very sick man.

"Embarrassing, isn't it?" said Bradley, from the bar.

James hadn't realized he'd been staring so hard. "Not particularly."

"Take my word for it," said Bradley. "That's one of the reasons I use the chair as much as I do. People aren't so inclined to look at you as if you were some kind of a freak."

"What's wrong with you?"

"Straight to the point. I like that. Are you really interested, or are you just making conversation?"

"I'm a terrible conversationalist."

"I'm dying, Mr. Reed. That's what's wrong with me."

"We're all dying," said James, wishing he'd never asked. He was spared having to make further conversation as Cooper announced dinner was served.

In the few minutes since James had last seen him, Fairman had managed to get quite drunk. He started to hold forth at the dinner table about how Australia was God's chosen land and no place else was worth a shit. Bradley, who was pretty drunk himself, didn't seem to mind, and as neither of the girls seemed to carry any weight in the household, Fairman plowed on. Even this wasn't able to spoil the dinner for James. Cooper might be one of the world's worst drivers, but he was a hell of a cook. The wine was as good as James had hoped it would be. He tried to make small talk with Jane, seated on his left, but gave up after ten minutes of monosyllabic responses. He tried exercising his charms on Betsy. He didn't have much luck there either. Her full attention was directed toward Bradley. James decided that, if one discounted the food, the dinner party was a dead loss. At least, it was until Karl Langer showed up.

Bradley had just announced that they'd take coffee and brandy in the living room when the front doorbell rang. What conversation there was stopped dead. Even Fairman, who was extolling the virtues of Bondi Beach over every other stretch of sand in the world, shut up. Nobody moved.

"Do you want me to get it," asked James, finally.

"Cooper will handle it," said Bradley.

"He's probably locked himself in the larder," said Fairman. But he made no move himself.

The doorbell rang once more. Without asking this time, James stood up and went out to the entrance hall. He opened the front door to Langer.

"Good evening, Mr. Reed." He looked the same as James remembered. Beautifully dressed, the scar on his face plainly visible in the light from the hall.

"Mr. Langer, isn't it?" He could see the monolithic shape of Michael, lurking in the shadows just outside the guest house.

"You lied to me, Mr. Reed."

James started to say something, but Langer cut him off with a small wave of his hand. "We'll discuss that later. Right now, I'd like to talk to Mr. Bradley."

"I'll see if he's in," said James.

He closed the door in Langer's face and walked back into the dining room. Nobody had moved. "The bogeyman's here. What do you want me to do?"

Both of the girls looked frightened. Fairman fidgeted in his chair. He seemed to be waiting for a source of adrenaline to start pumping. Bradley just sat there, his expression unreadable behind his dark glasses. "Ask him in," he said, finally.

As James headed back to the front door, the two girls started to get to their feet. "Stay where you are," said Bradley. "I'll talk to him in the living room."

James opened the front door to Langer again. He hadn't moved. But Michael had. He was standing just behind Langer, effectively blocking out the night sky. James figured if he'd not opened the front door, in another thirty seconds Langer would have had Michael huff and puff and blow it down.

"Come on in," he said.

He stood aside as Langer came indoors. Michael came in right behind him. "You too," said James. He pointed toward the living room. "In there."

Langer moved off without a word. Michael stayed where he was. It was a large entrance hall, but he made it seem crowded. James hadn't really gotten a good look at him the other night. The light had been bad, and he'd been drunk. Cooper's reference to Goldfinger's Oddjob came back to him. Only the man standing in front of him was bigger, uglier, and looked twice as dangerous. He didn't smell too good either. Apart from the remembered garlic and halitosis, he also exuded a strong body odor overlaid with cheap cologne. Obviously the limo he drove for Langer had efficient air-conditioning. If he'd been James's chauffeur, James would have insisted on a convertible.

"You want to wait in the kitchen?" James asked.

Michael shook his head.

"You'll excuse me, then. I'm in the middle of my dinner." He walked back into the dining room. The girls were still seated at the table. They were both watching Fairman who had produced his gun and was checking the clip.

"Where is he?" Fairman asked James.

"Langer's in the living room. The ox is in the hall."

Without sitting, James drained the last of the magnificent wine he'd been drinking with dinner. "Anybody need anything, I'll be in the guest house."

He walked back to the hall, stepped around Michael, and out the front door. Back in the guest house, he checked the shells in the shotgun, tucked it under his arm and walked out again. He skirted the house and took the side passage straight out to the beach. There, he unlocked the gate and walked up the steps that led to the terrace. He wasn't too concerned about being spotted.

With the lights on in the living room and darkness outside, the glass doors out to the terrace acted like a mirror.

Both Bradley and Langer were standing in front of the fireplace. Langer with his one walking stick, Bradley with two. Langer was talking and Bradley was listening. There were no fireworks, no excitement. In fact Langer was talking so quietly that James couldn't hear a word. Now Bradley shook his head vigorously. Langer continued to talk. Again Bradley shook his head. Now Langer raised his voice. At last James could hear something. He moved closer. It did him no good, Langer was talking in German. It was a language that James could neither speak nor understand. So he continued to watch. Although Langer had raised his voice, he hadn't lost his cool. For the next two minutes he continued to address Bradley, then abruptly he turned on his heel and limped out of sight toward the hallway, leaning heavily on his walking stick. Bradley remained where he was, looking after him.

Quickly James ran back down to the beach and through the side passage toward the front of the house. Michael and Langer were leaving. He watched them out the front gate, which they left open. Before he could reach it, he heard a car start up outside. By the time he peered out into the street, the limo had pulled away. He came back in and tried to close the gate. It was off its hinges. He remembered now, it had been locked. Michael had obviously done his huffing and puffing out here. He decided that he'd put the cost of a new gate on Bradley's account. He dropped off the shotgun in the guest house and went back to the main house. The doorbell was answered by Fairman with a gun in his hand and an aggressive expression on his face.

"Oh! It's you, sport."

As if you didn't know, thought James. The surprised recognition was as phony as the fake aggression.

"They've gone," said James.

"Just as well," said Fairman. "Come on in."

James came into the house.

"Great minder you're turning out to be," said Fairman. "First sign of trouble and you scarper."

"Self-preservation," said James. "Besides, I figured you could handle it."

"Bet your ass," said Fairman. He put the gun away into a shoulder holster under his left armpit. Shoulder holsters were strictly for guys who hoped they wouldn't have to use their guns. Anybody remotely serious kept their firearms in a holster clipped to their belt or just tucked into the top of their pants.

"Where's Bradley?" asked James.

"He went to bed."

"How about the girls?"

"In the living room."

James started in that direction. Fairman grabbed his arm. "If you're thinking of starting anything with Betsy, forget it. It's hands off in this household. The boss wouldn't like it. Neither would I."

"You're scaring me to death," said James.

In the living room, James was interested to see that Betsy had started on the brandy. She was standing behind the bar topping up a glass that already held a sizable slug. Jane was standing in front of the fire looking as though she couldn't make up her mind whether to pack her bags right away or burst into tears. James went straight to the bar.

"May I?" he said. He took the brandy bottle from Betsy and poured one for himself. Fairman had followed him in and was glaring at him from the doorway.

"Where were you?" asked Betsy.

"Protecting your rear," said James. Under cover of the bar he put the flat of his hand on what he claimed he'd been protecting. She pulled away, but not immediately. Now Jane announced that she too was going to bed. Without saying good night, she walked out past Fairman.

"How are you getting home?" James asked Betsy, quietly enough that Fairman couldn't hear.

"By cab," she said.

"I'll drive you," said James. "It might be safer. See you out front in ten minutes."

He drained his brandy and walked out.

"Stay cool, sport," he said to Fairman, as he passed him in the doorway.

Before leaving he stuck his head into the kitchen. Cooper was seated at the table enjoying the same meal he had served up earlier. James noticed he also had a bottle of Bradley's wine at his elbow, half empty.

"Great dinner," said James.

"That's what I do, man," said Cooper.

"Where were you when the bogeyman arrived?"

"Minding my own business. Same as always."

"Friend Bruce figured you were hiding in the larder."

"Yeah . . . well he would, wouldn't he? It's where he'd have liked to be."

"He's one tough hombre, that one."

"That's how they breed them down in Aussie land."

James declined the offer of a glass of wine. He said good night and went back to the guest house. Exactly ten minutes later Betsy knocked on his door.

"It's very kind of you to offer to drive me back to my hotel," she said, closing the door firmly behind her as she came in. She was already unbuttoning her dress as she headed for the bedroom.

"Did anyone ever tell you you look like Michael Caine?" said Betsy.

"Is that a fact?" said James. God, but he was dying to go to sleep. Her enthusiasm had only been outweighed by her ingenuity. He couldn't remember when he'd felt so wiped out. She was leaning up on one elbow plucking idly at the hairs on his chest.

She had sulked a little when he told her he wasn't up to a third dip into the honeypot, but she'd cheered up when he'd fetched her another brandy. As long as he was on his feet, she'd also asked him to put something romantic on the stereo. Now he was back in bed, wondering how he was going to peel her away from him so he could get some sleep.

"Was it as good as last night?" asked Betsy.

"Much better."

"What was wrong with last night?" A dangerous pout in her voice.

"Different. I meant it was different from last night."

Sinatra was announcing from the living room that it was a quarter to three and there was no one in the place when James heard a car backfiring. Then it backfired again. And once more. He pushed Betsy away from him and sat up.

"What is it?" she asked.

James held up his finger for silence. That was exactly what he got, complete and absolute silence except for Sinatra asking for one more for the road. Cars didn't backfire unless engines were running, and if engines were running, you could hear the bloody things. He started to climb out of bed.

"Where are you going?" asked Betsy.

"I need to check something out," he said.

She looked nervous suddenly. "There's something wrong, isn't there?" She started to get out of bed herself.

"Just stay where you are, Betsy, please. I'll only be a few minutes."

She watched him as he dragged on a track suit. "Can't I come with you?"

"Have another brandy. Soon as I get back we'll try something new."

"Kinky?" Her mind was off on another track now.

"Outrageous," he promised.

In the living room he fetched the shotgun from behind the bar. He'd unloaded it before he'd tumbled into bed. Now he reloaded and went outside. The night was as quiet and as dark as a tomb. From here he couldn't hear the sea. All he could see was a small area of the garden in front of him, lit by the light leaking from the guest house. He walked out to the road and looked left and right. Both of Bradley's cars were parked in the garage. As he had surmised, the stretch limo was too long to allow the door to be closed. The back stuck out three feet. The panel truck he had borrowed was tucked in close to the fence. Apart from that, nothing. He went back in and looked toward the main house. There were no lights burning. So . . . a car had backfired.

It was probably up on Pacific Coast Highway. No big deal. Sound traveled a long way at night. He tried very hard, but he couldn't convince himself. Keeping as quiet as possible, so as not to disturb Betsy, he went back into the guest house and collected the spare set of keys to the main house.

He needn't have worried about Betsy. The sound of a gentle snore was emanating from the bedroom. His promise of carnal delights to come had sent her straight to sleep.

He let himself into the main house through the side door. He switched on the kitchen lights. Cooper had cleared up before going to bed. The place was spotless. He prowled through to the entrance hall and into the living room. The door to the terrace was open. Without switching on the lights, he crossed the room and went outside. The gate at the bottom of the steps leading down to the beach was wide open. He came back into the living room, slid the door shut and locked it.

He was going to have to go upstairs. He didn't like the idea that Fairman might hear him creeping around. The Australian was the kind of guy who'd investigate a suspected intruder by shooting him first. Hoping that Jane had assigned everybody the rooms he'd suggested, he walked upstairs quietly and along the passage to Cooper's room. The door was open. He looked into the room. It was pitch dark. He whispered the name loudly. "Cooper?" No answer. After a moment, he felt his way into the room, heading toward where he knew the bed was located. His foot hit something. He stepped back and prodded it with his toe. He knew what it was before he switched on the light.

Cooper was lying flat on his back, arms stretched wide. He was naked. Most of the back of his head was gone. James could see bits of it on the wall six feet away.

Fairman and Jane had died together in the same bed. They had been making love when they were shot. Fairman's body was still sprawled across Jane's. There was a small hole in the back of his head. Jane had taken hers straight between her wide-open eyes. Three down, one to go.

The master bed had been slept in, but Bradley wasn't in it. The bathroom was empty. So too was the closet. The safe was open and empty. James checked the spare bedroom. He looked in the linen closet. He even went up the ladder to the sun roof. Then he went through the rooms he hadn't already examined; the dining room, the study, the utility room, and the small storeroom where he kept the beach furniture. Dead or alive, wherever Jonathan Bradley was right now, he certainly wasn't in the house.

3

James bypassed the local sheriff's department and called the LAPD. It was going to be their problem eventually. There was no point in going through a middleman. Besides, he had a friend there. The courts might well consider a man innocent until proven guilty. Homicide cops worked on the opposite principle. A lot of shit was going to hit various fans and he was familiar enough with police procedure to know that it did no harm to have an ally in the opposing camp. He asked to speak with Lieutenant Applethwaite.

It seemed that Applethwaite didn't work nights, could anyone else help?

Maybe he could talk to Applethwaite at home?

Sorry, not permitted to give out home numbers.

James asked if they'd call the lieutenant at home and ask him to call back as soon as possible. He gave them his name and number.

"It's the middle of the night, buddy," said the voice on the other end of the line. "The lieutenant's gonna kill me if I wake him."

"Take my word for it, he'll kill you if you don't."

He agreed to give it a try. But if he got his balls chewed off, he'd make it his personal responsibility to fuck up James's life from this point on. "One call to the DMV, buddy, and I'll have so many warrants out on you you'll get run in ten times a day."

James went back to the guest house. He'd promised Betsy something outrageous. She wasn't going to be disappointed.

She was still sleeping. He decided he'd let her stay that way. If he woke her up now and told her what had happened, there was no guarantee that she wouldn't bolt. He wanted her on hand when the police arrived. He knew the first thing they'd want from him would be an alibi. Betsy was it.

He unplugged the extension phone in the bedroom. He went back into the living room, shutting the door quietly. He was about to make some coffee when the phone rang.

"Whatever it is, it had better be the most important fucking thing in your life right now," said Ted Applethwaite. His voice was still clogged with sleep.

"You still with homicide?" asked James.

"Don't tell me! You've iced some chick who had the good sense not to go to bed with you."

"I didn't ice anyone. Somebody else did."

"Are you drunk?"

"Not particularly."

"Okay. So tell me." He sounded bored, but the sleep had gone from his voice.

"There are three stiffs in my house right now. All died from gunshot wounds."

"Jesus, James. You *are* drunk. Go fuck yourself."

The line went dead. James hung up. He went into the kitchen and put the coffee on. The phone rang two minutes later.

"Okay. I've taken a pee. I've had a drink. Talk to me," said Applethwaite.

James started to talk. After a couple of minutes Applethwaite cut in on him.

"Where are you calling from?"

"The guest house."

"I'll be with you in thirty minutes," he said. "And James, don't go back to the main house before I get there."

James agreed that he wouldn't.

While he was waiting for Applethwaite, James sat back in his desk chair, closed his eyes and, in his mind, walked back through the main house checking what he had seen and what he hadn't seen.

The gate at the bottom of the steps to the beach was open. Had he relocked it after his attempted eavesdropping on Langer and Bradley? He had been in such a hurry to get around to the front of the house when he'd seen Langer leave, he couldn't remember. Of one thing he was sure, the living room door onto the terrace hadn't been open when he'd said his good nights.

All the lights were out upstairs. Whoever had been wandering around either had switched them off after the massacre or had been using a flashlight.

It figured that Fairman and Jane had been shot first; the sound of the shot had awakened Cooper who had got out of bed and started from the room; he'd been blown away halfway to the door.

And, the sixty-four grand question, where the hell was the boss?

James couldn't remember seeing his walking sticks. Come to think of it, he couldn't remember seeing the wheelchair either. Sticks or wheelchair, it would be hard going along the soft sand of the beach and he sure as hell hadn't tiptoed out through the front gate. For one thing, James would have heard him even though his head had been buried between Betsy's ample thighs, and for another, all the transport belonging to the house was still where it was supposed to be.

He poured himself another cup of coffee and tried to remember if there was anywhere in the main house he hadn't searched. True, he hadn't looked in the closets or bathrooms of the secondary bedrooms. He hadn't looked in the garbage cans or the broom closet or the freezer. Neither had he pulled up the floorboards or torn out any of the walls. No doubt the police would do both. Fine fucking rental this one had turned out to be.

■ ■ ■

Fifteen minutes later, he heard a car pull up outside. He picked up the shotgun and stepped out of the guest house.

"Freeze, buddy, or I'll blow your balls off."

A young guy was crouched in the open gate. He was in the regulation police posture for blowing away miscreants, crouched, with the gun held straight out in both hands. "Drop the gun."

James bent to put the shotgun on the ground.

"I said drop it."

Keeping his fingers crossed that it wouldn't go off and blow off his legs, James did as he was told.

"Face the wall and spread your legs."

Again James did as he was told. It was easier than trying to explain.

The guy approached him carefully and patted him down. James became aware that he was reaching for his cuffs. "No cuffs," he said.

"Shut up and stick your hands behind you."

"Jesus, where did Ted Applethwaite find you?"

This threw him slightly. "What's your name, buddy?"

"Reed. James Reed. What's yours?"

"Detective Cortes, LAPD."

"Let me guess," said James. "Ted called you and told you to meet him here. You live closer than he does so you got here first."

"What of it?"

"I'm the guy who made the call. This is my house. I live here."

"Yeah! So what are you doing coming from the outhouse with a shotgun?"

"It's the guest house. And the shotgun was because we've had a spot of trouble round here tonight. Now why don't you put your gun away and come on in. We can have a drink while we wait for Ted to show."

Detective Cortes thought about it for a moment. Finally he accepted half of James's suggestion. He picked up the shotgun and followed him into the guest house, but he didn't put his gun away.

"Coffee or booze?" asked James.

Cortes was looking around. "What's in there?" he asked, nodding toward the bedroom.

"My bedroom." As if to confirm the fact, the door suddenly opened and Betsy walked out. Her body was so opulent that a naked Betsy seemed twice as naked as anyone else. She didn't even see Cortes.

"James. When are you going to start being outrageous?"

"We've got company, Betsy."

She turned and saw Cortes. It was a toss-up whose eyes were the widest. Cortes recovered first.

"Ma'am," he croaked politely.

Betsy remained rooted to the spot for a long moment, then she bolted back to the bedroom and slammed the door. She shouted from inside the bedroom.

"If your idea of outrageous is a ménage à trois, James Reed, you can forget it." She managed to make the sound of the key turning in the lock as loud as a falling portcullis.

Ted Applethwaite arrived ten minutes later. Cortes and James went out to meet him. He was a large, rather untidy man with a pockmarked face and an expression that seemed to say he'd seen practically everything and not much liked any of it. James knew him as one of a group of guys he played poker with a couple of times a month. While not exactly an "honest cop," he was the next best thing in that he was less dishonest than most. He was hardly out of his car when two other cars pulled up behind him. Out of them stepped a team of half a dozen technicians who headed for the main house like a small herd of buffalo.

"Get your asses back here," shouted Ted. "I'll tell you when you can go in." He saw Cortes. "Sam," he said.

"This guy says his name's Reed," said Cortes.

"It is."

"He says he lives here."

"He does."

Cortes moved closer and whispered something to Applethwaite.

"There usually is," said Ted. He looked at James. "Anyone I know?"

James shook his head. "Her name's Betsy Carmichael. She's English, and you'll want to talk to her later."

"I'll take her statement," said Cortes quickly.

"Why don't you do that," said Ted.

Cortes started toward the guest house, already sharpening up his hormones.

"Break it to her easy," said James.

"Break what easy?"

"What happened. She slept through it."

Cortes looked confused. "What *did* happen?"

Ted looked toward James and raised his eyes to heaven. "Forget it, Sam. We'll take her statement later. Okay, James, let's see what you got me out of bed for."

Ten minutes later, Ted Applethwaite turned the technicians loose. He and James walked back to the guest house. The door to the bedroom was still locked. James put his ear to the panel. Total silence. Either Betsy had gone back to sleep or she was waiting on the other side of the door, ready to defend her honor by braining the first man who tried to come in.

"You want a drink?" asked James.

Ted accepted a large Scotch, removed his topcoat and made himself comfortable. James had no idea how efficient a cop Ted was, but if the way he played poker was any indication, he was a good one. Play everything close to the chest and never tip your hand. "You're gonna have to do some repainting over at the big house," said Ted.

"No shit!" said James.

"But not before I tell you. Okay?"

"Naturally."

"So . . . what can you tell me?"

"You've already seen it all."

"Come on. You were a cop. Talk to me."

"They moved in today. They had one visitor this evening who stayed for about ten minutes."

"What do you figure's missing from over there?"

"I was told Bradley traveled with a lot of loose cash. I assume it was in the safe."

Ted nodded toward the bedroom door. "Where does she fit in?"

"You'd better ask her yourself."

"I'll do that. Can I have another drink?"

James refilled his glass.

"Good Scotch," said Ted. "So . . . any ideas?"

"Nope."

"Don't give me a hard time, James."

"I'm not trying to give you a hard time. I don't have any ideas."

"Sure you have. Let's hear them."

"Find Bradley. Then I'll start making some guesses."

"We're looking, buddy."

There was a knock on the front door. James answered it to Cortes who asked to speak to Ted. The two men spent a couple of minutes talking quietly outside. Then Ted stuck his head back in. "You wanna come see what we found?" he asked James.

Ted left Cortes in the guest house, in case Betsy emerged and decided to walk home. He and James walked over to the main house. Ted spoke to one of the men in the house, who pointed out toward the living room terrace. He and James walked onto the terrace. Someone had located the switch for the outside lights and turned them on. The illumination spilled onto the beach as far down as the water's edge. A couple of Ted's men were getting their feet wet. One was holding a powerful flashlight, aiming it seaward. The other was busy telling him where to shine it. He was holding two walking sticks.

"Charlie spotted them down on the beach soon as we turned on the lights," said the cop. He'd come up to the terrace when Ted had called him, leaving his companion to continue searching with the flashlight. "They were right down by the water's edge. A couple of minutes more they'd have been washed out to sea."

James identified them as the same type of sticks he had seen Bradley use. "Have you found a wheelchair?" he asked.

Ted nodded his permission for the cop to talk in front of James.

"In one of the upstairs closets. Guess he just walked down to the edge of the sea, then kept walking."

Ted told him to call the coast guard and have them mount a search at first light. "That about wraps it up," said Ted to James. "The poor guy wakes up to find his people have all been shot and his house robbed. It was too much for him to handle, so he takes a hike into the ocean."

"Open and shut," said James.

It fell to James to break the news to Betsy. Applethwaite had decided the time had come to get some kind of a statement from her. Not to confirm James's story, he hastened to say. He believed everything that James had told him. "Sure you do," said James.

"Look, you told me the lady's known Bradley for a long time. I need to start building up some kind of a background on the guy."

She wasn't waiting on the other side of the bedroom door with a blunt object. She'd gone back to bed. It took two minutes of hammering on the door to awaken her.

"Are you alone?" she asked, before she unlocked the door.

James assured her he was alone, nodding for Ted to move out of the line of sight. She opened the door to him carefully. "Has he gone?"

"Betsy, we've got to have a talk."

"Let's talk in bed," she said. She opened the door wide now. She was still naked.

"Really talk. Put some clothes on."

She disappeared and returned a minute later wearing James's terry robe, dragging a comb through her hair. As soon as she saw Ted she turned on James.

"You bastard," she said.

"He's a policeman," said James.

"They're the worst. I told you, I'm not into . . ."

"Sit down, Betsy, and shut up for a minute. Nobody's going to jump on you, I promise."

She looked at the two men though she didn't believe it for a moment, but she sat anyway.

James figured he'd best get his alibi on record first. "What time did we go to bed, Betsy?"

She looked toward Ted suspiciously.

"I really am a cop, miss," said Ted.

She turned back to James. "What've you been up to?"

"Just tell him, please. What time did we go to bed?"

"About eleven, I think."

"What time did I get up?"

"I don't know. Two hours later . . . when you heard that car backfiring."

James looked toward Ted. He nodded his approval. Maybe it was for James being able to handle two hours in the sack with Betsy.

"Now will somebody please tell what's going on?" continued Betsy. James told her.

After he had fetched her a large brandy and she had stopped crying, Ted took over. "Tell me about Mr. Bradley?" he asked.

"But where is he?" she wailed.

"We don't know yet. Now, please . . . talk to me." His voice was gentle, persuasive. There was an "I need your help" tone to it. James recognized a good cop when he heard one. He'd been that way himself once, as slippery as a bucketful of eels.

She told him more or less what she had told James, which was very little other than she and Bradley had been practically brought up together due to the proximity of their respective family estates. She didn't mention the name Glessen.

"James said there was a visitor earlier this evening. Do you happen to know who it was?"

"Karl Langer. Didn't James tell you?"

"He must have forgotten," said Ted. He flashed a disappointed look toward James.

"He did it," said Betsy.

"Did what?"

"Everything. I mean . . . it must have been him. He's been hounding Jonathan for years."

"Hounding him for what?"

"I don't know. I only know that he kept turning up wherever Jonathan was, him and that terrible man who works for him."

"We'll check him out," said Ted.

"Maybe I can help you," said James.

"That'll be a change," said Ted.

James gave him the number of Langer's car that he had memorized. Ted called the department and told them to put a trace on the car and get back to him right away. "What else can you tell me about Mr. Langer?" He glanced toward James. An edge crept into his voice. "Either of you."

"He's got pots of money," said Betsy. "I know that because I said to Jonathan once that if Karl Langer was causing him so much aggravation why didn't he just buy him off. Jonathan told me that Langer was richer than he was."

"What was wrong with Bradley?" asked James. If Ted minded James taking over the questioning, he didn't say so.

"He's been sick."

"With what?"

"I don't know. Just sick."

"AIDS?"

"Good heavens, no. At least, I don't think so." She thought about it for a moment, then shook her head. "No. Absolutely not." If she'd been to bed with him, her denial could be based on wishful thinking rather than hard knowledge. "He went off to Europe about two years ago. As far as all his friends were concerned, he just dropped out of sight. We used to talk about it . . . his friends in London . . . trying to guess where he'd gone. Someone said they saw him in Saint-Tropez; someone else claimed to have seen him in Marrakesh; I thought I saw him myself once in Rome. I called his name. Either he didn't hear me or it wasn't him at all. Anyway, all of a sudden I get this call from him from a private clinic just outside London. He said he'd been sick and he'd come home to recuperate. Would I like to visit. I went down there like a shot. My God! I hardly recognized him. He looked worse than he does now. I mean . . . talk about skin and bone.

He couldn't walk either. He'd broken both his legs in an accident."

"What kind of an accident?" asked James.

"Skiing, he said."

"What happened next?" Ted Applethwaite asked the question this time.

"I visited him in the clinic a couple of times. Next thing I knew, he'd checked out and disappeared again. That was about nine months ago. But this time he kept in touch. I got postcards from time to time . . . from all over. Then he told me he was coming here and if I happened to be in town he'd like to see me. I caught the first plane out."

The telephone rang. James picked it up. It was for Ted. He grunted into the mouthpiece a couple of times, made a note of something and hung up.

"The limo is owned by Glaner, Inc."

"What's Glaner? Apart from an anagram of Langer," asked James.

"We're looking into it," said Ted. He turned to Betsy. "Where are you staying, Miss Carmichael?"

"The Beverly Wilshire."

"I can get in touch with you there, right?"

"I think I want to go home."

"Not just yet," said Ted.

"You can't stop me." She thought about it for a second. "Can you?"

"I'm afraid I can."

"Oh." She looked as if she might burst into tears again.

"It'll just be for a few days," said Ted. "Until we can sort this mess out."

A triple killing; a disappearing act, possibly a suicide but more likely another killing; good luck, thought James.

Ted wouldn't let James take either of the Bradley vehicles, so he was forced to drive Betsy into town in the panel truck. If she minded, she didn't say so. She'd put on fresh makeup, smartening up her freckles. In fact, considering what had just gone down, she looked remarkably together. Just as they were leaving, Ted Applethwaite came out.

"Do you have your passport with you, Miss Carmichael?"

"It's at the hotel."

"There'll be a man there when you arrive. Would you give it to him please?"

"Can you do that? Take my passport, I mean."

"Yes ma'am, I can," said Ted.

"Perhaps I should call the consul."

"Maybe you should."

"My father's in the House of Lords."

"That must be very nice for him," said Ted. He went back inside.

As they drove up onto Pacific Coast Highway, James could see a police chopper and a coast guard vessel already starting their search for Bradley. He didn't think they were going to get lucky.

He parked the truck outside the hotel on Wilshire Boulevard. As promised, there was a cop waiting in the lobby. As Betsy asked for her key, the clerk pointed out a guy who was dozing in one of the lobby armchairs. He accompanied James and Betsy up to her room where she reluctantly handed over her passport. He gave her a receipt, thanked her politely and left.

"How long will they keep it?" she asked James.

"A couple of days." There was no point in telling her the truth.

"What am I going to do here for two days?"

"You could try Disneyland."

"Don't be facetious."

"I'm not. I suggest you pack your bags and check into another hotel. They've got one at Disneyland, which is about the most anonymous place you'll find for a hundred miles."

"Why should I check out?"

"For the same reason I'm not going home. We're going to be front-page news by lunchtime."

"You mean newspapers?"

"Newspapers, TV, wire services. There'll even be a couple of TV producers trying to buy your story to make into a movie of the week."

"That's terrible," she said. She looked as if she might start to cry again.

"Listen. If it'll make you feel any better, I'll check in to the same hotel."

"Why should that make me feel better?"

"We could do Disneyland together."

She sniffed back the encroaching tears and even managed a small smile. "I've never been to Disneyland."

"Neither have I," said James.

James watched her as she packed her bags. She had so much stuff she looked as if she'd emigrated to L.A. When she was ready he called the desk and had them send up two bellboys and a luggage cart. James stood with her as she paid her bill with a credit card. As she was signing the bill he drew her aside. "I don't trust those bellboys," he said. "Keep an eye on your bags."

"My credit card . . ."

"I'll get it."

She moved off to do as he asked. James went back to the desk and collected her credit card. He copied down the name of the issuing bank and the card number before giving it back to her.

Traffic had increased along Wilshire Boulevard. The majority of Los Angelenos go to work early. The doorman, who had come on duty since they'd arrived, was eyeing the panel truck suspiciously, wondering how long it would be before he could legitimately call the police and have it towed away. James threw Betsy's suitcases into the back and they drove to Anaheim.

"Soon as we check in I'll call Ted and tell him where we're at," said James.

"Do we have to?"

"Unless you want him putting out an APB."

She didn't know what that was, but she was sure she didn't want it.

James filled in the registration slip in the name of Mr. and Mrs. Peter Small of London, England. "A double room, sir?" asked the clerk.

"Adjoining rooms," said James. "I snore." He used his best English accent.

The clerk glanced at the registration slip. "Welcome to California, Mr. Small. Have a nice day," he said.

Upstairs James had the bellboy unlock the connecting doors. The rooms were neat, clean and impersonal. While Betsy unpacked, he called Ted at police HQ.

"Shit!" said Ted as soon as he came on the line. "I just heard the broad checked out of her hotel. I was gonna put out an APB."

James told him where they were and the reasons for being there. Ted promised to see the information wasn't leaked.

"Anything new?" asked James.

"We haven't found a floater yet," said Ted.

"Do you expect to?"

"I don't know what to expect, buddy."

"Are you going to keep me clued in on this?"

"What do you want to know?"

"Anything. Everything."

"You keep me clued in on the girl, I'll do the same for you."

"She's got a cast-iron, copper-bottomed alibi, for Christ's sake."

"I know. She was romping in the sack with you."

"So?"

"What's your alibi?"

"The same."

"What a coincidence," said Ted.

James and Betsy went down to the coffee shop where she ordered juice, coffee, bacon, eggs, toast and a side order of pancakes. Adversity sure didn't mess up her appetite. James ordered juice and coffee.

"What happens now?" she asked. He told her he was going to drive back into Beverly Hills. "You said you were going to take me to Disneyland," she complained.

"Later. Meantime stay in your room. Watch some TV. You might even be on yourself."

"Maybe I should dye my hair," she said. "So's people won't recognize me."

"I like it the way it is."

"Do you really. It's natural, you know."

"I know," said James. When he left her in the coffee shop, she was blushing again.

He arrived at Wise's office at nine fifty. "Bradley's gone, missing," James said to Wise.

"He only arrived yesterday," said Wise, not particularly interested.

"Now he's gone. And he's left a real mess behind."

"Listen . . . you've got all your rent in advance. He wants to take off and leave the place untidy, what do you care?"

James told him exactly how untidy the place had been left.

"You're kidding me, of course," said Wise.

James assured him he wasn't. Wise sat down behind his desk. Then he stood up again and went to the bar to pour himself a glass of water. His secretary hadn't changed the water jug since yesterday. Something dead was floating on the top of the glass. He looked at it for what seemed to be a very long time. Then he put the glass down and poured himself a brandy instead. He swallowed it in one long draught. Pulling a terrible face, he came back to his desk and sat down again.

"God! That's awful," he said. James didn't know if he was referring to the taste of the brandy or what he had just been told.

"Who put Bradley onto you?" asked James.

"An associate in London called me. Bradley was looking for a house. He remembered your ex-wife's place. I called her. She told me to call you."

"Who's your associate in London?"

The brandy had started to take a bite. It had dulled the shock and sharpened the suspicions.

"Why should I tell you?"

"Because I might be able to get you off the hook."

"What hook? What are you talking about?"

James wasn't too sure, so he tried making up the scenario as he went along. "The only people who knew Bradley was going to be at my house were you, your London colleague and me. One of us must have told Langer. It sure as hell wasn't me."

"I never heard of Langer till you asked about him the other day."

"I believe you. But I don't know about the cops. See, whoever told Langer could be considered an accessory."

"Come on! That's ridiculous."

James hoped the diplomas hanging on the office wall were for business management and not law. "That's the law, Mr. Wise. Take my word for it. The sooner you tell me the name of your contact in London, the safer we'll all be." All it needed now was for Wise to ask why, and James would be up shit creek.

"Barton, Carmichael and Phelps. At least, that's the name of the firm. My friend is Simon Wilson. He's a junior partner."

"What's his number?"

Wise gave it to him. "You're doing the right thing," said James. He started for the door.

"That word you used the other day?" said Wise. "Watcher?"

"Minder," said James.

"Some minder you turned out to be," said Wise.

Back in the pickup he tuned into an all-news station. The accident on the San Diego freeway had been cleared and traffic was now moving at its normal snail's pace; the White House denied everything; the weather was pretty good and going to get better; the L.A. Raiders had been slaughtered over the weekend, and, stand by for an update on the Malibu massacre. It turned out there was no update, but they repeated what they'd already put out. Three foreign nationals, names withheld pending notification of next of kin, were brutally done to death at the Malibu beach house formerly owned by movie star Katherine Long, who is best remembered for an Oscar-winning performance in *The Cheaters*.

The present owner of the property, James Reed, ex-husband of Katherine Long, is unavailable for comment. Another witness, a female whose identity has not yet been established, is also unavailable for comment. The police are understood to be trying to locate Jonathan Bradley in connection with the multiple slaying. Bradley, also a foreign national, is renting the former Katherine Long house. When contacted, a spokesman for Ms. Long told this station that Ms. Long has had no connection with the house for the past five years. Lieutenant Edward Applethwaite of the LAPD homicide division, when asked how his investigation was progressing, had no comment. Stay tuned to this channel for further updates.

James called Ted from the parking lot. "I'm back in town. Have you found Bradley?"

"Not yet."

"What about Langer?"

"We're still looking."

"Have you got somebody watching the airport?"

"We have."

"Have you checked the hotels?"

"Still doing it." An edge was creeping into his voice.

"How about that corporation, the one that owns the limo. What have they got to say?"

"There's nobody there. Seems they only come in a couple of times a week to pick up mail."

"Listen . . . you want a word of advice?"

"No," said Ted and hung up the phone.

So fuck you, Ted Applethwaite. James looked up Glaner, Inc., in the phone book. There was a Beverly Hills address, not more than three minutes' walk from where he was. He tried the number. There was no answer. He left the truck in the parking lot and walked the block and a half to the offices of Glaner, Inc.

It was a high-rise building, the street floor occupied by a bank. The directory in the lobby announced that Glaner, Inc., was in suite 1142. James joined a gaggle of secretaries in the elevator. They'd just been to the coffee shop in the basement and were carrying plastic cups of coffee, sticky donuts and danish pastries wrapped in paper napkins. They all got out on the tenth floor, leaving the elevator awash with the smell of cheap perfume and warm pastry.

James got out one floor higher. Suite 1142 was at the far end of the passage. Double doors with a discreet brass plate announced Glaner, Inc. James tried the door. It was locked. He banged on it. Nobody answered. It took him just thirty seconds to force the lock and slip inside. Mail was spread around the floor where it had fallen after being stuffed through the mail slot.

He ignored the mail as he came in. First things first. Rule one for being in a place where you weren't supposed to be was to locate a back way out. There wasn't a back way out. The suite consisted of an outer reception area, an inner office designed to be used by a couple of secretaries and an executive office that looked out across the rooftops of Beverly Hills. The whole suite was furnished with anonymous-looking medium-quality stuff that was probably rented.

James went through the place quickly. Nothing. No papers, no memos, empty filing cabinets, empty drawers. He went back into the reception area. He poked through the mail spread around the floor. Most of it was junk mail. There was an envelope from the owners of the building. There was one from Pacific Bell and another from SoCal Edison. There was one from a gasoline company. It looked like an invoice. He started to open it carefully, meaning to seal it back down after he'd checked the contents. Then he became impatient and ripped it open. He was right. It was an invoice for gas. Close to two thousand dollars. That was a lot of gas, enough to drive the stretch limo to New York and back. Or enough to fly a private airplane from here to practically anyplace.

He didn't bother resealing the envelope. He stuck it in his pocket instead. He redistributed the mail around the floor and let himself out of the office.

James called the gas company and asked for the accounts department. A girl came on the line wanting to know how she could help.

"I've got a problem with a bill," said James. He gave her the account and invoice number. She asked him to hold while she punched it up on her computer.

"What seems to be the problem, sir?" she said finally.

"I didn't order any gas," he said.

"My records show the fuel was ordered and pumped on the tenth of this month."

"That's only last week. How come you got the bill out so fast."

"We're computerized, sir," she said smugly.

"I'm not paying it," said James.

That threw her. She put him through to her supervisor. "What seems to be the problem, sir?"

James made a great deal of noise disclaiming all knowledge of the charge. This generated a fair amount of activity at the other end of the line and the supervisor's supervisor took over.

Finally, five minutes later, James thanked them politely for their trouble and hung up. He now had the information that the fuel had been ordered by Captain Wyman, who was authorized to sign for fuel on the Glaner account and, as usual, the aircraft had been fueled at Burbank Airport the moment it had landed. He called Burbank Airport and asked to speak to someone in traffic control. He was put through and eventually told they weren't permitted to give out the type of information he was seeking.

"I just want to know if it's taken off yet," he said.

"I can't tell you that," said the guy on the line.

"Try looking out the window," said James. "Either it's there or it's not."

"I'm not permitted to divulge—"

"It's my aircraft, for Christ's sake," cut in James.

"What's your name?"

"Glaner."

"Hold on, please, Mr. Glaner."

When he came back he sounded nervous. "Are we to assume you didn't authorize the departure, Mr. Glaner?"

"I authorized it," said James. "I just wanted to know they'd got away okay."

"Yes sir." The guy sounded relieved. The airport wasn't going to be blamed for a missing aircraft. "They filed their flight plan at six A.M. They took off at six thirty."

"For New York," said James.

"No sir. Mexico City."

"Of course," said James. "I forgot." He thanked the guy and hung up. Ted Applethwaite could keep a man at LAX until the cows came home, he wasn't going to run into Langer. He started to call Ted with the news, then he thought the hell with it. Let him find out for himself. That's what he was paid for. He walked back to the parking lot, collected the panel truck and drove back to Anaheim.

Betsy was in her room glued to the TV screen. "We were on TV," she said.

"We were on the radio too." James had listened to the news during the drive. There had been no further updates. "What are you watching?"

"I'm waiting for a news flash."

"They're not going to interrupt the afternoon soaps for anything as trivial as a triple killing." He crossed in front of her and switched off the TV. "Who's Simon Wilson?" he asked.

"He's a good friend of Jonathan. At least, he was when Jonathan still had friends."

"The kind of friend he'd call if he was in trouble?"

"He can hardly call Simon if he's dead," she said with a certain amount of venom.

"On the other hand, if he does call friend Simon, we'll know he's *not* dead," said James patiently.

She thought about it for a moment. "You're right."

"So give him a call."

"Simon?"

"Sure Simon. Ask if he's heard from his old buddy. You'll be doing him a favor. Chances are he hasn't heard what's happened. Better to get the news from you than hear it on the breakfast show."

"I don't have his number."

"I do," said James. He gave her the number he'd extracted from Wise.

"That's the office," said Betsy. "I know because I call Daddy there. Simon certainly won't be there now. It's the middle of the night in London."

James checked his watch. In fact, it was about ten thirty P.M. in London. "Do you have a home number for him?"

She didn't.

"We'll get it from Information. Where does he live?"

"In the country somewhere." She didn't know exactly where except it was about forty minutes out of London.

"How about Daddy? Would he know?"

She doubted it. Senior partners didn't carry around the home phone numbers of junior partners.

"Try," said James.

She tried calling Daddy at home. There was no answer. "What happens now?" she asked.

James had been up all night. "I'm going to bed."

"God! How can you think of sex at a time like this."

"I wasn't," said James. "But I'm open to offers."

She switched on the TV again and he went to bed.

She woke him a couple of hours later. "You're wanted on the phone," she said.

It was Ted Applethwaite. "Thought you'd like to know. The members of the fourth estate seem to have lifted the siege on your house. I've still got a man there, he just phoned in."

"Is he staying?"

"There's no need." James thanked him and hung up.

"What was that about?" asked Betsy, who was standing at the end of his bed, trying to look as if she weren't interested in his phone conversation.

"The lieutenant says it's okay for me to go home."

"Did he say anything about my passport?"

"Your name didn't come up."

"You're not going to leave me here alone?"

"You can come with me."

"I don't want to go back there," she said. "It's too frightening."

James thought it was frightening too. Not for the same reason as Betsy. He had a sneaky feeling that maybe there might have been some unfinished business left over from last night. After all, Betsy had said it herself, she could have been in Jonathan's bed. Maybe somebody else had known it too.

"Okay. We've paid for the rooms. We'll stay here," he said.

She liked that idea fine.

At first, Betsy had wanted to go out to dinner. Then she caught the five-o'clock news on TV. The local station had done a good job. There was coverage of the house, swarming with police; there was a photograph of "James Reed, the owner of the house"; and there were two or three shots of Katherine Long, "the movie-star ex-wife of James Reed, former owner of the property." After all, this was Hollywood. A picture of a movie star was a big plus to any story. But everything was dressing. There had been no breaks in the case. A reporter stated that the motive for the killings must have been burglary because, he had been reliably informed, Mr. Jonathan Bradley was known to travel with items of considerable value. As to the whereabouts of Mr. Bradley, the LAPD had mounted a massive search, involving, among others, the coast guard.

One of the neighbors was interviewed on camera. James knew him vaguely. He lived half a dozen houses up the beach. Nothing like this had happened in the neighborhood before and he, for one, was going to double-check all the locks before he went to bed tonight.

"Perhaps we won't go out," said Betsy, after the newscast. "Someone might recognize you."

James ordered a meal from room service. Betsy asked him to order a bottle of brandy too.

At ten thirty he announced he was tired and was going to bed. He closed the connecting doors, undressed and showered. He came out of the bathroom wrapped in a towel to turn down the bed. There was an apologetic tap on the connecting door and

Betsy came in. She was wearing something diaphanous and carrying the half-empty bottle of brandy.

"I can't sleep," she said. Considering he'd only left her ten minutes ago, it wasn't surprising.

"Can I stay with you?" she asked. She caught his expression. "We don't have to . . . I mean . . . there's no need to . . ."

"In that case," said James. "Be my guest."

She was out of her robe and into the bed before he could switch off the overhead light. As he climbed under the sheets, she made a grab for him. He told her it had been one hell of a twenty-four hours. He truly didn't know if he had the energy to do anything but sack out. She accepted his decision and offered to give him a massage . . . just to relax him. He'd always been a sucker for a massage. A real turn-on. So he was as surprised as she must have been when he woke up seven hours later.

4

There was nothing fresh on the early news. They watched it while they ate a room-service breakfast. As soon as they had finished, he told her to call Simon Wilson in London. He would listen in on the conversation on the extension line.

"Barton, Carmichael and Phelps," came the voice from six thousand miles away.

Betsy asked to speak to Simon Wilson.

"Mr. Wilson's office," came another voice.

"This is Betsy Carmichael, Miss Cremin. Is Simon there?"

"Oh, Miss Carmichael, isn't it awful. It was on the news this morning. I told Mr. Wilson when he came in . . . I said I certainly hope Miss Carmichael's all right."

"I'm fine, thank you. Is he there?"

"I'll put you through right away."

There was a short pause before a clipped, very British voice came on the line. "Betsy! Where are you?"

"I'm in Los Angeles."

"I called your hotel. They said you'd checked out. Have you spoken to your father? He's very concerned."

"I'll talk to him later. Listen, Simon, has Jonathan called you?"

There was a short pause on the other end of the line. "I thought . . . he's dead, isn't he?"

"They don't know that for sure. That's why I wanted to know if he'd called."

"No, he hasn't. But if he's not dead, where is he?"

Betsy looked toward the other side of the room to where James was listening on the extension. "What do you want me to say?" said her expression. James shrugged. It made no difference. "I don't know where he is. Nobody does," said Betsy, back into the phone.

"I think you should come home right away," said Simon.

"I can't. The police have taken my passport. They say I'm a witness."

"We'll see about that," said Simon. "Hold on a second."

A minute later another voice came on the line. Deeper, more authoritative. James remembered the type of voice well, even after fifteen years. It was the kind of voice that emerged from a bewigged figure in scarlet robes seated on a judge's bench or from a senior government minister announcing to the public that he knew what was best for them. It took five hundred years of upper-class breeding to perfect those rounded tones.

"Elizabeth. This is your father. You will go straight to the British consulate in Los Angeles and wait there until you hear from me. Is that understood?"

"Yes, Daddy." She sounded around seven years old.

"I shall call Moynebee at the Foreign Office. He'll take care of everything."

"Yes, Daddy."

"There's a good girl. I'll see you tomorrow." The line went dead.

They both hung up their respective phones. "I take it Daddy's quite a big wheel," said James.

She shrugged. She'd never given it much thought. "Is there a British consulate here in Los Angeles?" There was. If there hadn't been, James didn't doubt Daddy's ability to have one opened right away just to take care of his daughter.

"Can you drive me there, please?"

She still sounded like a little girl. A not particularly happy little girl.

"What's bothering you?" asked James. "Daddy's going to take care of everything."

"I didn't get to go to Disneyland."

Daddy had worked very fast. By the time they reached the consulate, word had come through from the Foreign Office in London that Betsy was to be taken in as soon as she arrived. An excessively cheerful young Englishman apologized profusely that the consul himself wasn't around to welcome her, but he hoped he'd manage to make her comfortable. He helped James unload her luggage.

"Be careful," Betsy said to James, before he climbed back into the truck.

"You too. Keep in touch."

She looked as if she might burst into tears any moment. "I think you're super," she said. She kissed him and ran into the consulate. Just before he drove off, the Englishman who'd unloaded the bags came running out of the door.

"I say. Hold on there a jiffy."

James wound down the window.

"Thanks awfully for helping with the bags, driver," said the Englishman. He tipped James one dollar.

Burbank airport was normally twenty minutes' drive from the consulate, but the rush-hour traffic was still on the freeways. It took James forty minutes. He parked the truck and started to ask questions. Half an hour and a hundred dollars later, he knew that the Glaner, Inc., aircraft had left yesterday morning with its regulation crew of two and two passengers, a guy with a limp and another guy who looked like somebody's bad dream. They had arrived at the airport in a stretch limousine that had been turned over to a man who was waiting for it. The only knowledge James had bought for his hundred dollars was that Bradley hadn't flown out of Los Angeles with Langer. Not that James believed he had. But it was worth knowing just the same.

Maybe Ted Applethwaite had been right when he said the press had lifted the siege on his house, but James wasn't taking any chances. He parked the truck a quarter of a mile away and walked to the house along the beach. Fortunately the showery weather was keeping the locals away from their surfside constitutionals. James didn't want to bump into anyone he knew and have to start apologizing for ruining the neighborhood. He let himself in through the rear gate and went straight to the guest house. Somebody had fixed the front gate. The police probably.

His answering machine was blinking steadily at him. Its message capacity was full. He knew what they'd be before he checked them. Would he call the L.A. *Times*, the *Herald Examiner*, ABC, NBC, CBS, Channel 5, Channel 9, three publications he hadn't heard of and the *National Enquirer*. There were half a dozen hang-ups, a message to call Gloria and another to call Katherine. He wiped the machine clean and reset it. Then he called Roger's Engine and Body Shop.

"Shit, man!" said Roger when James identified himself. "What's going down at your place?"

"Is my car ready?"

"I mean . . . like wow!"

"My car?"

"Crazy, man!"

"For Christ's sake, Roger. Is my car ready?"

"Oh, sure. You want me to bring it over?"

"I'll pick it up."

"No trouble, Mr. Reed. I can be there in fifteen minutes. Hey! Maybe you'll show me where it happened."

"I'll be with you in half an hour," said James. He hung up.

He walked over to the main house and let himself in. The police had left the place looking like a garbage tip. They'd searched the house and then searched it again. James had no idea what he was expecting to find that they could have overlooked, but he looked anyway. There was a chalked outline on the floor of the bedroom where Cooper had died. There was still a lot of dried blood and God knows what else on the wall. Most of Cooper's belongings were still hanging in the closet. Knowing the police would have been there before him, James went through the pockets anyway. Then he looked in the drawers and the cabinet in the bathroom. Nothing. It was the same in Fairman's room. The bed had been stripped and they had taken the mattress and the covers. There was a dried bloodstain on the floor.

The whole upstairs was going to have to be redecorated, even if it was only to remove the stink of death. James knew the death smell was only in his mind, but it was still overpowering.

Bradley's stuff was scattered around his dressing room, some of it still in the suitcases that there hadn't been time to unpack. James went through everything quickly, realizing it might have been better to do all this before he'd called the police. There was nothing of the remotest interest.

He almost didn't bother with Jane's bedroom. He knew he'd find nothing. But he went in anyway. The police had been through there too, they hadn't made such a mess of it. Her clothes were hanging neatly in the closet. The blouse she had been wearing the day she'd arrived was in the dirty clothes basket along with a pair of pantyhose, panties and bra. She had set out some personal things on the nightstand, a small alarm clock, an antique snuffbox containing wax earplugs, a pretty little potpourri jar and silver-framed photograph of a middle-aged couple standing in the front yard of a small English seaside bungalow. James wondered briefly if they'd heard the news yet. He was about to leave the room when he realized that something was missing. Cooper had told him Jane was nurse as well as secretary. Okay, if she was a nurse, where was her medical stuff? Among other things, she gave Bradley his shots. Vitamins, uppers, downers and, if he'd read Bradley correctly, some of the hard stuff. There had to be a medical bag with needles and vials and cotton balls and disinfectant. He went through the room again quickly. There was nothing. Maybe the police took it.

Bradley's two automobiles were still in the garage. James tried the doors. They were locked. He hadn't seen any keys during his tour of the house, which probably meant the police had taken them. He was going to have to ask Ted Applethwaite what he was supposed to do with the cars and the rest of Bradley's stuff.

He drove to Roger's place. His car had been resprayed more or less the same color.

"Four hundred bucks," said Roger.

"You told me three fifty."

"As long as it was here, I checked under the hood."

"What did you find?"

"Take my word for it, Mr. Reed. You don't want to know. Next time she dies on you, give her a decent burial."

Sam Cortes was waiting when he got back to the house. "The lieutenant wants to see you," he said.

"Tell him I'll be down later."

"He wants to see you now. I'm to take you in myself."

"You take me in, you'll have to bring me home."

"The way the lieutenant's talking, I wouldn't bank on coming home."

"Have you got some kind of a warrant?"

"You're not gonna give me a hard time are you?"

"I'm not going to give you anything. Tell Ted I'll be down to see him later."

Cortes started to look confused. "Listen, he'll chew out my ass if I don't bring you in right now."

James thought about it for a moment. There wasn't much point in being perverse just for the sake of it. "Okay. I'll go see him now. But I'll take my own car."

Cortes agreed, reluctantly. He looked at James's car as they walked out. "I'll be behind you all the way," he said.

"You worried I might try to give you the slip?"

"I'm worried your car's not gonna make it."

Ted Applethwaite was real pissed off. "Sit down," he said to James, as Cortes showed him into the office. "Beat it, Sam." None too happy, Cortes went out and closed the door. Ted took out a pack of cigarettes, stuck one in his mouth and struck a match on the THANK YOU FOR NOT SMOKING sign on his desk. He puffed angrily for a moment.

"I thought you'd given up," said James.

"I give up every week. Then someone like you comes along and I get started again." James could see Ted needed no prompting, so he kept his mouth shut. "I ought to lock you up for withholding information," said Ted. James still didn't say anything. "Why didn't you tell me this guy Langer left the country?"

"I only just found out," said James.

"You're a liar. You knew yesterday. You leaned on some poor schmuck out at Burbank."

There didn't seem to be much point in denying it. "Are you pissed off because I found out before you did?"

"I'm pissed off because you're sticking your nose where it doesn't belong. You're not a cop, so do me a favor and stop trying to act like one."

"I've got a personal interest," said James.

"You sure have, buddy. If I didn't know you personally, you'd be behind bars by now. A number-one suspect."

"Come on! You heard my alibi."

"Some fucking alibi. A flaky Brit broad who could be as deep in this as you are."

"You don't believe that."

"Maybe I didn't an hour ago. But I've just had a telephone call, buddy. The broad has gone to ground in a foreign consulate. Hands off, Mr. Policeman, or you could start a diplomatic incident. I mean, what kind of shit is that unless she's got something to hide? And if she's got something to hide, I figure the same goes for you."

James had to agree it was a good line of reasoning. "I don't have anything to hide," he said.

"Is that a fact? So how did you know about the airplane out at Burbank?"

Maybe it wouldn't be such a good idea to admit to illegal entry of the Glaner offices. "It wasn't too hard."

"What kind of an answer is that?"

James figured it was time to start leaning on his rights. "It's the only one you're going to get. And unless you've got a good solid reason for keeping me here, I'm leaving." He started to get to his feet.

"Sit down, for Christ's sake." Ted was still angry, but James could sense that it wasn't directed at him any longer. Maybe it hadn't been from the start. He just happened to be handy. He sat again. "Anything strange strike you about this case?" Ted asked.

"Practically everything."

"We've got a triple killing on our hands, maybe four, we don't know yet. Why aren't the media still swarming all over? Shit, the bodies aren't even cold yet."

The same thought had crossed James's mind, but he'd been too concerned with other things to bother with it.

"You want to know what I think?" said Ted. "I think there's some heavy pressure being applied. I mean real heavy."

"What kind of pressure?"

"Government. Diplomatic. International. You name it."

"Come on, Ted. You know as well as I do. When it comes to the press, official pressure to lay off works the opposite way. They get twice as nosy and three times as offensive."

"Depends where the pressure's applied. Think about it, buddy! Half the newspapers and TV stations in the country are owned by foreigners. Okay, so some of them have taken out American citizenship, that's the law. But they're just the high-profile guys. Don't try to tell me that a lot of the so-called proprietors aren't just front men for the money. And the money's German or Japanese or Arab. Shit, they own most of everything else. The important real estate; the goddamn farms in the Midwest; majority shareholdings in industry and airlines and oil outfits; they've monopolized the auto and the electronics industries. I kid you not, James, there's a fucking great sign hanging over these United States. It reads SOLD."

It was an interesting premise, but James had lost the drift. "What's that got to do with the case?"

"I'll tell you. Some foreign government doesn't want a big hoo-ha made of our little case. Don't ask me why, I don't know. So they call Mr. Big, who's a national of theirs, and they tell him to lean on his people over here. At the same time, he will call his big buddies in Berlin or Tokyo or London, tell them you rub my back, I'll rub yours. Maybe even call the United States Treasury . . . tell them unless they apply some governmental pressure then maybe all these foreign big wheels will withdraw the money they've got on deposit over here, all six hundred billion dollars of it. We're not asking much, Uncle Sam. Let the media cover the story, by all means, but don't blow it up too much, and let it die quietly."

"Why should they do that?"

"I told you. I don't know. But I've been doing some checking. Bradley, for instance. Know who he is?"

"His father's a banker."

"His father is the biggest banker in Europe, buddy. London, Paris, Berlin, Switzerland. You name it. Wait till I tell you what bank I'm talking about?"

"Glessen."

Ted started to look angry again. "Shit! You knew! Why didn't you tell me?"

"It didn't seem relevant."

"Is there anything else you don't consider relevant? Like Langer for instance."

James shook his head. "I don't know anything about Langer."

"You knew he'd left the country." James couldn't argue with him there, so he said nothing. "I rang my wife's cousin. The schmuck's a professor of economics in one of those colleges back East. He's written a couple of books about international money men. I asked him about Langer. It's not common knowledge, but it seems friend Langer owns the Glessen banks . . . all of them."

That *was* news to James. He wondered if Betsy knew and, if she did, why she hadn't mentioned it.

"So the way I figure it," Ted continued, "this guy Langer has got some kind of a hard-on for Bradley. Business maybe. Maybe something personal. He talks to him. Maybe tries to straighten it out. Bradley doesn't go for it. So he offs Bradley. At the same time he has to off the others because they're witnesses. He knocks off some bread from the house to make it look like a burglary. Then he flies out, makes a couple of phone calls when he gets home to get the publicity quieted down. What do you think?"

"I think it stinks."

"Why?"

"If Langer's the big wheel you say he is, he's not going to do a thing like that himself."

"So he pays somebody to do it for him. You can get your own mother killed in this town for a hundred bucks."

"So where's Bradley?"

"Feeding the fish."

"Why didn't they knock him off in the house with the others?"

"He gave them the slip and ran down to the beach."

"He couldn't run to the toilet."

"So maybe he was taking a midnight stroll. That's where they found him. They killed him there and threw him in the ocean."

"I still think it stinks."

Ted sighed. "So do I. But that's the line I'm gonna take."

"Whose idea is that?"

"What do you care? Listen, I'm a public employee. Five years from now I can start drawing a pension. The way things are going right now, my pension's gonna buy me a pack of cigarettes and a gallon of gas, but it's all I'm gonna have unless I can get me a job on the outside. I've been told jobs on the outside are gonna be very thin on the ground if I fuck up this investigation."

"Told by who?"

"What difference does it make. So I'm not gonna fuck it up. I'm gonna make my report . . . person or persons unknown . . . motive, robbery. Who knows, we might get lucky and some fisherman will land Bradley on the end of his line."

"And Langer gets away with it."

"He's out of my jurisdiction."

"Haven't you ever heard of extradition?"

"It would be easier extraditing the Pope."

James thought about it for a moment. "Is that why you asked me down here? To tell me this shit?"

"I asked you down here to tell you to lay off. If you don't, maybe the person or persons unknown won't be unknown anymore. *Capisce?*"

"Loud and clear," said James. "Can I go now?"

"Sure you can go. Next week, my place."

James didn't understand. He said so. "Our poker school, buddy. Next week, it's my turn."

"Right. See you next week," said James.

Sam Cortes was waiting outside Ted's office. He looked a little surprised when James came out. "Where you going?" he asked.

"Put your cuffs away, Sam. I'm going home," said James.

He was halfway back to the beach before he remembered he hadn't asked Ted whether or not any of his guys had found Jane's medical bag.

There were a couple of messages on his machine when he got home. One was from Betsy. "I'm at the airport. My plane leaves in ten minutes. I just wanted to say thank-you again. Perhaps . . ." James could hear somebody say something to her. "I'm just coming," she said. Then back to the phone. Whatever she had been going to say, she'd changed her mind. "I hope you'll be all right." She said good-bye quickly and hung up. The other message was from Roger. James had forgotten to sign his check.

There was nothing to eat in the fridge. James was about to drive to the market when he remembered Cooper's shopping expedition. Sure as hell nobody over at the main house was going to need the stuff. The house still smelled of death. He opened some of the downstairs windows before going through into the kitchen.

Apart from what Cooper had used for the last supper, everything was still there. He found a plastic bag and started to help himself from the fridge. Raiding his tenants' food reminded him that he should have asked Ted what he was supposed to do with all the personal effects still in the house. He'd call him tomorrow. He checked the freezer. There was enough food in there to last him a month. He chose a couple of bottles of wine and went back to the guest house, where he started to cook himself supper.

He was just sitting down to eat when the phone rang. He answered it carefully, without identifying himself.

"This is Sam Cortes."

"Jesus, Cortes. When are you going to get off my back?"

"The lieutenant's on his way to Marina del Rey. He wants you to meet him. They've fished out a floater. Maybe it's Bradley."

"Maybe it is. What's it got to do with me?"

"You're the only one who knows what he looks like. Meet him at the coast guard dock soon as you can." The phone went dead.

James reached Marina del Rey forty minutes later. He asked around and finally located the coast guard dock. Ted Applethwaite was in the small office talking football with one of the duty officers. He saw James through the window and came out to join him. He looked tired. "Thanks for coming," he said. He led James toward the end of the jetty where there was a coast guard cutter tied up. A couple of guys were hosing down the deck. On the jetty, close to the gangplank, was something draped in oilcloth. Nobody seemed to be taking any notice of it. Water splashing from the deck hoses beaded across the oilcloth.

"Watch it, fellas!" called Ted. He pulled back one end of the oilcloth and looked at James.

"Well?"

James looked down at the body. "What do you want me to say?"

"Is it Bradley?"

James looked again. The corpse must have been in the water a long time. Apart from general wear and tear caused by submersion, some predatory fishes had been at work. His or her own mother would have had trouble identifying it. Hair was gone; features mostly nibbled away; eye sockets empty; flesh bloated; only one thing was clear, this had been a short, fat person.

"No," said James.

"Are you sure?"

Something in the tone of Ted's voice made him look again. It still wasn't Bradley. "Is it male or female?"

"Would I be asking you if it was Bradley if it was female?"

"I don't know, Ted. Would you?"

Ted looked as if he was about to lose his cool. He controlled himself and repeated the question. "Is it Bradley?"

It was no skin off his nose. "Maybe," said James.

"I need more than a maybe."

"What exactly do you need, Ted?"

"I need an identification, for Christ's sake. Now tell me this is Bradley and we can all go home."

Right! And your pension is safe and you'll find yourself a nice job when you retire doing security work for some big international corporation. And why not, you've paid your dues.

"It's Bradley," said James.

"Are you sure?"

"Don't push your luck." James turned and started back along the jetty.

After a few yards Ted caught up with him. "Thanks," he said.

"You're welcome. What do you want me to do with his stuff?"

"Whose stuff?"

"Bradley's. The stuff he left at my house."

"As far as I'm concerned, you can help yourself."

"What do I say if he comes back."

"He's dead, James. You've just identified the body. Right?" He wasn't exactly begging, but it came pretty close.

"Right," said James. He started away. Then he remembered something. He turned back to Ted. "Any of your guys find a bag at the house?"

"What kind of a bag?"

"Something that a doctor might carry around . . . or a nurse maybe."

"Nothing like that," said Ted. "Why?"

"Just curious. Can I go home now?"

"Sure you can. Remember, my place next Tuesday."

James went home.

He tried heating up his dinner. It wasn't successful. He ended up tipping most of it down the garbage disposal. The wine was okay, though. He finished one bottle and debated whether he should open the second. It was no contest. He opened it. He was about to pour his third glass when the phone rang. He didn't want to talk to anyone right now, so he switched on the answering machine. It picked up the call right away. First his own voice announcing that he wasn't in right now and if the caller would care to leave a message he'd get right back to them, then an empty silence as if the person on the other end was debating whether to commit themselves. Finally, "Mr. Reed, this is Karl Langer. I'm calling long distance. Would you be kind enough to . . ."

James picked up the phone, which switched off the machine. "Reed here," he said.

"Good evening, Mr. Reed. What can you tell me about the events that recently took place?"

"I was about to ask you the same thing," said James, starting to wish he'd taken it easy with the second bottle of wine.

"If I knew anything, I'd not be wasting your time," said Langer. The tone of his voice said "*my* time." "All I know is what I have heard on the news bulletins."

"Then you know as much as I do," said James.

"If I thought that was the case, I'd not be asking you these questions. Has anything been discovered yet about the whereabouts of Jonathan Bradley?"

"I've just got back from identifying a body," said James.

There was a long silence from the other end. James could hear the echoing emptiness of the transcontinental connection. "And?" said Langer, finally.

"You can read about it in the papers tomorrow."

"I'd prefer that you tell me."

"I identified the body as Bradley. Is that what you want to hear?"

"I want to hear the truth."

"It wasn't Bradley."

Another pause. "Then why did you say it was?"

"Expediency," said James.

"For whom?"

"I was under the impression it was for you, Langer. Case now closed. RIP Jonathan Bradley."

"I think you and I should have a talk," said Langer.

"That's what we're doing, isn't it?"

"A personal talk. Face to face."

"I don't like Mexico City."

"I'm not in Mexico City."

"I didn't think you would be," said James.

"So why did you say that?"

"That's where you were supposed to be going at six o'clock the other morning."

"Did the police tell you that?"

"All my own work," said James.

"Do you mind telling me how you went about it?"

"A small bribe. A little larceny, and a lot of lying."

"Can you be more specific?"

What's he going to do? thought James. Sue me? He gave Langer a rundown of how he'd burglarized the offices of Glaner, Inc., and the follow-up that led him to Burbank Airport where he'd got the information that Langer had flown to Mexico City.

"Interesting," said Langer. "But there's nothing sinister about it. I frequently instruct my air crew to file a misleading flight plan. It helps to preserve my privacy. However, it reinforces a decision I've made about you. I'm in Zurich at the moment. I could meet you in London or Paris. Your choice."

"I think I'll stay right here," said James.

"It could be to your advantage."

"Mr. Langer, at the risk of using a cliché, I don't like people who get away with murder. Only in your case the cliché is meant literally."

"You honestly think I was responsible?" said Langer.

"Certainly. And I was hell-bent on trying to prove it."

"What changed your mind?"

"I haven't changed my mind. It's just that I realized I was flogging a dead horse. Nobody cares. Nobody gives a goddamn."

"That's where you're wrong, Mr. Reed. I care very much.

That's why I want to talk to you. If you won't come to Europe then I shall come to Los Angeles. I shall be there day after tomorrow."

"If it's just to tell me you're not responsible, Langer, don't bother. You can lie to me just as easily over the phone."

"I have no reason to lie to you. You said it yourself. Nobody cares. I could tell you here and now that I killed those people and there's nothing you could do about it."

He was right, of course. "Look, Langer, it's over. The official line is that the killings were done by an overenthusiastic thief. You say you didn't do it. Okay. Everybody seems happy to agree with you."

"It wasn't a thief," said Langer. "I know things were stolen, but that had nothing to do with the murders or with the disappearance of Bradley."

"You know this, or you're guessing?"

"I know it, Mr. Reed."

"So, what do you want with me?"

"I'm interested in locating the real culprit. I think you can be of assistance."

"What's wrong with the police? That's what they're paid for."

"I don't wish to involve the authorities."

James started to consider what was being said. It was too complicated to rush. "Give me a number and I'll call you back," he said.

"Certainly," said Langer, without hesitation. He gave James an eight-digit telephone number. "I'll wait for your call," he said and hung up.

James started to pour himself another glass of wine. Then he changed his mind and made some coffee instead. The coffee didn't help so he went for a walk. Some kids had lit a bonfire a few hundred yards down the beach. James could see them outlined by the firelight. The sound of Tina Turner bounced toward him across the water. He wasn't looking for company right now so he walked in the opposite direction. It was twenty minutes before he headed back to the house. The party along the beach had livened up. More fuel had been thrown on the fire and the music was louder. James reckoned it wouldn't be long now before one of the neighbors called the law. He let himself into the guest house, made a fresh pot of coffee and called Zurich.

Langer answered the phone himself. "Yes, Mr. Reed?"

"Let's make it London," said James. "Day after tomorrow, providing I can get a flight."

"I'll see that you get a flight," said Langer. "Somebody will be in touch with you later today."

"It's ten thirty already," said James.

"I'm sorry. Here it is seven thirty A.M. Tomorrow then. You will be met at the airport. A hotel will be arranged."

"Nothing too fancy. I can't afford it."

"I shall be paying," said Langer. "And Mr. Reed, what prompted you to change your mind?"

"Do you really want to know?"

"I wouldn't ask if I didn't."

"I still think you might have done it. If you did, I want to nail you for it."

James heard something suspiciously like a chuckle on the other end of the line. Then again, it could have been a bad connection.

"I'll see you the day after tomorrow," said Langer. The line went dead. Now James finished the second bottle of wine.

He was awakened by the phone at eight thirty A.M. "Mr. James Reed?" A woman's voice.

"I think so," said James. Never believe anybody who told you good wine didn't give you a hangover.

"This is the offices of Glaner, Incorporated. I have your reservation for you. Do you have a pencil?" James stumbled out of bed and fetched a pencil and a scribbling pad. He ought to be angry at being dragged out of bed at this hour, but for the woman to be on the phone so early must have meant she'd been up half the night following Langer's orders. "Okay," he said to the phone.

"TWA seven sixty, departing LAX at five thirty-five this afternoon. I'll have a car pick you up at your house at four P.M. The driver will have your ticket. A car and driver will meet your flight at London Heathrow. Estimated time of arrival eleven thirty A.M. tomorrow. Accommodation in London has been arranged."

"Where?" said James. He didn't really care, but he thought he ought to contribute something to the conversation.

"I'm sorry, but I don't know that," said the woman on the line.

"Would you tell me if you did?" said James.

"I'm sorry?"

"Or doesn't Mr. Langer want me to divulge my forwarding address?"

"I don't understand," she said.

"Don't worry about it," said James. "Neither do I."

At four o'clock on the dot somebody rang his front gate. "Car for Mr. Reed," said an immaculately dressed chauffeur. James grabbed up his suitcase, checked that he had his passport and locked up the guest house. The chauffeur handed him an envelope as he got into the rear of the limo. He looked inside. There was one first-class ticket, Los Angeles to London. The fact that he had been booked first class impressed him. But any pleasure that he might have felt was dispelled by the realization that it was a one-way ticket.

5

Flight 760 landed at London's Heathrow ten minutes ahead of schedule. James peered out of the window as they taxied to their arrival gate. The sky was clear blue, not a cloud in sight. Great! He wasn't going to need the overcoat he didn't own. Then the captain announced that the outside temperature was five degrees Celsius, have a nice day. James passed through immigration, and after a fifteen-minute wait, he collected his bag. He walked through the green section of customs unchallenged. Outside the customs hall people were waiting to meet friends and relatives. James didn't have either. What he did have was a young Negro dressed in a light brown chauffeur's uniform holding up a sign with his name on it. He caught the chauffeur's eye as he headed for the main exit, indicating that he was, in fact, James Reed. By the time he reached the exit, pushing his way through embracing couples, the chauffeur had moved around and was waiting for him.

"Mr. Reed. My name is Roland. Allow me to take your bag."

He followed him out of the terminal to where a Rolls-Royce was waiting in flagrant violation of all parking regulations. Next to the Rolls stood a man wearing an airport security uniform.

"Thank you, Mr. Waring," said Roland. "I shall be returning about four P.M. Terminal three. The flight from Zurich."

"I'll be off duty by then. I'll leave word."

Roland thanked him politely. He opened the rear door for James before putting the suitcase in the trunk. As he got in behind the wheel he took an envelope from his pocket and passed it to James. "I was asked to give you this, sir."

James opened it, wondering if it might be his return ticket. It contained ten fifty-pound notes.

"What's this for?" he asked.

"I have no idea, sir." The car pulled away from the curb without a sound. James hadn't even heard the engine starting up.

James tried talking to Roland for the first five minutes. Then the monosyllabic replies started to get on his nerves so he shut up. Whatever services Roland was paid for apart from driving, talking wasn't one of them. They reached the Cromwell Road in twenty minutes. James remembered the area well, it had been part of his manor when he was a cop. What he didn't recall was the hotel outside which they pulled up. It was located in one of the garden squares between the Cromwell and Fulham roads and looked like all its stately terraced neighbors. As the Rolls slid to a stop, a discreetly uniformed man came out of the building and down the steps to the sidewalk. He had the rear door of the Rolls open before James realized they'd arrived. "Good morning, sir. Welcome to Struther's."

Roland handed over James's suitcase from the trunk, touched his cap to James and climbed back into the car. As James mounted the steps to the front door, the Rolls was already half a block away. A discreet brass plate on one side of the entrance announced that this was STRUTHER'S. Apart from that, there was nothing to show that the building was any different from any of the others in the square. The entrance hall looked more like the living room of a stately home than a hotel lobby. There wasn't even a front desk. As James came in, a black-coated, pin-striped man appeared from God knows where. "Take Mr. Reed's bags to two oh four," he said to the uniformed guy. Then he turned to James. "Barlow, sir. I am the assistant manager. If there is anything you require please don't hesitate to let me know. This way please."

James's suitcase had disappeared through a door under the main staircase. Barlow led him to an elevator concealed behind carved wood doors that looked like they might have been looted from Versailles.

"This place is new, isn't it?" said James as the elevator started upward.

"We have been open for six years now, sir."

"Bit small for a hotel, isn't it?" said James, remembering the size of the place from the street.

"We have the two buildings on either side of this one, sir. Five in all. That gives us room for twenty suites."

Five houses of this size should have provided a minimum of sixty good-sized rooms. Some hotel, thought James.

"Incidentally sir, should you be returning here at any time by taxi, it is quite possible that the driver will not know the name Struther's. I suggest you ask for the street address."

"An anonymous hotel," said James.

"That's how we like it, sir," said Barlow.

The elevator doors opened onto a wide carpeted corridor with double doors on either side. Every few yards along both walls stood an antique table or chest. On each of them was a vase of fresh flowers. The walls were paneled, and while James knew very little about paintings, those that were hanging along the corridor looked as though they'd be more at home in the National Gallery. Barlow led the way to 204 and, opening the door, stood back for James to precede him. The suite consisted of a living room, a large bedroom, a bathroom, a dining room and a small kitchen. James reckoned if he could sell the furniture and pictures he'd make enough money to retire. "Are there any messages for me?" he asked Barlow.

Barlow looked upset, as though he was personally responsible for James not getting any messages. "No sir, I'm sorry. Were you expecting anybody in particular?"

"A guy named Langer is supposed to be contacting me."

He brightened up again. "Mr. Langer will be here later this afternoon, sir. I'll inform him you have arrived."

"Is he staying here?"

"But of course, sir. He has his permanent suite on the top floor."

"He uses the hotel often, does he?"

"He *owns* the hotel, sir."

That figures, thought James.

After Barlow left, he made another inspection of the suite. Behind the bookcase in the living room he found the bar, and behind the mirror in the bathroom, he found the sauna. There was nothing in the kitchen except dishes and cutlery, enough to serve a sit-down dinner for twenty people. But he couldn't eat the plates, so he called downstairs and asked for a room-service menu.

"We don't have menus at Struther's, sir. You tell us what you'd like and we will prepare it for you."

Supercilious sod, thought James. "I'd like some smoked salmon, a steak and a green salad."

"T-bone, filet or rump, sir?"

"New York," said James. Sort that one out!

"Fifteen minutes, sir." The line went dead.

James drew a bath. There was no bathtub in the guest house at home, just a shower. He'd almost forgotten what it was like to soak in an outsized tub of hot water. He was still wallowing like a contented seal when there was a tap on the bathroom door.

"Who is it?"

"Your lunch is served, sir."

He climbed out of the tub and wrapped himself in a terry robe he found hanging behind the door. A place had been laid up for him at the head of the dining room table. As he came in a waiter emerged from the kitchen carrying a plate of smoked salmon. He placed it in front of James.

"What wine would you like, sir?"

James said he'd leave it up to the waiter, who disappeared back into the kitchen and reemerged with a bottle of white wine wrapped in a linen napkin. He poured James a glass and stood back while he tasted it. "How do you prefer your steak cooked, sir?" he asked, when James had pronounced the wine drinkable.

James told him he liked it rare. The waiter went back into the kitchen. James heard the rattling of pots and pans. At Struther's, room service obviously meant more than that. Here they actually cooked the meal in the suite. Whatever else Langer did, he sure owned a classy hotel.

After lunch James took a walk. Once-familiar places weren't even recognizable any longer. A couple more high-rise hotels; a supermarket where once had been half a dozen small, family-run stores; half a block of Victorian houses demolished to make room for studio apartments; and the movie theater he'd frequented, now a bingo hall. He remembered there was an afternoon drinking club somewhere in the neighborhood, a place he'd busted on more than one occasion. He couldn't even find the street, let alone the club.

The sun was still shining but it was very cold. After fifteen minutes he hailed a taxi and asked to be driven to Harrods. There he bought himself a topcoat, using money the chauffeur had given him. Maybe it was intended for something else, but he doubted it. Langer struck him as being the kind of man who invested heavily up front to make it difficult for a person to turn him down later. But if he thought five hundred quid and a couple of days in a fancy hotel was going to buy James Reed into doing something he didn't want to, then he was dead wrong. More or less.

Barlow was right. The taxi driver he hailed outside Harrods had never heard of Struther's Hotel. James gave him the street and the number.

"No hotel there, guv, take my word." When he discovered he was wrong, he grew truculent, as though the whole thing were James's fault. As James came into the hotel, Barlow appeared suddenly.

"Mr. Langer has arrived, sir. He asked me to tell you he expects you for dinner at nine. Informal."

"Where?"

"In his apartment, sir. It's on the fourth floor."

"What number?"

"There's only one apartment on the fourth floor," said Barlow.

"Tell him I might be a little late," said James, heading for the elevator. No point in having the hotel staff think he was at Langer's beck and call, even if he was.

Jet lag hit him quite hard around six. He decided he'd take a nap. When he woke, it was eight forty-five. He doused his face in cold water, brushed his teeth, pulled on shirt and pants, topped it with a sweater and took the stairs to the fourth floor. The same type of corridor up here, but with only one door leading from it. No number on the door. James looked for a bell, couldn't find one, so he knocked. He glanced at his watch. It was exactly nine o'clock. So much for being late. The door was opened by Michael. James's arm and foot gave a small retroactive twinge of pain as if to remind him to behave himself.

If Michael remembered their last meeting, he gave no sign. In fact he gave nothing at all. He just pulled the door wider and stepped back. James assumed this was an invitation to enter and walked in.

Langer's suite looked the same as James's only bigger. Langer himself was standing at the far side of the living room talking softly into a telephone. He finished his conversation quickly and hung up. He took his walking cane from where it was propped against the table and limped across the room toward James.

"Good of you to come, Mr. Reed." He didn't offer to shake hands. "Please, sit down, make yourself comfortable."

James settled back in a leather armchair. Michael had disappeared. His place had been taken by the same waiter who had served James lunch. "Would you care for a drink, sir?"

James said he wouldn't. Langer didn't even have to ask. The waiter brought him a thin Scotch and water before disappearing as quietly as he had materialized.

"Your health, Mr. Reed," said Langer. He took a tiny sip of his drink before putting his glass aside. "You're comfortable here, I trust."

"I won't know if I'm comfortable until I discover what I'm doing here," said James. "Incidentally, what's the money for?"

"You are here at my request. I could hardly expect you to pay for anything yourself."

"Walking-around money."

"Exactly. If you need more, ask Barlow."

"That sounds as if you expect me to be around for some time."

"That will be up to you, of course. After you hear what I have to say." He took another sip of his drink. "I would like to tell you a story," he said. "It's quite a long story, so I hope you'll bear with me."

"Maybe I should have that drink after all."

"Certainly. Just ring the bell by the fireplace."

"I'll help myself," said James. He mixed a Scotch and water at the bar, making it as light as Langer's. "I'm all ears," he said to Langer when he was sitting again.

"How well did you know Jonathan Bradley?"

"Not at all. He arrived at my house. I had dinner with him. He disappeared leaving death and destruction in his wake."

"You know something of his background?"

"Banking family. Father came to England after the war. Changed his name from Glessen to Bradley. Junior didn't take to banking so he went off and became a playboy. Got sick. Came to Los Angeles to recuperate."

"I assume Miss Carmichael gave you this information," said Langer.

"Most of it."

"As far as the broad strokes are concerned, it's accurate. Did she at any time mention the name Marianne?"

James shook his head.

"It's not surprising, I suppose. Poor Betsy always hoped to marry Jonathan Bradley. If it hadn't been for Marianne she would probably have achieved her ambition."

"The other woman," said James.

"In a manner of speaking. Let me tell you about Marianne." He paused for a moment as if examining what he was going to say before he committed himself. "You understand that English is not my native language. Sometimes I have difficulty in expressing myself the way I would like. I find I don't understand the nuances. So when I tell you that Marianne was all things to all men, I hope you understand what I'm trying to say."

"If you're trying to say that Marianne was a knockout, you're doing okay," said James.

"A knockout." Langer thought about the expression for a moment. "Yes, she was a knockout. Anyway, Jonathan fell in love with Marianne . . . no, that doesn't express it correctly . . . Jonathan Bradley became besotted with her. If she had asked him to cut his own throat, he would have done it quite happily. In fact, in a manner of speaking, that's exactly what she did do." He took another sip of his drink. "Jonathan Bradley met Marianne about three years ago. Up to that time his life had been exactly what one would expect from the eldest son of an old banking family. Educated in England, with a year of business school in America, followed by short periods working in various sections of the Glessen banks around Europe. In a couple of years he would have returned here to London to be groomed eventually to take over from his father."

"I heard you owned Glessen's."

"Where did you hear that?"

"Is it supposed to be a secret?"

"Not at all. But it's what you might call specialized knowledge, of little interest or concern to anyone not connected with banking."

"I have no interest in banking."

"But you do in me? You still think I'm responsible for what happened in Los Angeles?"

"You haven't come up with anything yet to change my mind."

"If you truly believed I had anything to do with it, you'd hardly have taken the risk of meeting me here alone."

"I took out some insurance," said James.

"What kind of insurance?"

"If I don't contact certain people at certain times . . . that kind of insurance." It wasn't true, but there was no way Langer could know that.

Langer thought about it for a moment before deciding to ignore the implications. "So, there was Jonathan Bradley all set for a successful banking career. Then he met Marianne. At the risk of sounding melodramatic, he fell completely under her spell."

"It happens," said James.

"Indeed it does. I know from experience."

It was difficult to imagine Karl Langer falling under anybody's spell. "So what was the big deal? He was free, white and twenty-one. Why didn't he marry the lady and settle down to raise a family of little bankers?"

"She was already married, and her husband wouldn't agree to a divorce. So she and Bradley ran off together. He left behind a promising career, she a grieving husband."

"Mr. Langer, I don't know about the circles you move in, but where I come from, it happens all the time."

"I agree. It's a commonplace occurrence. But let me finish. Jonathan Bradley was . . . is . . . a weak person. He is easily led. Marianne is the opposite. She is also wilful. She destroyed him, both physically and mentally. Not right away. It took two years approximately. At the end of that time, Bradley was completely dependent on the hard drugs she had introduced him to."

James had been right about Bradley. He was on the hard stuff.

Langer continued. "Then, just over a year ago, she met somebody else and she left Bradley. She and her new lover disappeared completely. She and Bradley were living in Marrakesh at the time. When he was unable to find her after a month, Bradley tried to commit suicide."

"Let me guess. He jumped off a high place, only it wasn't high enough."

"He was under the influence at the time, I believe. He sustained multiple fractures to both legs. As soon as he was able to walk again, he resumed his search for Marianne. He still believed he couldn't live without her."

"Was he still looking for her when he came to Los Angeles?"

"Mr. Reed, take my word for it, the only eventuality that will stop him trying to find her, is death."

"His or hers?"

Langer glanced at him briefly for a moment. "Either, I would imagine."

"I'm only asking because maybe that's why he wants to find her. Women don't have a monopoly on the 'hell hath no fury' syndrome."

"Not in this case. Believe me, all he wants is to persuade her to return to him. He will promise her anything. Do anything. That is the effect Marianne has on the men who are unfortunate enough to become attracted to her."

James started to take another drink from his glass and realized it was empty. He went to the bar and mixed himself another, a little stronger this time. He came back to his chair and sat down. "I assume you haven't finished," he said.

"No. What I have told you up to now is fact. Now I am going to enter the realm of supposition. Not guesswork, mark you, but supposition based on certain things that have come to light over the past few days. But first, let me go back slightly. During the time Jonathan and Marianne were together, he sold a large number of his shares in the Glessen Bank. He was perfectly entitled to do this. At that time, they were his to dispose of any way he wished. They came from a trust set up by his grandfather. The average market value over the period he disposed of this stock was about forty-seven dollars per share. He divested himself of his entire holding, seven hundred and fifty thousand shares in all."

James started to calculate quickly but he always had trouble if there were more than three zeros.

Langer helped him out. "Approximately thirty-two million dollars."

"That's a lot of cash. What did he do with it?"

"He certainly spent a great deal. But even with the lifestyle he and Marianne were leading, it would have been impossible to spend that amount of money. I have reason to believe that he opened a number of bank accounts in false names."

"Why would he use false names?"

"When his family realized what he had become, and the influence Marianne had on him, they started to take steps to have him declared legally incompetent. It wasn't difficult, given his dependence on drugs. That effectively meant all his assets were placed under the jurisdiction of the courts. He saw this coming, so he cashed out his inheritance. By the time the courts were in a position to freeze his assets, everything was gone. Except, of course, the bank accounts and deposit boxes that nobody could locate, because only he knew where they were. That is, until three days ago."

James guessed they were about to get to the nitty-gritty. He hoped it wasn't going to take too long because he was beginning to feel hungry. Somebody must have read his mind because, at that moment, there was a tap on the door, and the waiter announced that dinner was served.

Where James's dining room would probably have seated a dozen, Langer's had room for twenty. Two places had been set at one end of the long table. Another waiter had appeared to assist the first. As one of them emerged from the kitchen, James caught sight of a chef at work among the pots and pans. "I hope you like caviar," said Langer as they sat down.

James liked it a lot. He also liked the vodka that was served with it, so cold it stuck to the roof of his mouth. But he knew that Langer was far from finished, so he refused a third. Besides, he wanted to leave room for the wine, which he knew would be great.

Langer was one of those people who didn't like to talk about important things while eating. Small talk was okay, but anything beyond that was going to have to wait until the coffee. James wasn't very good at small talk, and Langer didn't seem to have any at all, so after James had commented on the wine and Langer had informed him it came from one of his own vineyards, dialogue disappeared from the menu and the meal passed in almost total silence. Coffee and brandy were served in the living room. Once the waiter had done his thing and faded away, Langer took up his story as if there had been no break at all.

"Three days ago, two hundred and fifty thousand dollars was withdrawn from a bank in the Bahamas. The withdrawal was made by a man who seemed to be quite ill. I have reason to believe that it was Jonathan Bradley."

"What reason?" asked James. Finally it was getting interesting.

"I have been trying for a long time to locate the various bank accounts that Bradley opened. A difficult task, you'll agree."

James wasn't going to agree to anything, so he kept quiet.

Langer went on. "I have influence in a number of what are referred to as 'offshore' banks. It was this kind of bank that Bradley would have used when he was opening his accounts. Over the past six months I have located three that I believe could be Bradley's."

"How did you do that?" You never knew when a lesson on offshore banking might be useful.

"I looked for accounts that were opened during the period that Bradley was disposing of his inheritance. Accounts that consisted of a single sizable deposit, with no subsequent withdrawals. Accounts where the depositor was not known personally to the bank. I say I located three, in fact there were eight initially. Five turned out to belong to others. The three remaining, I was still monitoring."

"How?"

"Through a senior employee at each of the banks in question. They were instructed to inform me of any withdrawals from the account."

So much for the confidentiality of banking, thought James. He helped himself to another brandy without asking and sat down again. "Okay," he said. "Let's assume you're right and it was Bradley. What about it?"

"I want you to find him for me," said Langer.

Maybe he shouldn't have poured the second brandy. Still, he didn't have to drink it. He sniffed at it a couple of times, he rolled it around in the glass, he sniffed at it again. The hell with it. He took another swallow. If Langer was waiting for him to say something, he was going to have a long wait.

"No doubt you want to know why," said Langer, eventually.

"Not particularly," said James. "But no doubt you're going to tell me. At the same time, you could try telling me why the hell you're asking *me* to do this when you've obviously got enough money and influence to employ Scotland Yard, Interpol and probably the FBI and CIA as well."

"Let's take the second part first," said Langer. "I would have thought my choice was self-evident. One, you know what Jonathan Bradley looks like. Two, as an ex-policeman, you have certain technical expertise. Three, I believe you have a personal stake in the matter; it was in your home that those killings took place. Four, I know by your movements over the past few days that you want this matter cleared up; the fact that you tried to follow my trail proves that. Five, you will be well recompensed."

"And six, you're probably planning something highly illegal which, if anything goes wrong, you can lay on my doorstep."

"I assure you that what I am planning is not illegal. I just want him found."

"How much money can you spend, for Christ's sake?"

"I don't understand."

"What difference is a few more million going to make to your lifestyle?"

"It's not the money, Mr. Reed, I assure you."

"So what is it? According to what I heard, and I quote, you've been 'hounding Jonathan Bradley for years.' "

"That sounds like something Betsy Carmichael might have said."

"It doesn't matter who said it. It's true, isn't it?"

"I have kept in close touch with him, I agree."

"Why?"

"There's really no reason for you to know that."

James drained his glass. "You're right," he said. He got to his feet. "Thanks for dinner. I'll see myself out." He started for the door.

"Sit down, Mr. Reed. Please."

James liked to think it was the "please" that did it. In fact it was the hulking frame of Michael that suddenly appeared in the doorway, looking as impassable as the Matterhorn. How the hell had Langer caused him to materialize so quickly? In any event, James returned to his chair.

"Hear me out. Then, if you still wish to leave, you may do so," said Langer. "It is not Bradley I am interested in. As far as I am concerned he can rot in whatever pit he chooses to sink into."

"You've lost me," said James.

"It is not Bradley I wish you to find, it is his companions."

James stopped looking at Michael. If Bradley was traveling with companions, it was six-to-four they were the killers. "Who are they?"

"There is a man, his name is Alain Christophe. And there is a woman."

"Does she have a name too?"

For a moment, James didn't think he was going to get an answer.

"Marianne," said Langer, finally.

"The same Marianne who dumped him."

"When she deserted Bradley, she did so with Christophe."

"What prompted their reemergence?"

"When Marianne left Bradley, she took with her the jewelry she owned and as much cash as she could lay her hands on. Perhaps a couple of hundred thousand dollars. I believe that money has been exhausted and she and Christophe are now trying to gain possession of some of the millions that Bradley hid away when he and Marianne were together. They need Bradley to gain access to this money because only he knows where it is deposited and only he is entitled to withdraw it."

"So they killed the people in the house and snatched Bradley?"

"That is what I think happened, yes."

"If Bradley was chasing round the world looking for her, why didn't she just pick up a phone and say 'Here I am, come get me'?"

"Bradley isn't capable of getting around on his own. He needs help."

"He was paying three people to help him."

"One of them was also on my payroll. It is my belief that they suspected as much, but they didn't know which one. So, to keep me from being informed of their whereabouts, they killed all three."

James was sufficiently interested by now that he didn't even notice that Michael was no longer looming in the doorway.

"Now they say to Bradley, 'Go get us some money.' "

"Yes."

"If I was Bradley, I'd tell them to go fuck themselves."

"But you're not an addict, Mr. Reed."

He was right. Control his supply, and they'd got him. They'd even taken along Jane's medical bag to keep him quiet on the first leg of the journey.

"But you still haven't told me why you want to nail Christophe and the woman."

"That needn't concern you."

"Sure it concerns me. For all I know, you might want them dead. I could wind up an accessory to murder."

"I don't want them dead. Take my word for it."

"Why should I take your word for anything."

Langer thought about this for a moment. Then he made up his mind.

"Would you fetch me that picture over there? The one on the piano."

James fetched the picture. Silver-framed, it was of a younger Langer, dark-haired, with no scar, and obviously nothing wrong with his leg because he was on skis. He had his arm around a girl who could have been his daughter. She was looking straight into the camera, smiling. She was quite attractive, but nothing special. Langer was smiling down at her, ignoring the camera. From the look of his smile, he was ignoring everything else too. A truly doting father, thought James, as he handed the photograph to Langer.

"This was taken five years ago," said Langer. He'd aged so

much; James had figured ten at least. "Zermatt. We were on vacation." He looked at the photograph for a long time without saying anything. He had that expression people wore when they were looking at photographs or mementoes of long-dead loved ones. Finally he handed the photograph back to James.

"This is Marianne," he said.

It seemed that Langer was the husband she deserted when she took up with Bradley. He had tried to get her back, but she was one of those women who, once they had made up their mind, nothing or nobody could change it. She'd told him she was in love with Jonathan, and when he tried to restrain her by force, she'd pushed him down a flight of stairs, breaking his leg. While he was helpless on the floor at the foot of the stairs, she'd fetched a pair of scissors from her bureau and tried to stab out his eyes. He'd managed to fend her off until a servant, attracted by the noise, had come out to see what the master and mistress were up to now. By the time Langer was out of hospital, with a permanent limp and a scar, Marianne and Bradley were long gone.

"You forgot to mention your ex-wife was a psycho, to boot," said James.

"She's not my ex-wife. We're still married."

"I suppose you'll be telling me next you want her back."

"Exactly," said Langer.

It was after midnight when James got back to his own suite. He felt as wide awake as he had ever been. He poured himself a brandy and switched on the TV. Then he remembered he was in England. All-night TV was only for American insomniacs. Still, it didn't much matter, he had enough on his mind to make up a dozen melodramatic soaps of his own, each scene slightly more bizarre than the last. Here was Karl Langer, principal banker to half of Europe, rich as Croesus, as powerful and as influential as some heads of government, chasing after a woman who'd not only dumped him, but had tried to carve his eye out as a going-away gift. Then there was Jonathan Bradley, scion of an old banking family, turned into a drug addict and a partial cripple for the rest of his life, chasing after the same woman. Some lady!

Langer hadn't wanted James to take the framed photograph of himself and Marianne, but had found another for him. It was a studio portrait taken, according to Langer, about six months before she deserted him for Jonathan Bradley. James examined it, trying to see something that Langer, Bradley and, presumably, the man Alain Christophe might have seen. She looked around twenty-eight years old, with dark hair, a slightly oriental tilt to the eyes, a small nose, a generous mouth, an attractive smile. Pretty, certainly. But he saw far prettier on the beach or on the street every day of his life. Maybe he'd been wrong to ask for a photograph. Langer had immediately assumed that he'd accepted his proposition.

"I'll let you know tomorrow," James had said.

Langer had tried to pin him down.

"Tomorrow," he'd repeated.

Langer had agreed to meet him for breakfast. Michael had loomed once more to show him out.

Ever since his breakup with Katherine, James had made a business of not becoming involved. One of his girlfriends had compared him once to a rogue elephant, who stood outside the herd viewing everything with a jaundiced eye, concerning himself only when it directly affected his own well-being. The only argument he had with this theory was being likened to an elephant. He accepted the rest. He wasn't particularly proud of it, but neither did he see any reason why he should change. So, why had he agreed to meet Langer in the morning? Why hadn't he called the airline and booked himself on the next flight home?

Another acquaintance of his, also female, had told him that he had an infinite capacity for believing the lies he told himself. He'd told her there wasn't much point in telling lies to oneself if one *didn't* believe them. He had failed in his accepted task of minding Bradley; his home had been desecrated; he wanted to see justice done; he needed the money; he was bored and not doing anything right now; surely enough lies to justify meeting with Langer again tomorrow. Just before he tipped over the edge into sleep, he came up with another one. He was intrigued to meet this woman who could inspire such devotion from the men she destroyed. At least, he assumed that too was a lie.

"I'll give it a try," he said to Langer. "But there are conditions." They were having breakfast in Langer's suite.

"I assumed there would be," said Langer. He was dressed this morning for business in a dark suit, a white silk shirt and a discreet tie. He looked as if he might be going to chair a meeting of the board.

"One, no interference; two, access to all the information you have and, three, your word that nobody gets hurt."

"Why should you be concerned what happens to any of them?"

"It's just that if, after I find them, they come to a sticky end, I'm not about to be charged as an accessory."

"I too have a condition," said Langer. "No results, no payment. You may spend whatever is necessary, but only when you inform me exactly where I can find them do you get paid your fee."

"How much?" said James.

Langer shrugged. "Whatever you think reasonable."

"Fifty thousand dollars," said James.

"Agreed," said Langer, far too quickly.

Okay, thought James. Now we know where we are. Langer had no intention of paying him. That either meant that he was going to involve James in some illegality he was planning, or he didn't expect James to be around to collect.

"Would you be kind enough to fetch me the file from the top drawer of the desk?" asked Langer. James fetched the file and handed it to Langer, who opened it and unclipped a couple of credit cards. He handed them to James. "These can be used for your expenses. They each entitle you to draw up to one thousand dollars per day. Should you need more, there is a telephone number you can call." James looked at the cards. They were both issued by a Swiss bank he'd never heard of, and they were both already made out in the name of James Reed.

"You were pretty sure I'd go along," said James.

"I'm an excellent judge of character."
Boy, are you in for a surprise, thought James.

He spent the rest of the morning going over the file. Of the two remaining bank accounts that Langer suspected might belong to Bradley, the first was in the Channel Islands in the name of John Peterson. It had been opened with a single deposit of $500,000 just over eighteen months ago. Since then it had earned interest at a rate of five percent. The penalty for using shadowy banks was obviously a low rate of interest. Apart from the quarterly additions of the interest, there had been no activity. The second account was at a bank in Monaco. Name, Henry Robinson. Two hundred fifty thousand dollars deposited about three weeks after the Channel Island bank. As before, no activity in the account other than the addition of interest. Here it was only three and a half percent. Secrecy in Monaco cost more than in the Channel Islands.

James checked the Bahamian account that had been cleaned out three days ago. Two hundred fifty thousand dollars deposited around the same time as the others by a Mr. Charles Johnson. The whole amount withdrawn and the account closed. Peterson, Robinson and Johnson; if they were all Bradley's accounts, he'd been pretty unimaginative with his aliases. Penciled at the top of each of the three reports was the name of the bank official with whom Langer had a direct link.

There was a sketchy biography of Alain Christophe accompanied by a photograph taken at a costume party. It showed a dark-haired man in his mid-thirties with a slightly beat-up face and a smile that somehow contrived to be attractive and repellent at the same time. He was dressed as a matador and he had his arms around two girls, both in costume, one a harem girl and the other a flamenco dancer. They were both pretty in a vacuous kind of way, and both were obviously enjoying themselves. Neither of them was Marianne.

The biography read like something from a French B movie. Born Marseilles 1953. Brought up in an orphanage; served time as a juvenile for petty theft and pimping; charged on three separate occasions in his early twenties, assault with a deadly weapon, dealing in narcotics and murder; cleared of all three charges due to unavailability of prime prosecution witnesses, two of whom had never been seen or heard of since. Married in 1980 to Marie Duchene; marriage annulled six months later. Married again in 1982 to Margerethe Van Gotha, only child of P. Gotha, diamond dealer of Amsterdam. Wife dies in 1984 of an overdose of drugs. (Christophe was suspected of providing the drugs but nothing was proven and he was never charged.)

Those were the facts. Whoever had dug up the report had added something of his own. "Christophe can best be described as a sociopath. He is extremely attractive to women, especially those of masochistic tendencies. He is clever and can be dangerous." This was the guy that Marianne had left Bradley for. What was he able to give her that Bradley couldn't? It certainly wasn't money. Maybe the clue was in the "masochistic tendencies." Perhaps Marianne liked being knocked around. No doubt Bradley would have obliged had he been asked, but a make-believe sadist was no substitute for the real thing. James made a note to ask Langer about Marianne's sexual preferences. He'd probably lie, thought James, but he'd ask anyway.

There was also a short, factual biography of Marianne Langer, nee Brooks. Born 1957. Father English, mother French. Educated in England; later moved to Paris to complete her education. Married Karl Langer in Zurich in 1982.

The remainder of the file was a fairly detailed report of where Bradley and Marianne had spent their time together up to when she ran off with Christophe. There were some gaps in the schedule, but whoever Langer had employed to keep tabs on them had done a pretty good job. Langer was some glutton for punishment, decided James. His wife runs off with a guy, and for the next three years he has them followed all over the world. Maybe he figured Marianne would dump Bradley eventually, and he wanted to be around when that happened, hopefully to pick up the pieces and get her to return to hearth and home.

She dumped Bradley, sure enough, but took off with a two-bit French gangster. This time she managed to bury herself so successfully that even Langer's people couldn't find her.

Now, if Langer knew what he was talking about, she had put in a brief appearance, created major pandemonium and gone back to ground. How the hell was James expected to find her? And for what? He didn't for one moment believe that Langer wanted her back as his wife. So what did he want of her? He thought about it for a long time. Then he put the file in his desk drawer and after calculating the time difference he called the Bahamian bank and asked for Mr. Clavell, the name penciled on Langer's list.

There was a slight confusion at the other end of the line. Apparently Mr. Clavell was dealing with a client right now. "Tell him Karl Langer wants to talk to him," said James.

Clavell came on the line thirty seconds later. "Mr. Langer? Clavell here. What can I do for you, sir?"

"My name is Reed. I'm calling on behalf of Mr. Langer. He sends you his best regards, incidentally."

"Please be so kind as to reciprocate. How can I help you, Mr. Reed?"

"I need some information on the Johnson account that you were monitoring for us."

Clavell lowered his voice a little. "You understand, of course, that whatever I tell you must be treated with the strictest confidentiality." Even flaky offshore banks didn't take kindly to having a viper in their own bosom. Clavell was worrying about his job.

"You have my word, Mr. Clavell."

"The account was closed four days ago. Mr. Langer already knows that."

"How was it closed?"

"Mr. Johnson came to the bank and withdrew his money personally."

"Without prior notice?"

"Ah! I see. We normally require fifteen days advance notice of such a withdrawal. In this case, we waived that provision."

"Why?"

"Mr. Johnson was willing to pay the penalty we imposed for early withdrawal."

"What penalty?"

"Fifty thousand dollars."

James wondered briefly how he could get into the offshore banking business. It sounded like a real moneyspinner. "Did you deal with Mr. Johnson personally?"

"I did."

"What proof of identity did he give you?"

"He didn't need any. I remembered him from his last visit, when he made the original deposit."

"Tell me about that."

"It's a long time ago, Mr. Reed. What do you want to know?"

"Whatever you can remember."

"He came into the bank and asked to deposit two hundred and fifty thousand U.S. dollars."

"He had it with him?"

"In an attaché case. I opened the account for him and he left."

"How was he?"

"I don't understand you."

"Did he seem . . . normal? Fit, healthy?"

"Absolutely. I remember him as an extremely likable young man, full of exuberance. That's why I was so shocked at the change that had taken place since I last saw him. He's a very sick man, Mr. Reed. I can understand why he needs the constant attention of a nurse."

"She was with him at the bank?"

"Most solicitous. A caring young woman."

"Was there anybody else with them?"

"Only their driver. I helped the nurse walk Mr. Johnson to his car. It's as well I did. A policeman was trying to move the car on. It was illegally parked. I think I was able to prevent an unfortunate incident."

"What kind of incident?"

"The driver was refusing to move, the policeman was insisting. I took care of it."

"How did you do that?"

"Our policemen are not well paid, Mr. Reed. I was able to . . . persuade him to settle the matter with just an on-the-spot fine for illegal parking."

"What did the driver look like?"

"Just a driver."

"European?"

"Certainly. A native driver would have had more sense than to argue with a policeman."

"You've been very helpful, Mr. Clavell. Thank you."

"Any time I can be of further service to Mr. Langer, I trust he'll let me know."

"Absolutely," said James.

At ten minutes past five Langer called from his suite to say he was about to leave for Stockholm. James went upstairs to see him.

Michael admitted him to the suite. The young black chauffeur who had picked James up from the airport was waiting in the entrance hall in case he was needed to take down any bags of money or gold bars or whatever Langer carted around with him when he traveled. Langer himself was on the telephone in the living room when James came in. He was talking in German, so there was no point in trying to eavesdrop. He finished his call, glanced at his watch, then limped over and sat in the same chair he had sat in yesterday evening.

"Please make this as short as possible, Mr. Reed."

"Do you have anybody trustworthy in Nassau?"

"For what purpose?"

"I need some legwork done."

"Why not do it yourself? That's what I'm paying you for."

"You're paying me for results. I don't deliver, I don't get paid. So technically, as of right now, you're not paying me for anything."

"I stand corrected," said Langer coldly. "Now let me repeat the question. Why don't you go to Nassau yourself?"

"I've got other things to do."

Langer waited for him to enlarge on the statement. James let him wait. "You don't like me very much, do you, Mr. Reed?" Langer said finally.

"I don't like you at all," said James.

Langer considered this for a moment before deciding to let it pass. "No, I don't have anybody like that in Nassau. Is it important?"

"It could be. But I'll take care of it," said James. "Tell me about Mrs. Langer's sexual proclivities."

If Langer was in any way offended by the question, he didn't show it. "Why?"

"It might help."

"I fail to see how."

"Christophe is a sadist. Maybe that's what she wanted and she wasn't getting it at home."

"You're asking if Marianne is a masochist?"

"That's what I'm asking."

"I told you, Mr. Reed. Marianne is all things to all men."

"That's not much help."

"I'm sorry. It's all I can give you." He glanced at his watch again. "Now, unless there's something else . . ."

James said there was nothing else for the time being.

Langer gave him a telephone number. "Any time you need to contact me, call this number, tell them where you can be reached and I'll get back to you within the hour. Now I must go."

"Have a good trip," said James.

Back in his suite, James worked out the time in Los Angeles and called Ted Applethwaite at the office. The switchboard asked him to hang on while they located him.

"Make it fast," said James. "This is long distance."

"Where's long distance?" asked Ted, when he came on the line.

"London."

"We're supposed to be playing poker tomorrow night."

"That's why I called," said James. "I didn't want you to worry when I didn't show."

"Ha!" said Ted. "Why did you call?"

"You owe me a favor."

"So?" Suspicious now.

"Have you got any old buddies retired in Florida."

"Californians don't retire to Florida."

"Let me put it another way. Have you got anybody you can trust in Florida?"

"I might. What do you need?"

"Some legwork in Nassau."

"Nassau isn't in Florida. Don't they teach geography at limey schools?"

"I'm not paying ten bucks a minute to listen to your smartass remarks," said James.

"If I know you, you're not paying for the call at all," said Ted. "Tell me what you need."

James told him. "I'll call you back in fifteen minutes," said Ted. "Collect."

He called back in ten. It seemed that one of Ted's wife's cousins lived in Miami. According to Ted, he was a medium-bright kid of twenty-one, and right now was on Christmas vacation from college where he was learning to be a lawyer. He'd welcome a couple of days in the Bahamas, especially if he could earn a few dollars at the same time. "I'd do it myself if I could swing the time off," said Ted.

"Go sick," said James.

"I was sick last week for the Raiders game in San Diego." Ted read back what James had told him, just to check that he had the facts right. James took down the name and address of the cousin, promised to wire the kid one thousand dollars first thing tomorrow morning, said good-bye and hung up.

It was too late to call the banks in Jersey or Monaco so James called Betsy Carmichael instead. "What on earth are you doing in London?" she wanted to know.

"I came to see you," said James. "How about dinner tonight?"

"I've already got a date, but I'll break it."

James didn't try to dissuade her. "I'll pick you up at eight," he said. "Nothing dressy." He called downstairs to Barlow. Where could he rent a car? Barlow said he would arrange it. "Charge it to my room," said James.

"Naturally, sir," said Barlow.

He bathed and dressed in the smartest clothes he had brought with him from Los Angeles. Maybe if he kept his Harrods topcoat on, they'd let him through the front door of a restaurant. Then he had a better idea. He called room service and told them he would be requiring dinner for two this evening, please have the chef choose the menu, the sommelier could do the same with the wine. Nine o'clock would be just fine.

At seven thirty he went downstairs. He collected his car keys and was shown to a discreet BMW parked right out front of the hotel. He had a little trouble discovering how to start it; the flashing instrument panel confused him. Back home in his car, the only things that flashed were the warning lights. When eventually he had the engine running he couldn't find the lights. By the time he'd located them, the doorman had fetched Barlow.

"Is there any problem, sir?"

James assured him there was no problem, and drove off up the wrong side of the street.

Betsy lived in Hampstead, deepest Yuppieville. It was a large old house that had been converted into half a dozen apartments, each one of which probably cost ten times as much as the original house. Betsy was ready and waiting, probably because he arrived fifteen minutes late. She didn't seem as pleased to see him as she had sounded on the telephone. Maybe the date she'd been forced to break had given her a hard time. She invited him into the apartment for a drink. "Unless we're late for the dinner reservation," she said.

James assured her they weren't late and accepted her offer of a glass of wine. Apparently there was no hard liquor in the place. The apartment was large, light and feminine. In one corner of the living room was a desk holding a typewriter and some neat stacks of unused paper.

"What's the typewriter for?" asked James.

"My job," said Betsy.

"I didn't know you had one."

"I edit manuscripts for a couple of authors I know. A girl's got to work."

"It must pay well," said James. "This is a nice apartment."

"Actually the house belongs to Daddy. I rent from him."

"Very convenient," said James. "May I . . . ?" Before she could answer either way, he walked through into the bedroom. Neat, tidy, with a double bed occupied by at least a dozen teddy bears. A framed photograph of Jonathan Bradley was on her nightstand. He could see the bathroom leading off the bedroom.

He came back into the living room. "Yes, very nice," he said. "Now drink your wine and let's go eat."

"Am I dressed all right? You did say casual."

"You look very sexy," he said. He was gratified to see she hadn't lost her ability to blush. In fact, she didn't look very sexy at all. She was wearing a shapeless smock-type dress in a non-descript color, with flat-heeled shoes. James assumed it was the "in" fashion for this week. He didn't like it. Instead of a topcoat, she draped herself in what looked like an old army blanket. Only when he put his arm around her shoulder as they walked to the door did he realize it was cashmere.

"Where are you taking me?" she asked, as she buckled herself into the front seat of the car.

"Somewhere special," he said.

She managed to restrain her curiosity until they reached Swiss Cottage. "What brought you to our fair city?" she asked, far too casually.

"I was homesick," said James.

"I seem to remember you saying if you never saw London again it would be too soon."

"I don't remember saying that."

"Words to that effect."

"I must have been drunk," said James.

"I thought perhaps you might have come for the funeral."

"Who's being buried?"

"Jonathan of course. They're flying his body in tomorrow."

Some poor American John Doe was going to get a slap-up burial in a foreign field, thought James. "Are you going?" he asked.

"Of course."

"I'll come with you."

She thought about it for a moment. "All right," she said reluctantly. She didn't much like the idea, but being a lady, she couldn't think of any way to avoid it.

They pulled up outside Struther's. The doorman appeared to take the car. "What is this place?" asked Betsy as they walked up the steps.

"My hotel."

"I thought we were going out to dinner."

"I didn't say that. I just asked if you would have dinner with me." For one moment he thought she might turn around and walk off. It was all right sharing a hotel suite in California. All kinds of free and easy things went on over there, especially at Disneyland. But this was home territory. The rules were different. But curiosity got the better of her. Once she'd set foot inside the lobby, she was a goner. "What a smashing hotel," she said. "Funny I've never heard about it."

"It's very exclusive," said James. He thought for a moment that she was going to ask "So what are you doing here?" But she didn't. As they headed toward the elevator Barlow stuck his head out from wherever it was that he spent his time. "Good evening, Mr. Reed. Madam."

"Don't you ever go home?" asked James.

He managed a smile. "Struther's *is* my home, sir. Have a pleasant evening."

"We'll do our best," said James.

If the lobby had impressed her, the suite knocked her eyes out. "It must be hideously expensive," she said after she'd made a quick tour, possibly to check if there was a back way out should James decide to come on strong before she'd consumed the requisite amount of brandy. He agreed that it was expensive. "To think, the first time I saw you I thought you were the handyman."

There was already a bottle of champagne in an ice bucket set out on the bar. James opened it and poured two glasses.

"What shall we drink to?" said Betsy.

"Whatever you like."

She thought about it for a moment. "Let's drink to friendship," she said, finally. That would do to be getting on with, thought James. They drank to friendship. James called down and told them to serve dinner. While they were waiting they had another glass of champagne and Betsy told him what a terrible time she'd had since she'd last seen him . . . I mean, having to get out of America practically in somebody's diplomatic bag . . . then the reporters at the airport . . . Daddy had sent Simon to meet her . . . he was very efficient, he managed to smuggle her out the back door, so to speak . . . Daddy had wanted her to go straight down to the country but she'd decided she'd prefer to stay in town . . . Simon had been very good, making sure nobody bothered her for the first couple of days.

"Are you and Simon an item?" asked James.

"Good heavens, no," she said. "He works for Daddy." Proper English ladies didn't date the help.

"Is he going to be at the funeral?" asked James.

"Certainly. He was one of Jonathan's best friends."

"Maybe you'll introduce me."

"Why?" She sounded suspicious. James suspected she and Simon were more of an item than she wanted to admit.

"I'd like to meet him."

"Then so you shall," she said, holding out her glass for a refill. Then the waiter stuck his head in from the dining room and announced that dinner was served.

James allowed her to chatter on during dinner, only contributing to the conversation when she showed signs of flagging. He made sure that he kept her wine glass topped up. Between the entree and the dessert she accused him of being very naughty because he was trying to get her tipsy. In fact he was, but not for the reasons that she believed. He asked the waiter to serve coffee in the living room.

"I'd love a small brandy if you've got one," she said, after the waiter had left.

James fetched her a brandy and one for himself. He made hers a small one. He had no objections to what brandy drinking did to Betsy, but business before pleasure, and he didn't want her incoherent. At least, not yet. "How come you and Jonathan never got married?" he asked.

She shrugged. "One of those things, I suppose. Too much like brother and sister."

"It wasn't because of Marianne then?"

"That bitch wouldn't have . . . I don't remember telling you about Marianne."

"Where else would I have heard it?"

She considered this for a moment before deciding it wasn't important. "She had nothing to do with us breaking up. Whatever anyone else thought."

"Did you know her well?"

"I met her a couple of times."

"What was she like? A woman's point of view."

"Frightful. I mean, really dreadful. She just threw herself at poor Jonathan. It was the drugs of course. I mean, he'd never have run off with a woman like that if she wasn't providing him with something he'd come to depend on, poor darling."

She was certainly doing that, thought James, though he doubted it was drugs. In London they could be bought as easily as cigarettes. "Did she have any friends that you know about?"

"Anything in trousers. It was revolting the way the men drooled all over her."

"Girlfriends?"

"You must be joking!" She was getting drunk, but not *that* drunk. "Why are you asking all these questions about Marianne?" she asked suspiciously.

"Jonathan Bradley was killed in my house. I want to see justice done." He made it sound very sincere.

Betsy's eyes widened. "You're working on the case. Why didn't you say so before? That's right . . . you used to be a policeman didn't you?" Then she became suspicious again. "Why aren't you back in Los Angeles where it happened instead of wasting your time asking questions about Marianne Langer?" Then her eyes opened really wide. "You think she had something to do with it, don't you? Oh, please God you're right and you catch her and they hang her." She was a real liberal, was Betsy. She thought about it a little longer. "Why would Marianne want to kill Jonathan?" she said. "I mean, what would she stand to gain?"

"I didn't say it, Betsy. You did."

"Did I?" She thought about it for a moment. "Please can I have another brandy?"

James fetched her another brandy. "Maybe I should take you home soon," he said.

"There's no hurry. How long are you going to be in London?"

"A few days. Where's the funeral going to be?"

"At the local church. You can drive down with us." Her original reservations over his attending the funeral seemed to have been dissolved by the alcohol.

"Who's us?"

"Simon and me. You wanted to meet him didn't you?"

James agreed that he wanted to meet Simon Wilson, but he didn't want to be trapped way out in the boonies without means of getting back to London. "I'll take my own car," he said. "I'll follow you."

"Please yourself," said Betsy. "Where's the loo?"

James pointed her in the direction of the bathroom. When she came back she had put on a new face. "Would you like to go dancing?" she asked.

James would have been hard-pressed to think of anything he would have liked to do less. "I'd love to," he said. "But I have to get up real early in the morning." Now she's going to ask for another brandy and start taking her clothes off, thought James. *Qué será será*. Instead, she asked him to drive her home. He called down for the car and ushered her out before she could change her mind.

She didn't stop talking on the drive back to Hampstead, saying practically nothing at all. Such a drag, Christmas is just around the corner again; what was James doing for Christmas?; maybe she'd go to Klosters again this year; she really must tell her friends about that wonderful hotel James was staying at; Daddy was an absolute pain when she got back from America; if James wanted to see any shows while he was in town she had a good friend who could get seats for anything. He let it wash over him, grateful that she seemed to have forgotten Marianne Langer entirely.

"I'll call you about the funeral," she said as they pulled up outside her house.

James gave her his number and walked her to the front door. Forty minutes later he was back at Struther's getting ready for bed.

He was wide awake at six thirty A.M. His body clock still hadn't adjusted to London time. He dressed in a pair of jeans, a sweatshirt and sneakers and went for a jog. It was another cold day. Later it was going to be bright; right now it was only just getting light. The streets were comparatively empty. People didn't go to work in London as early as they did in Los Angeles. He pounded the pavements for twenty minutes and got back to the hotel at seven fifteen. For once, Barlow didn't appear the moment he walked into the lobby. Upstairs he called down for some breakfast and started to plan his day. At nine A.M. he called the London branch of the Swiss bank that issued his credit cards and instructed them to transfer one thousand dollars direct to Ted's wife's cousin in Florida. Then he called Barlow and asked for the name and number of a reliable travel agent. He called the agent and told him that he needed to go to Jersey today, what was the best way to go about it? Two hours later he was on a flight out of Heathrow Airport.

James had been to St. Helier, the capital of Jersey, once before. It still looked like an English seaside town with French overtones. The bank he was looking for was just off Broad Street and, from the outside, looked as if it might have been used by Charles Dickens. Inside it was more up to date. There was a small counter with two tellers' windows, one of them unmanned.

Ninety-five percent of Jersey banking was done by mail or telex.

A very small proportion of people owning bank accounts in Jersey ever came near the place. As a European tax haven, it didn't compare to Switzerland or Luxembourg, but it did all right for itself. He asked the girl behind the teller's window if he could speak with Mr. Roget. He was asked to wait, while she disappeared into the back of the building and reappeared a couple of minutes later accompanied by a middle-aged man with a creased face and a suit to match. Only when James dropped Langer's name did Roget unlock a door at the side of the counter and ask him to step through into a small, untidy office. How could he be of assistance? James told him that he was acting on behalf of Mr. Langer and was interested in the John Peterson account.

"I must check with Mr. Langer himself before I divulge anything," said Roget.

"Go ahead," said James. "I'll wait."

James's ready acceptance to the suggestion was sufficient for Roget. "Please go ahead," he said.

"How much notice would you need if Peterson wanted to close out his account?"

"In what way, close his account?"

"Say he wanted to pitch up here and take it in cash?"

"Over half a million dollars?"

"Humor me."

"Seven days minimum."

"Would you be prepared to waive that?"

"I couldn't even if I wanted to. We don't keep large sums of cash in this branch. I'd need at least seven days to obtain the funds."

"So, if you hear from Peterson, you could let me know."

"I could let Mr. Langer know."

"Check it out with him. He'll okay it."

Roget agreed he would call Langer and, if Langer agreed, he'd contact James direct. James gave him the number of Struther's.

"What identification would you need from Peterson?"

"Providing he came here personally, none. I know what he looks like. I opened the account for him eighteen months ago."

Same modus operandi as in Nassau. But this time, James was

going to have an edge. Seven days' notice if Bradley decided to empty out the account. He could be waiting on the doorstep. He thanked Roget for seeing him. An hour later he was on a flight back to London. He could have done the whole thing on the phone.

As he drove back into London from the airport, the commuter traffic was streaming out of the city. Contrary to expectations, it hadn't been a bright day. It had snowed lightly. Come tomorrow it would melt into sludge, but right now it made everything look clean and bright. There was a message waiting at the hotel. Would he please call Betsy Carmichael.

"The funeral's tomorrow," she told him. "Are you sure you don't want to drive down with us?"

James said he'd be outside Betsy's house at ten A.M., the time that Simon Wilson was going to pick her up. He'd follow them down.

"What are you doing this evening?" she asked. "I'm having a few friends in for cocktails. You'd be more than welcome."

He suspected Betsy's friends might be from the same mold, Sloane Rangers and their boyfriends or husbands. He told her he had a business meeting, but he'd try to get along later. There was no point in not keeping one's options open. He went out to an early dinner at a little restaurant he'd used a lot in the old days. It had changed. What had once been a friendly place with dark wood floors and paneled walls had become a trattoria, all white marble, modern art and indifferent waiters. The menu was handwritten and barely decipherable. The clientele, all of whom seemed to know the maitre d'hotel personally, were young enough to make James feel even older than he was feeling already, which was at least ten years older than he actually was. On the way back to the hotel he felt depressed, mourning the passing of the London he'd known. Then he decided that maybe London was the same, he was the one who had changed. This depressed him even more. He went to bed early, and for the first time since he had arrived in London, he slept like a log.

■ ■ ■

At exactly ten A.M. he parked the car outside Betsy's house and rang the doorbell of her apartment. "We'll be right down," said Betsy over the intercom. It seemed that Simon Wilson had arrived five minutes earlier. She was so determined that he assimilate this fact, James knew he'd been there all night. He was a tall, slim, sandy-colored man in his late thirties. Everything about him was limp, from his small mustache to his handshake. "Terrible business," he said to James, after the introductions.

James agreed it was a terrible business.

"Bloody Americans," said Simon. "I don't know how you can stand to live in the place. People getting shot and stabbed and raped all over the place. Damned barbarians."

There were times when James would stoutly defend his adopted country. Right now, he couldn't be bothered. Simon was a throwback, the kind of Englishman who believed everybody born east of Dover was a wog, while everybody born on the other side of the Atlantic was beyond even that pale. They headed for their respective cars. Simon's was a Porsche. For one moment it looked as though Betsy might choose to ride with James, but Simon was holding the door of his car open. "Come on, old girl. Bad form to be late for a funeral." He looked toward James. "I'll keep my speed down, old boy. Wouldn't want to lose each other, would we."

They left the motorway at Oxford. Whereas yesterday's light fall of snow had turned to muck in London, here it still carpeted the fields and hills, softening what, at this time of the year, could be a very bleak landscape. James found himself quite enjoying the drive. It seemed a lifetime since he'd last driven through the English countryside. At least that hadn't changed. The car was warm and comfortable. It had come equipped with a cassette player and half a dozen classical tapes. Mozart wasn't exactly what James would have chosen, but it soothed the angst that had been his constant companion for the past couple of weeks. By the time they arrived in the village of Upper Chipping, he was feeling almost human.

Upper Chipping, so named to distinguish it from Lower Chipping, was one of those English villages that look as if they'd been designed solely for the American tourist. Tiny houses of Cotswold stone and thatched roofs lined both sides of the street. Some of the ground floors had been converted into shops selling Olde English Antiques of doubtful age and origin. James followed Wilson's car through the village to the church at the far end. Long before they reached it, James could see that parking was going to be a problem. The Bradleys were important people in the neighborhood, the eldest son was going to get a slap-up sendoff. There were over forty vehicles parked along both sides of the narrow road leading up to the church. James found himself a spot and managed to park without doing too much damage to his fenders. Wilson was driving his own car, so he was more careful. It took him ten minutes to find a place.

Eventually he and Betsy joined James and they walked the couple of hundred yards to the church together. As they arrived they could see that the first act was over. People were coming out of the church and heading off around back to the final resting place. They were a mixed bunch. Some of them looked as if they could have arrived on horseback. There was a sizable sprinkling of city types. After all, Bradley, Sr., was a big-time banker, and bankers were very important people in the business world. The investment of a few hours in the country on what was normally a working day might pay dividends when it came to negotiating a future loan.

"Which are the parents?" James asked Betsy as they joined the crowd. Betsy pointed out an elderly couple walking together without touching each other. Mrs. Bradley looked distraught. Mr. Bradley just looked angry. "And yours?" said James.

"Over there." She pointed out another couple. As she did so, they saw her and waved. "Let's join them."

The three of them joined Betsy's parents. Her mother was what James would describe as "a fine-looking woman." A slim, slightly angular face, naturally fair hair, good features and light blue eyes. She was dressed entirely in black, as were a lot of the guests. She managed to look chic where most of the others just looked depressing. Betsy's father matched the voice that James had heard over the phone. A large, clean-shaven man with cold eyes and a permanent expression of superiority that only came with the genes. Betsy introduced them to James.

"Grateful for what you did for my daughter," said Carmichael, without a trace of gratitude in his voice.

"I was glad to be able to help, sir." The "sir" came out automatically. After all these years, James's background still reacted subconsciously. The aristocracy weren't the only ones whose genes were passed on intact. He was surprised he hadn't tugged his forelock.

Betsy's mother was more gracious. Either that, or she'd become adept at conversing with the lower classes. "She's told us so much about you," she said to James. "Heaven knows what she would have done if you hadn't been there."

If he hadn't been there, Betsy would probably have been tucked up in her hotel bed and remained completely uninvolved. He didn't think it was a good idea to mention it.

"Morning Simon," said Carmichael. "You bring Betsy down?"

"Yes sir. Good morning, Lady Carmichael. Terrible business."

Betsy's mother agreed it was a terrible business. James sensed she didn't much like Simon Wilson. She turned to Betsy. "Come dear, you walk with us."

Betsy moved off with her mother and father, leaving James and Simon together. "Meant to thank you m'self for taking care of Betsy," said Simon, as they fell in behind the Carmichaels. "She told me all you'd done for her." Not all, thought James. "Damn good of you to fly over for the funeral," Simon continued. "After all, it's not like you knew poor old Jono all that well."

"I didn't know him at all," said James. "He rented my house."

"Is that a fact?"

"Sure it's a fact," said James. "You arranged it."

"Not me, old boy."

"You called Stephen Wise in Beverly Hills and asked him to find a rental."

"You're right," said Simon, as though he'd just learned something new. "I did."

"And Wise called you back and told you he'd found just the place."

"He did, as a matter of fact."

"And you called Karl Langer and told him all about it. Who else did you tell?" By now they'd reached the outer edge of the group around the grave. Somebody shushed at them angrily. James could see that Simon was pretending to listen to the vicar drone on, while he sorted out his reply. Obviously he couldn't come up with anything he considered suitable because as soon as the short graveside service was over, he started to edge his way through the crowd that now hemmed them in, trying to put as much distance between himself and James as possible. Realizing he wasn't going to lose James that way, he took refuge in the bosom of the Carmichael family, who were straggling away from the graveside with the rest of the mourners. Where he came from, one didn't discuss awkward subjects in the presence of outsiders, especially if they were ladies. So he placed himself strategically between Betsy and her mother. He'd forgotten James didn't come from the same place.

James fell into step on the other side of Betsy. "Apart from Langer, who else did you tell about my house?" he asked.

Betsy looked at him. "Are you talking to me?"

"To Simon," said James.

"This is damn bad form, old man. It's not the time or the place to—"

"You told Karl Langer?" said Betsy to Simon. There was an edge to her voice that James hadn't heard before.

"Of course I didn't."

Betsy's mother looked confused. "Is this something that I should know about?"

"No," said Betsy. "I think it's between James and Simon. Come on, Mother." She detached herself from Simon and walked away with her mother. Once more, Simon was left alone with James.

"You're after Betsy aren't you?" said Simon. "I guessed it all along. You're trying to antagonize her against me."

"If I was trying to do that I'd have asked you about Marianne."

Simon and Betsy were well-suited. He blushed too. Only with

him, it wasn't so much a blush as the blood draining from his face leaving high spots of red on his cheekbones. Considering how the remark had affected him, he pulled himself together remarkably quickly. Only the high spots of color remained. "I've no idea what you're talking about," he said. He continued down the path toward the front of the church, without breaking his stride.

James stayed in step with him. "I'm glad. Accessory to murder is a pretty heavy thing to have to deal with. See you around." He quickened his pace. He wasn't at all surprised when, after a couple of yards, Simon caught up with him.

"I suppose you have some grounds for that slanderous statement."

"I didn't slander anyone. I just said I was glad, for your sake, that you hadn't been in touch with Marianne Langer."

"You implied that if I had, I might be guilty of something."

"It's hypothetical," said James. "You haven't, so you're not."

"What if I had? Hypothetically, of course."

"Then you and I should have a little chat."

"I've got to go to the Bradley house . . . pay my respects to the parents."

"I'm in no hurry."

"There's a pub in the village. The Green Man. I'll see you there in an hour."

"It'll be a pleasure," said James.

Simon was more than an hour. In fact, he was nearer two. James was just beginning to think he wouldn't show when he walked in. He looked as if he might have had a couple of drinks already, probably to prime himself into the right state of mind to deal with this bounder.

"How was the wake?" James asked him.

"I didn't meet you to engage in small talk," said Simon. "If you've got anything to say to me, I suggest you get on with it. But just allow me to remind you, we have very stringent laws in this country. It's not at all like America." He didn't actually say "you nasty common little man," but he didn't need to. It was plain in the tone of his voice and his attitude. He'd built himself a fine head of steam, and he had decided the best way to handle things was from a position of superior breeding. It had worked fine for three hundred years, no reason why it shouldn't continue to do so.

"Would you like a drink?" asked James.

"No I would not like a drink. I want nothing from you."

"Suit yourself," said James. He moved over to the bar and ordered himself another Scotch.

"Sorry, sir. We've just called time."

He'd forgotten about the English licensing laws, where it was okay to get drunk between eleven and three, but not between three and six.

"How long before you chuck us out?"

"Five minutes," said the landlord. That ought to do it, thought James. He walked back to where Simon was fuming by the window.

"Just tell me where you got in touch with Marianne Langer, and we can all go home," he said.

"I don't know Marianne Langer."

"Sure you do! Which way did she swing for you? Were you the hitter or the hittee? Or maybe you're not into pain either way. Maybe she ran around the room in her underclothes and then let you chew on them. Or are you one of those guys who likes to be chained up and have his supper from a doggy bowl? How about the knotted twine trick? She had to have come up with something that you weren't able to get any place except from a hooker. I'm intrigued to know what it was."

"You're disgusting," said Simon.

"So is murder. Now just tell me how and when you got in touch with her and I promise not to tell Betsy Carmichael a thing."

"You would too, wouldn't you?"

"You'd better believe it," said James.

He did believe it, but he still didn't say anything. James gave him another push. "I don't think Daddy would like it much."

"Bastard," said Simon. The reference to Daddy had gotten to

him. However, he still wasn't quite ready to give up. "I think you and I should step outside."

For a moment James figured he wanted to talk without risk of being overheard by the other late drinkers.

"Whatever," he said. He downed his drink and started for the door.

Simon was right behind him. "I'm going to thrash you within an inch of your life," he said. My God! The man was taking him outside for a fight. He'd obviously had more to drink than it seemed, certainly a lot more than James, who would go to practically any lengths to stay out of a fight. He stopped and turned toward Simon, meaning to try to talk some sense into him. Simon misinterpreted the sudden movement. He swung a roundhouse punch at James that connected solidly because it was the last thing James had been expecting. He stumbled backward, tripped over a table and landed flat on his back amid a pile of broken glass and spilled beer. Simon loomed over him. "Had enough?" he said, flexing his ego. James climbed to his feet one step ahead of the landlord who had emerged from behind the bar with a cricket bat in his hand.

"Out," said the landlord.

"I'm on my way," said James.

"The both of you."

"He provoked me," said Simon.

"I don't care what he did. Out, or I'll call the police."

James headed for the door, brushing shards of broken glass out of his coat. Simon followed him. He must have felt ten feet tall because as soon as they were out of the door he continued to come on strong. "Don't you ever let me see your face again," he said.

"Give it a rest," said James.

"There's plenty more where that came from."

"Listen, I don't want to hurt you, but one way or another I'm going to get some answers," said James.

"You haven't had enough, have you?" This time he actually said it. "You nasty little man."

"Yes I have," said James. He hit Simon once. A straight,

stiff punch in the diaphragm. The air exploded out of him like he'd been punctured with an ice pick. The only reason he didn't collapse was because James moved round quickly and grabbed him under his armpits. He led the white-faced Simon toward his Porsche, where he lowered him face-down across the hood. Simon was still desperately trying to get some air into his lungs.

"You'll feel better in a minute," said James.

In fact, it took five minutes before Simon was able to say anything. "I'll have you arrested for assault," was the best he could manage.

"Come on," said James. "Half a dozen local boozers saw you hit me in there." He moved a little closer and lowered his voice. "What they're not going to see is the wreck I'm going to make of your face if you don't start talking." He realized he sounded like a cheap gangster movie, but he was fast running out of patience. Also the side of his face hurt where Simon had hit him. Maybe Simon had seen the same movie because James's threat did the trick.

"All right. What do you want to know?"

"Marianne Langer?"

"She telephoned me at the office a couple of months ago and said she was in town and she'd like to have lunch with me. There didn't seem any harm. She told me she was interested in contacting Jonathan. She wanted to try a reconciliation."

"You believed her?"

"Not at first."

"Why did you change your mind?"

"She convinced me."

"Let's see if I've got this right. You were banging her brains out and she was telling you she loved it. It was the best she'd ever had . . . please do it some more, but while you're doing it, tell me where Jonathan is because it's him I really love."

"She was going back to Jonathan because she felt sorry for him. She felt responsible for his condition."

"So as soon as Wise told you about the house he'd rented, you called her and gave her the address."

"I asked her not to go. Fortunately she listened to me, or she'd be dead herself by now."

There's plenty of time for that, thought James. "Any plans for seeing her again?"

"That's none of your business," said Simon. He was obviously beginning to pull himself together.

"Let me guess. She told you she'd be in touch, and you shouldn't try to contact her because she didn't know where she'd be."

"Now that Jonathan's dead, she'll contact me," said Simon with complete conviction.

"Don't hold your breath," said James.

All he was able to get from Simon Wilson was a Paris telephone number. There was no address. There wouldn't be much of a problem running the address down, but he didn't expect it to yield anything. He was halfway back to Oxford when a light started to blink at him. He was running out of gas. He pulled into a self-service station and filled up. From there he called Struther's to see if there were any messages. A Mr. Roget had called him from Jersey; Mr. Langer had called; and would Mr. Reed be dining at the hotel this evening? He told them Mr. Reed would be dining out. He paid for his gas, and five minutes later he was on the road again.

If Jersey had called it had to be because they'd had word from Bradley, hopefully that he was going to pitch up at the bank seven days from now and draw out his money. The further the whole thing progressed, the more Langer's theory about who had done what to whom seemed to hold up.

James passed a motorway intersection with a sign to London Airport. Why didn't he forget the whole thing and jump on the first available flight back to Los Angeles? Everything was clean back there. The police might still be pretending to look for the killer. After all, you just didn't close the file on a triple or quadruple slaying. But, sure as hell, they weren't looking very hard. Also, the sun was undoubtedly shining back there. He had become awfully accustomed to sunshine. So why didn't he point the car at Heathrow and call it a day?

Four reasons. One, the money; two, he was still pissed off at his house being turned into an abattoir; three, he had screwed up in his job as Bradley's minder and now had a chance to set it right; and four, before all this had started he'd been bored clear out of his skull.

There was a fifth reason, one with which he was just flirting around the edges. He didn't want to delve into it too deeply yet because he hadn't had the guts to analyze it. But whichever way you sliced it, it came out the same way. He just couldn't wait to meet Marianne Langer.

6

James called Langer as soon as he arrived back at Struther's. No, he had nothing to tell Langer. No, that didn't mean he'd made no progress, it just meant he had nothing to tell Langer.

"Were you successful in Jersey?" asked Langer.

"Don't tell me. You own travel agencies as well," said James. "Or is it Mr. Barlow?"

Langer didn't even bother to answer. "Please keep me informed," he said, and hung up.

James called downstairs and asked to speak to Barlow. "I'll be checking out tomorrow," he said.

If Barlow was surprised, he gave no indication. "Very well, sir. Just let me have your forwarding address before you leave and I'll make sure all your messages are passed on to you. Will you be keeping the car?"

He told Barlow he'd hang on to it for the remainder of his trip.

Just before he went out to dinner, Betsy called him. "I thought I'd see you after the funeral," she said.

"I had to get back to town."

"Simon disappeared too. I had to cadge a lift. What was going on between you two?"

"Nothing important," said James. "But if you've got any secrets you want kept, don't tell them to Simon Wilson."

"Is this something Daddy should know about? Simon does work for him, after all."

"I don't think Daddy has anything to worry about."

"But I do. Is that what you're saying?"

"It depends on your plans. But I wouldn't advise buying a trousseau."

"Simon means nothing to me. I told you that." There was a slight pause. "There's another woman, isn't there?" The choice of phrase, "another woman," gave her away. She *did* have plans for Simon.

"There may well be," said James.

She wanted to know more, of course. "How do you know?"

"Men's talk," said James.

"You're being beastly," she said.

James refused to be drawn out. After she'd hung up, he wondered why he'd bothered to warn her against Simon at all. Live and let live was his motto; never become involved. Simon might make her a good husband, even if he did have the hots for Marianne Langer. He finally figured he'd told her because marriage to Lord Carmichael's daughter would be something that Simon Wilson would really dig. Right now his face still hurt from Simon's blow and anything he could do to make things difficult for Simon was okay with him.

He had dinner at a curry restaurant five minutes' walk from the hotel. It was a good meal, in spite of the fact that it gave him heartburn. He burped his way back to Struther's, stopping at a late-night grocery store to buy some Alka-Seltzer. Tomorrow he was going to have to find someplace else to stay. It was a drag, but he didn't want Barlow getting on to Langer reporting every move that he made. He believed a time was going to come when he'd need to go to ground. Struther's wasn't the place to jump off from.

■ ■ ■

He checked out at nine A.M. He promised to let Barlow know where he'd be as soon as he was located. He signed a hotel bill that looked like the national debt. He had his bags put in the back of the car and told the doorman he'd be back to pick up the car later.

He walked to the Cromwell Road and reserved himself a room at one of the high-rise hotels that the city planners had permitted to blot this particular section of the landscape. It was clean, functional and anonymous. He told the reservations clerk that he would be paying for the room in cash. He didn't want Langer tracing him through his credit cards. And no, he had no idea how long he would be needing the room. London was pretty empty this late in December. The clerk told him he could have the room at least up until Christmas Eve, at which time he would have to leave because the hotel was fully booked for the festivities.

James had forgotten about Christmas. But this was nothing new. Since he and Katherine had split up, Christmas had become just another day, only remarkable because everything was closed. He walked back to Struther's, overtipped the doorman and drove the half mile to his new hotel. They showed him a place to park where the chance of getting a ticket was minimal, and his bags were taken up to his room. It was on the twelfth floor. From here he could see across the rooftops to Hyde Park. To his right was the Albert Hall, looking like some giant flying saucer about to take off.

It was now ten A.M. Banks were open. He called Roget in St. Helier.

"Mr. John Peterson has given seven days' notice of his desire to close his account," said Roget.

"How did he do that?" asked James.

"He telegraphed the bank."

"From where?"

"Caracas, Venezuela."

They were certainly covering a lot of territory. Maybe there'd been an account in Caracas that Langer's people hadn't been able to unearth.

"Did he give any indication when he'd be in?" asked James.

"Just that he wanted to close the account. It could be any time after seven days from yesterday."

"Thank you, Mr. Roget. I'll be in touch." Great! He'd be in touch. What was he supposed to do? Seven days from now start lurking outside the bank on a day-to-day basis? He could be there for days waiting for Bradley to show. That was always assuming John Peterson *was* Bradley. Out of the eight accounts Langer had pinpointed, five of them had turned out to be false alarms. This one might go the same way and John Peterson could turn out to be just another tax dodger with half a million dollars of funny money he wanted kept hidden for whatever reason. Still, he had seven days to find out.

He called Ted Applethwaite in Los Angeles. "Jesus H. Christ," said Ted. "It's two o'clock in the morning."

"I'll make it up to you," said James.

"Bet your ass, you will. What do you want?"

"I've moved house. When your wife's cousin can't get me at the old number, I figure he'll call you."

"So?"

"Take down my new number."

He had to wait while Ted clambered out of bed and fetched a pad and pencil. James heard a female voice complaining. Finally Ted came back on the line. "Mary says she's sorry she ever had a second cousin," he said.

"Serves her right for being dumb enough to share a bed with you," said James. He gave him his new number.

"Why didn't you leave a forwarding address where you were last at?" asked Ted.

"I've gone to ground."

"What are you up to in London anyway?"

"Revisiting my roots," said James.

"Do us all a favor. Replant them over there," said Ted. He hung up.

James walked to the nearest bank he could find. There, he collected a thousand dollars cash on each credit card. "I'd like to open an account," he told the teller. He filled in a couple of forms, and deposited the money in his new account. "See you tomorrow," he told the teller.

As he let himself back into his room, the phone was ringing. He picked it up. "Mr. Reed?" asked a male voice.
"Who wants to know?"
"John King." It was Ted's wife's second cousin calling from Nassau.
James introduced himself.
"Ted gave me your new number," said King.
"You just called him?"
"Ten minutes ago."
Ted was having one hell of a night. "How are you getting on?" asked James.
"You tell me," said King. "Got a pencil?" James confirmed that he had a pencil. "Okay. I did what you asked. I checked the traffic tickets at the police station. That cost me a hundred bucks. I got me the number of the car that was ticketed outside the bank. Another hundred. I traced the car back to one of the local rental agencies. Fifty this time. I asked to see the rental contract. Another fifty. I went to the address on the contract, a crummy little hotel just outside town, and talked to the desk clerk. Twenty-five bucks."
"Why did he come so cheap?" asked James.
"He works in the private sector," said King. "It's government officials who cost the big bucks. He told me the group I was asking about stayed at the hotel for one night only. They flew in late on Tuesday, rented the car on Wednesday morning, spent a couple of hours away from the hotel, came back, packed and left that afternoon. They registered under the names of Mr. and Mrs. St. Claire, and Andrew Potter . . . he was the one who was sick."
"Did the hotel check their passports?"
"Two French, and one English . . . Potter's."
"You've done a good job," said James.
"I haven't finished yet. The desk clerk overheard St. Claire

making airline reservations. It cost me another twenty-five to find out where to."

"You blew the last twenty-five," said James. "Caracas."

King sounded a little disappointed. "Sorry," he said.

"Don't worry about it."

"I'm not. So, three hundred and fifty bucks to buy the information. Round-trip ticket Miami-Nassau, three hundred. Hotel one twenty a night. Then there's my food and—"

"What's the bottom line?" said James, cutting in.

"You want I should go to Venezuela and keep tabs on them?"

"Would you be able to find them?"

"Do they take bribes in Caracas?"

"Guaranteed."

"You keep the bread coming, I'll find them."

"They may have left already."

"Then I'll find out where they've gone."

Not for a moment did James think it was going to be as easy as King was suggesting, but it was worth a try. It was no skin off *his* pocketbook, Langer was picking up the tab. "Okay. Go for it," he said. "I'll cable you another fifteen hundred care of American Express in Caracas."

"Great," said King. "I'm already booked on the noon flight."

"Pretty sure of yourself," said James.

"You didn't go for it, I cancel the flight. One more thing. We've only been talking expense money up to now. What about my time?"

"What do you figure it's worth?"

"I won't charge for my sack time, just my running-around time. I figure fifty an hour should cover it."

"How many hours have you put in up to now?"

"Sixteen, seventeen. I've got it written down. Don't worry, you'll get an itemized bill. It'll be deductible."

"Ted was right about you. You're going to make a hell of a lawyer," said James.

Now he had names. Passport names. The St. Claires and Andrew

Potter. Marianne and Christophe had prepared for the trip well in advance. They'd known they'd need a passport for Jonathan. With Christophe's flaky connections in France, there would have been no problem buying one. He went downstairs to the hotel lobby. There was a travel desk in one corner, near the gift shop. James asked the girl who was manning it how he would go about flying from Jersey to Caracas. After he had explained to her where Caracas was, she dug out a couple of airline directories and eventually came up with the information that he would have to do it through London, via one of the international airports in the States. New York; Chicago; Houston; Miami. There were others. Would James like a list? But he'd heard enough. To get to Jersey they were going to have to come through London. If the kid could get a trace on them in Caracas, well and good. James could be there at London Airport when they flew in. If he couldn't, things might turn out to be a little more complicated. Twenty-three or twenty-four thousand people passed through Heathrow on an average day. He didn't much fancy the idea of hanging around outside customs and immigration checking them all out.

He went back up to his room. From there he called Jersey Airlines and asked to speak to Customer Service. A bright young male voice came on the line.

"How can we help you, sir?"

"I want to find out if a Mr. Andrew Potter has a flight reservation to Jersey."

"Is this Mr. Potter speaking?"

"No," said James.

"Then I'm sorry, sir. We're not at liberty to give out that information."

"Very well," said James. "Don't say you haven't been warned."

"About what, sir?"

"It's Doctor," said James. "Dr. Reed. Mr. Potter is a patient of mine. But if you're not allowed to give out—"

"What exactly is wrong with Mr. Porter, Doctor?"

"It's Potter. I've been treating him for schizophrenic paranoia.

He's been threatening for weeks to run away to Jersey. Now I've lost him and I think he might be doing just that. But if you feel you can handle it, I'll—"

"Is he dangerous?"

"Most of the time he seems perfectly normal. Quiet as a lamb. There's a fifty-fifty chance you won't even know you've got a paranoid schizophrenic aboard. But if worse comes to worse, here's what you should do. As soon as he starts to scream, just—"

"Pardon me, Doctor. Would you hold the line a moment."

He was back in about three minutes. "If we let you know as soon as the reservation is made, will you be able to do something about Mr. Potter?"

"That's why I called you. He'll be traveling with a Mr. and Mrs. St. Claire, incidentally."

"Are they patients of yours too?"

"Not yet."

The airline promised to call James the moment Potter or the St. Claires came anywhere near them.

"You won't regret it," said James.

He called the bank in Monaco, listed in Langer's file, and asked to speak to M'sieu Janiello. Somebody else came on the line and identified himself as M'sieu Dubois. 'Ow could he be of service? James asked about the Henry Robinson account and was told that account information was strictly private.

"I'm speaking on behalf of Mr. Langer," said James.

"I do not care if you are speaking on behalf of the president of the United States. We do not divulge such information."

"Karl Langer. You've heard of him, I suppose."

"Who in the banking world has not?"

"Are you sure I can't speak to Mr. Janiello?"

"Janiello is no longer with this bank," said Dubois. He hung up. It seemed that Langer's man in the bank had either left or been fired. James was going to get no help from that direction. This meant that everything now depended on Jersey. Blow that, and he'd have lost his quarry for good. Not such a bad idea, he thought. Maybe then I can go home.

He had one more thing he needed to do today. He picked up

his car from where the hotel had told him to park it. There was a ticket under the wiper, which he threw away. He headed west out of town on the M4, past the airport and another thirty-odd miles, where he took the turnoff toward Basingstoke. Long before he got there, he turned off on a minor road signposted to Little Wycherly. If you weren't looking for it, you could drive through the village without even seeing it. Half a dozen small houses, a general store and a pub.

It was the pub he wanted. The Queen's Arms was unattractive enough on the outside not to be frequented by tourists out for a day in the country. The place looked as if it had been deserted years ago. James pulled into the graveled forecourt. As he climbed out of the car it started to rain. It was that cold, misty drizzle that made you believe it wasn't truly raining, but which soaked you clear through in about five minutes. It was just past five P.M., so the place wasn't open for business. James came in under the small porch and looked for a doorbell. There wasn't one, so he hammered on the door. For a long time nothing happened. Then, as he continued to bruise his hand, he heard a disagreeable voice from the other side of the door. "All right, all right, I'm coming for Christ's sake!" There was the sound of bolts being drawn back, and the door was opened from the inside by a stout, middle-aged man who looked as if he might just have gotten out of bed. He wore old flannel trousers held up by suspenders over a striped pajama top. His feet were encased in woolly slippers in the shape and color of two pandas. What hair he had stuck up in all directions. "What do you want?" he asked with absolutely no interest in any possible answer.

"I was just driving past your fine hostelry and I thought I might partake of some of your great English hospitality," said James in the broadest American accent he could muster.

"Jesus Christ," said the man. "We're closed."

"Surely you'd make an exception for a traveler from the United States of America."

"I hate Americans," said the man.

"You must be one of those English 'characters' I read about in my guidebook. They say the countryside is full of them."

"Fuck off," said the man. He started to close the door.

James stuck his foot in it. "You're not going to disappoint me, are you?" he said.

"I'm going to break your fucking foot if you don't take it out of my door."

"Same old Fred, all charm and old-world courtesy."

The man looked at James closer. "I left my glasses upstairs. Blind as a fucking bat without them."

"I used to make bets. Fred Carter won't manage more than two sentences without using the word *fuck*. I always won."

"Jim? Jim Reed?"

"Fresh from the colonies," said James.

Fred pulled the door open. "Come in. How are you, my old mucker. How long is it? Five years?"

"Closer to ten," said James as he came in.

Fred shut the door and relocked it. "Jim Reed! I'll be . . . ! I thought you were dead."

"I'm living in California."

"Way I hear it, it's the same thing."

"Don't knock it until you've tried it," said James.

"God's teeth, you're looking good."

"You too," lied James. "How have you been?"

"O-fucking-kay. Yourself?"

"Can't complain."

"Read something in the papers about you a couple of years back. You and that film star you married got divorced. I said to a couple of the lads, 'Mark my words, there's nothing over there for Jim boy no more. He'll be back.' "

"And here I am," said James.

"Shit! Have a drink!" He went behind the small bar. James looked around. The place was as depressing on the inside as it was on the out. Bare floorboards, hard benches, beer-stained tables, a dartboard sharing one of the walls with a large sign proclaiming the licensing laws and another sign stating NO GAMBLING. "What'll you have, Jim boy?"

James asked for a Scotch. He walked over to the bar as Fred poured two drinks. Fred had been one hell of a policeman in his day, a real neighborhood bobby, friendly with all the local shopkeepers; checking the brakes on the kids' bicycles; warning the street hookers at least half a dozen times before pulling them in; only writing sufficient traffic tickets to keep up with the station quota. Then the neighborhood started to change as black families moved in. The station began to receive complaints about Fred. He was coming on a bit too strong, making free and easy with his nightstick, putting the boot in. Fred, it seemed, was a racist. They pulled him off the street and made him a sergeant, sticking him behind a desk where they thought he could do minimal damage to community race relations. But somehow Fred always managed to turn up wherever there was a disturbance and thump a few heads, providing they were black. Finally, even the force, which was renowned for taking care of its own, had to disown him. He was retired early. He was able to buy this pub mainly because nobody else wanted it. Here he was able to expound his racial theories, which were close to Hitler's, to local farmworkers who didn't listen and who wouldn't understand what he was talking about even if they did. James had never liked him in the old days, and he didn't think there was any reason to change his attitude now. But he needed something from Fred, so he insisted they both have a second drink, which he paid for. Then he explained to Fred what he needed.

"I don't know about that, Jim boy," said Fred. "Sounds a bit dodgy."

James told him how much he was willing to pay.

"No problem, old son," said Fred.

He took James upstairs and showed him what he'd be getting for his money. James prowled around and made a couple of suggestions that Fred agreed he would take care of. "When's all this going down?" Fred asked.

"Sometime in the next few days," said James, hopefully.

"I'll be ready, old son," said Fred. They went back downstairs for another drink. Fred opened the bar at six. He needn't have bothered because nobody came in. James told him he needed to get back to London. "One other thing you can do for me, Fred," he said. "I need the name of a dodgy quack."

■ ■ ■

It was dark when James got back to London. The light rain had turned to sleet. James parked the car in the same place where he'd got the ticket. Maybe lightning wouldn't strike twice.

There were no messages at the desk. He went upstairs to his room and took a bath. Lying in the tub, he realized it was the first time he'd been warm all day. Christ, how he hated this climate. At eight P.M. he took a cab to Shepherd's Bush, where he paid it off and walked the last five hundred yards to his destination.

Dr. Quigley's waiting room was full when James walked in. Two old men with terrible chest problems were seated on straight-backed chairs, coughing and wheezing their way through their cigarettes; a young man with spiky blue hair, dressed in leather, was clutching the hand of his girlfriend, who was highly pregnant and had a streaming cold; a harassed-looking woman in her thirties was trying to calm a screaming infant; and a young man in the corner looked as though, if he didn't get a fix within the next five minutes, he'd dissolve all over the floor.

James stood by the outside door, marveling at the efficiency of socialized medicine. After five minutes, the door to the main surgery opened and a woman shuffled out, collected her coat and left. A moment later the doctor stuck his head out. "Who's next?" One of the old men started to get up from his chair. The doctor caught sight of James. "Are you on my panel? Can't see you unless you're registered."

"Private patient," said James.

Paying customers were a rarity in these parts. "Sit down," said the doctor to the old man. "I'll be with you in a minute." Then, to James. "Come in."

James followed him into the surgery. Dr. Quigley was a large man with long hair combed sideways in a futile attempt to cover a shiny pink scalp. He was dressed in an ill-fitting dark blue suit with enough leftover food on the jacket to feed an average-size family for a week. As he sat down, he lit a cigarette from a burning stub that he took from an overflowing ashtray on his desk. "What's wrong with you?" he asked.

"I need some methadone," said James.

"Are you a registered addict?"

"It's for a friend."

"Is he registered?"

"If he was, I wouldn't be here," said James. "I'll pay the going rate."

"Who gave you my name?"

"Another friend," said James.

Dr. Quigley thought about it for about three seconds. "How much do you need?"

"A couple of weeks to start with."

"Cost you a hundred quid. That's for the prescriptions. The methadone you pay for where and when you buy it." He wrote out four separate prescriptions. One for Smith, one for Jones, one for Brown and one for Grey. He handed them to James. "Don't go doing all your shopping in the same place," he said. James counted out five twenty-pound notes and passed them over.

"Tell the next one to come in," said Dr. Quigley as he pocketed the money.

As James came out into the waiting room, the old man whose place he'd usurped was having a coughing fit. The blue-haired punk took advantage of the situation and, grabbing his pregnant girlfriend, went through into the surgery before the old man had recovered sufficiently to light another cigarette. The kid who looked like he had needed a fix had disappeared altogether, probably in search of a reliable pusher. James could still hear the infant screaming when he was twenty-five yards down the street.

He went to two pharmacies. Both of them were closed. He didn't want to travel up to the West End to the all-night places. Tomorrow would have to do. He hailed a cab and asked the driver to take him to Struther's. The cabby had never heard of it. James told him where it was.

"No hotel there, guv!"

"Take me there anyway," said James.

" 'Strewth," said the cabby as James paid him off. "This is a new one on me."

As James came into the lobby, Barlow shot out of his office as if he'd been waiting all day for just this moment.

"Good evening, sir."

"Any messages for me?" asked James.

"There was a call from Nassau this morning. As you didn't give me any forwarding instructions, I was unable to help." He made it sound like a personal affront.

James ignored the implication. "Anything else?"

"A Miss Carmichael telephoned you."

"Thank you," said James. He started for the door.

Barlow caught up with him. "Perhaps . . . if you could let me know where you're staying . . ."

"I will as soon as I'm settled," said James.

Back in his hotel room, he called Betsy. "Why did you move out of that super hotel?" she wanted to know.

"I couldn't afford it any longer," said James.

"Pooh! I was looking forward to another dinner there."

"How about dinner anyway?"

"I can't tonight. I'll call you tomorrow. What's your number?"

"I don't have a phone," said James. Betsy might tell Simon who might tell God knows who. There was no point in hiding if you were going to hang out signposts. "I'll call you," he said.

"Promise!"

"Scout's honor," said James. He hung up and wondered what he was going to do with the rest of his evening. It was just past nine thirty. He wished he could remember the name of the drinking club he was always busting in the old days. It had been a fun place. Maybe the hotel doorman would know. In the meantime, he felt like a drink right now. He called downstairs for a bottle of Scotch and some ice. When it arrived he poured himself a stiff one and put his feet up for a few minutes. The next thing he knew the phone was ringing, dragging him out of a dreamless sleep. It took him a full minute to work out where he was. He rolled over and looked at the bedside clock. Five thirty A.M. He groped for the phone, dropped it, picked it up and stuck it to his ear.

It was Ted Applethwaite. "Are you sleeping?"

"Is that why you called? To get your own back?"

"That's not why I called," said Ted. "I want you to be wide awake before we talk." He sounded serious.

"Hang on," said James. He stumbled off the bed, poured himself a stiff Scotch and downed it in one swallow. It made him gag, but it woke him up. He sat on the bed and picked up the phone again.

"Okay. I'm awake."

"Did you send the kid to Venezuela?"

"Why?"

"Just answer my question."

"He suggested it, I agreed."

"What was he doing for you?"

The word *was* had an ominous ring. "What's happened?"

"He's dead is what happened. I just had a call from Mary's sister in Miami. They'd just gotten off the phone with the U.S. embassy in Caracas."

"How?"

"The local law figure he was trying to make a drug buy and got too smart with the local dealers. They messed him up, then they killed him."

"Messed him up how?" The slug of Scotch had turned to solid iron halfway to James's stomach.

"This is between you and me, understand? Soon as I heard the news I called Caracas myself and spoke to a guy at the embassy. He didn't tell the parents, but apparently they burned holes in him before they knocked him off. Not cigarette holes. Blowtorch holes."

"Shit!" said James.

"Yeah. But that's no help, buddy. What did they need from him that they got to do something like that?"

"I've no idea." The lie came without him having to think about it.

"What was he doing for you down there?"

"Following up on Nassau. Jesus Christ, I didn't even want him to go."

151

"He went anyway. For what?"

"He was trying to find Bradley for me."

There was a long silence on the other end of the line. "Bradley's dead," said Ted finally.

"Sure he is. I identified the body. Remember? You told me to."

"I asked."

"Told. Asked. What the hell difference does it make. You knew it wasn't Bradley as well as I did."

"Did Bradley have anything to do with the kid getting knocked off?"

"No," said James.

"You sound real sure about that."

"I am."

"So who?"

"The couple who snatched him. The same couple who went through my house making like exterminators."

"Names?"

"I don't know." This lie came out as easily as the first.

Another pause from Ted. "Has this got something to do with why you're in London?"

"Maybe."

"Don't give me the 'maybe' shit. Is Bradley the reason you're in London?"

"Yes," said James.

"Where's the bread coming from?"

"What bread?"

"The bread you've been throwing around these past few days. And don't try to tell me it's your own money. Somebody's financing this caper. I want to know who it is."

"I'm sorry, Ted. I can't tell you that."

"Can't?"

"Won't. But if it's any consolation, one way or another I'm gonna nail them."

"It isn't. Yeah, well maybe it is, for me. But not for his mother and father."

"I've got to ask you something, Ted. It could be important."

"Well?"

"Did the guy from the embassy tell you how bad he'd been burned?"

"Not enough to kill him."

"Enough to make him talk?"

"That's for you to find out, buddy," said Ted. A moment later the line went dead.

James climbed out of the clothes he'd slept in and took a shower. The hotel wasn't accustomed to guests showering or bathing at five forty-five A.M.; the water was barely warm. He came out of the shower and called for room service. He was told they didn't come on until six thirty. He pulled on a pair of jeans, a sweatshirt and sneakers and went for a jog. It was pitch dark still and bitterly cold. He ran hard and fast through the empty streets, arriving back at the hotel twenty minutes later. He didn't feel any better, just warmer. Up in his room, he stripped off and took another shower. This time when he called for room service he was able to order himself some coffee and juice.

How had they got on to the kid? Thinking about it, James could come up with any number of ways. They could have left word in Nassau that they be informed if anyone asked any questions about them, either at the hotel or the bank or the car rental agency. If John King had started asking questions as soon as he arrived in Caracas, the same could have applied. A few dollars spread around the airport or a couple of the hotels was all that it would take. So they pick the poor bastard up, take him someplace quiet and ask him some questions. Who are you working for? How much does he know? Who's paying him? And to make sure they get the right answers, they use a blowtorch. Shit! Why hadn't he told the kid thanks and go home to Miami. But he hadn't and he was going to have to live with it. John King had died for it.

James asked the waiter who brought his juice and coffee to bring him the same again in half an hour, this time with something to eat. The juice wasn't freshly squeezed. It was made out of a concentrate and it left a slightly bitter aftertaste. The coffee was hot and strong, it left an aftertaste too, just as bitter. He tried a swig of Scotch to wash it away. Then he realized the bitter taste had nothing to do with his breakfast. It was of his own making.

His second breakfast arrived. He was slightly surprised to find he had no trouble in eating what he'd ordered. Okay, so what had King told them, and what were they going to make of it?

I'm working for James Reed.
Who the hell is James Reed?
I don't know. My second cousin's husband put him on to me.
Who's your second cousin's husband?
He's an L.A. cop.
Is Reed a cop?
I don't know. He lives in London.
What did Reed want you to do?
Find you.
How did you do that?
I asked questions in Nassau.
How did Reed know about Nassau?

He wouldn't have been able to answer this one. Maybe they burned him a little about here.

What else does Reed know?
Your passport names.
Does he know where we're heading next?
No, or why would he pay me to find out?
That means we're still clear to go to Jersey.
So knock off the kid and let's be on our way.

Maybe this last answer was wishful thinking on James's part. Otherwise he was going to be up the creek without a paddle. They would disappear completely. They'd keep Jonathan alive a few more months while they raided more of his bank accounts. Then, when they figured they'd got themselves enough bread to live happily ever after, bye-bye Jonathan. After all, nobody was going to miss him. He was already dead in Los Angeles and buried in Upper Chipping.

■ ■ ■

James got Fred Carter out of bed to answer the phone.

"It's the middle of the fucking night, Jim boy," said Fred. It was just after eight.

"The quack worked out fine,'" said James.

"You didn't have to wake me to tell me that."

"I woke you because I need another favor. How are your contacts up here in the Smoke these days?"

"I steered you to Quigley, didn't I?"

"This is a bit heavier." As well as being a bigot, Fred had been a bent copper. Nothing heavy, but he knew where a few skeletons were buried and had kept quiet about them. Some villains had been spared doing time after making certain arrangements with Fred. But only providing their misdeeds had nothing to do with sex crime in any shape or form. Fred had the straitlaced morality of the English working classes. It was okay to beat up on your neighbor, but don't mess around with his wife or daughter.

"What do you need, Jim boy?"

"Where can I get a shooter?"

"You should have told me yesterday. You could have borrowed one of mine."

"What have you got?"

"A couple of fine twelve-bores. You can shoot any fucking thing on four legs with those beauties."

"You ever try sticking a shotgun in your pocket?"

"Ah! A real shooter." There was a moment's pause. "What would you be needing that for, Jim boy?" He sounded doubtful. He might be retired, but he still had the British policeman's ingrained antipathy toward firearms.

Maybe James should tell him he wanted to go out and start a race riot: that would do the trick. "Five hundred American dollars," he said.

"I don't know, old son." Still doubtful.

"That's just for you. I'll pay the going rate for the merchandise. I want to rent some muscle too."

"What kind of muscle?"

"Someone to keep an eye on my back."

"I'll make a couple of calls. You get back to me in about an hour."

At nine thirty he left the hotel and walked to the same bank he had used yesterday. The teller welcomed him like an old friend. He drew another two thousand dollars against his credit cards and deposited half of it in his newly opened account. The balance he pocketed with the thousand dollars he was still carrying. He thanked the teller politely and said he hoped he'd see her tomorrow.

There are four pharmacies in Kensington High Street. James had one of his prescriptions for methadone filled in each one. The last gave him a spot of trouble, saying he couldn't read what the doctor had written.

"$C_{21}H_{27}NO$," said James. "Methadone."

"Ah," said the pharmacist. "You're a chemist?"

"I'm a heroin addict and if I don't get my fix soon I'll get violent."

The pharmacist was in such a hurry to get rid of him that he overread the prescription and gave James double what the doctor had written.

He phoned Fred again as soon as he got back to the hotel. "Any luck?"

"I don't know, Jim boy. I've been out of action a good few years now. Things change fast. This address I'm going to give you, it's not one-hundred-percent reliable."

"What's the catch?" asked James.

"No fucking catch. It's just that the fellow I know who knows the fellow who knows the fellow you need to see, he says he's not sure the geezer's still in business. You could hike all the way over there and find the place has been turned into a fucking boutique or a curry restaurant."

"I'll take that chance," said James. He took down the address.

"It's gonna cost you a monkey."

"Dollars or pounds?"

"Pounds. You're back home now, my old son." At the current rate of exchange £500 worked out around $950. He could walk into any sporting-goods store in L.A. and buy the same thing for about $100. "That don't include the ammo," Fred continued. "Now listen to me, Jim boy," said Fred. "When I said a fellow who knows the fellow who knows the fellow, I wasn't kidding. This ain't your A-number-one straight from the horse's fucking mouth. So tread very softly and carry a big stick. I told 'em you were a paddy, incidentally."

"Why did you do that?"

"The Irish are always trying to buy shooters."

"Thanks, Fred," said James. "You can go back to bed now."

"Too fucking true," said Fred.

Just to be on the safe side, he decided to call Jersey Airlines again. He asked to speak to the same representative he'd spoken to last time. "This is Dr. Reed. Anything on Mr. Potter?"

"No, sir. He hasn't made a reservation through us."

"The St. Claire's?"

"No, sir. Of course, they may be planning to go by boat." He sounded as if that would make him really happy.

"He suffers from seasickness," said James. "You won't forget to call me, will you?" said James. The rep promised he'd not forget.

James had already considered the boat angle. Now he considered it again. It wasn't likely. The people he was looking for would want to be in and out of the U.K. as quickly as possible. Doubly so, now they'd learned somebody in London was looking for them. The flight to Jersey took about an hour. The boat trip, over six hours. It was just too long to hang about in one place. At least, that's how James was figuring it. Maybe he'd turn out to be wrong. He started to count the other areas where he might also be wrong. He reached a round dozen without any problem. On this basis, one more wasn't going to make much difference.

The address Fred had given him was in the Docklands. In James's memory the Docklands had always consisted of empty warehouses, fronted by grimy streets and backed by an equally grimy

River Thames. The river was still pretty foul, but the developers had been at work since he'd last visited the area. There were still long streets of warehouses, but they were no longer empty. They'd been converted into apartments, some of which were selling for over half a million dollars. But there still remained small oases of the past where the developers hadn't moved in; a few grubby little stores surrounded by four or five streets of houses, half of which were boarded up, the remainder looking as if they should have been condemned in Dickens's time.

"You sure you got the right address, guv?" asked the cabdriver as he pulled up. It was a fair question. The house was one of a terrace, differing from its neighbors only by virtue of its graffiti. FUCK EVERYBODY was painted across the front of the building in letters a foot high. This wasn't one of your artsy-craftsy spray-can jobs. Bright red paint, applied with a broad brush, the individual letters leaking over each other. It looked like somebody had disemboweled the house. James checked the number and announced this was the place.

"You want to wait for me?" he asked the cabby.

" 'Ow long you gonna be, guv?"

"I've no idea."

"Then if it's all the same to you, I'll be on me bike." He was eyeing a group of half a dozen youths loitering halfway up the street looking like extras from a Mad Max movie.

James paid him and he drove off. Even his vehicle seemed to sigh with relief.

James's knock on the front door went unanswered. He tried peering through the window that fronted directly onto the pavement. There was dirty net curtain hanging inside. He could see nothing of the interior. He tried knocking again. Still nothing. He was about to give up when a motor bike pulled up at the curb behind him. "Hey! You the mick?" said the rider. Apart from the fact he was a large man, nothing else could be made of him. He wore heavy motorbike gear, topped with the kind of helmet worn by Darth Vader. James owned up to being the mick.

"Hop on," said the rider.

James gathered his Harrods overcoat around him like a fastidious woman in a hooped skirt, and climbed aboard. He'd hardly settled his bum on the pillion seat when the bike took off fast. Screw his overcoat. He grabbed the man in front of him before he was thrown backward off the bike.

After five very hairy minutes the bike turned under a large arch into the center of a warehouse complex that had already been converted into residential use. It pulled up outside the main entrance. James climbed off the bike. "Penthouse two," said the rider. A moment later, he'd driven off again. The whole operation seemed a little melodramatic, but as a way of checking out whether or not James had come shopping on his own as opposed to trailing a posse with him, it served its purpose.

The main lobby was done in large potted plants and bleached wood. There was a huge window at the far side giving an impressive view of the river and the City beyond. James rang for an elevator. When it arrived, he pressed the button for the penthouse floor. There was somebody waiting for him as the elevator doors opened on the top floor. James found himself back on familiar territory. Here was the kind of villain he'd known well in the old days. A large man in his middle thirties, clean-shaven, hair neatly trimmed. He was wearing a dark gray pinstriped suit, a light cotton shirt and a tie. The clothes were top quality, the kind of wardrobe that would be worn by a stockbroker or insurance executive. Yet, to the experienced eye, the man still managed to look like an East End villain. Maybe it was the fact that he was a shade over six feet tall and the suit was designed to diminish the muscular build of his body rather than enhance it. His eyes flicked over James quickly. Apparently he was satisfied with what he saw.

"What do we call you?" he asked.

"How about Smith."

"That'll do." He started toward one of the two apartments located on this floor. James followed him. "You don't sound Irish to me," he said, just before they reached the door.

"You don't sound cockney to me," said James.

He didn't actually smile, that would have been out of character, but his face creased a fraction. He knocked on the door and it was opened immediately by another man who looked like he'd been cloned from the first. "Smith," said James's escort. The second man said nothing. He just indicated with a nod of his head that it was okay for James to come in.

The inside of the apartment was spacious. The entire back wall was glass, leading onto a wide terrace overlooking the same view James had seen from the lobby. The main room was clean, functional and not particularly attractive. It looked like a Swedish furniture store before opening time. The man told James to wait. He didn't invite him to sit. He disappeared through a door and James heard the rumble of voices. When he reappeared, James thought he was still on his own. Then he realized that somebody had come into the room behind him, so small that he had been completely hidden behind the bulk of the larger man. Now he stepped into the clear. He was about five feet six inches tall, and almost as round at the middle. He was totally bald, closer to seventy than sixty. He looked toward James. "Smith?" he said.

James smiled broadly. "How are you, Solly?" Immediately the younger man was on his guard. This recognition wasn't part of the scenario he was prepared for. The older man came closer to James, pulling a pair of horn-rimmed glasses from his jacket pocket. He put them on and peered up at James like a shortsighted owl. "I don't believe it," he said, finally. "Sergeant Reed. How are you, my boy?"

"I'm fine, Solly. You look good."

"Ah! Getting old. Come sit down. You wanna drink? Henry, get Sergeant Reed a drink. You remember my boy Henry. Henry, say hello to Sergeant Reed and thank your lucky stars he ain't on the force no more or you'd most likely be doing a stretch up the Scrubbs."

The large young man nodded briefly toward James. "What'll you have?"

"A Scotch would be fine."

"Don't pour him none of the cheap stuff," said Solly. "Nothing but the best for Sergeant Reed."

"Do me a favor, Solly. Enough with the 'sergeant.' "

"What do you want I should call you? Mr. Smith?"

"James'll be fine."

"So sit already, tell me what you been doing the past five years."

"It's ten years."

"Don't tell me. I don't want to know. Look at this place. Taken me near seventy years to buy me a place like this. Now I got it and time's going so fast I'll be dead before I even find out where the toilet is." Solly Seligmann had been a market trader when James had first come across him. He sold "genuine antiques" from a stall in Portobello Road. Half of his pieces had been stolen, the other half he bought from a manufacturer in Taiwan. Gradually the stolen goods had come to predominate his trade and, eventually, he had graduated into a full-time fence. He had prospered, because he got the reputation of giving every villain a fair deal. Ten percent of the market value, take it or leave it. James had busted him on more than one occasion. Then, when he transferred to the drug squad, he'd made a deal with Solly. He'd keep the law off Solly's back if Solly would stay out of the drug business and let him know when he heard of any drug deals going down. Solly didn't like drugs in any shape or form, not from any moral standpoint, but because the risk/return ratio was too high. So it was an arrangement that had suited both parties.

"It's a nice place," said James. "Business must be good."

"So-so. I got me a couple of drinking clubs, a casino or two, bits and pieces of some racehorses, a car dealership and property. Have I got property, my boy. That's where it really happened. Property. I own this building. And the one next door. And a couple more the other side of the river. If I'd known about property when I was young I'd be a millionaire by now."

"You are," said Henry from the bar.

"Don't listen to him," said Solly. "Okay, I've got some moola put aside. But millionaire! Maybe next year, God willing I should live so long."

"Sounds like you've gone legit, Solly," said James.

"It's a matter of degree, my boy. I don't fence no more and I run an honest casino. But let me tell you something about the property business. There's more bent geezers buying and selling property than you'd meet at the dog track on a Saturday night. Perhaps they ain't breaking no written laws, but if I'd've been that bent in the old days you'd've had me off the street fifteen times a day. So, maybe I gotta lean on some geezer occasionally, but we don't nail their kneecaps to the floor no more. We do it polite. You're looking at an honest man, my boy."

"I've never bought a gun from an honest man," said James.

Solly shrugged. "So I make mistakes. Tell me, what do you need with a shooter?"

"Can you get me one?"

"You're here, ain't you? But you know me, I don't like shooters and I don't like the people who use them, not unless they've got good reasons."

"If you don't like them, why'd you agree to sell one to Mr. Smith?"

"I was told Mr. Smith was Irish. What's an Irishman going to use a gun for? He's going to use it to shoot another Irishman. The Irish are thick as planks, so he's going to get caught and sent up. That way we've got two less Irishmen cluttering up the streets. I consider I'm doing a public service if I can sell a shooter to an Irishman. But you're not Irish. So what do you need with a shooter?"

"Do you trust me, Solly?"

"Of course I trust you, my boy."

"So trust me," said James.

Solly thought about it. Meanwhile Henry brought James his drink.

"So don't I get a drink?" said Solly.

"The doctor said you ain't allowed."

"So who listens to that quack? I'll have the same as what Sergeant Reed's drinking."

"Then you get it yourself, you silly old bugger," said Henry. He turned and walked out of the room.

"Kids. Who knows from kids these days. You got any kids?"

"No."

"You married that famous movie star, beautiful, bright, rich. And you don't have any kids! What are you, meshuga?"

"We're divorced a long time now. Kids would have made it worse. What about the gun, Solly?"

"I heard you want some muscle too? Do me a favor. Take my boys along. They're driving me crazy the way they hang around. How old do kids have to be before they leave home?"

"I may not need them. But it'll be good to know they're on call," said James.

Solly looked at him for a long moment. Then he reached out and patted his knee. "It's good to see you, my boy. Brings back memories of the good old days."

"What was good about them?"

Solly thought about it. "At least I could still get it up," he said. "Wait here."

He stood up and walked out of the room. As he did so, Henry came back in.

"You want another drink?"

James said that he didn't. "That your brother out there?" he asked.

"That's Mike."

"Your Dad thinks it's time you both left home."

"Stupid old sod. I've got a nice house in the country with a wife and two kids. Mike's got the same. What do we need with nursemaiding an old man who should know better. He's a grandpa, for Christ's sake, why don't he put on some slippers and start behaving like one? Oh no, not him. Because he can't forget he was once a villain, he's got to go on doing dodgy stuff . . . like selling you a shooter. And as long as he's still into that, there's gonna be guys out there waiting to put the boot in. If me and Mike don't mind the stupid old fart, who's gonna take care of him?"

"Where's your mum? She used to know how to keep him in order," said James.

"She died three years ago."

"I'm sorry," said James. "She was a nice lady."

"Who was a nice lady?" Solly had come back into the room carrying a briefcase.

"Sharon," said James. "Henry just told me she died."

"That she did." Solly looked around the penthouse. "She never even got to see this place." He thought about it for a moment. "Probably a good thing. She'd have filled it up with all that overstuffed junk her mother left her." He sat down beside James and opened the briefcase on his lap. Inside was a Colt .45 automatic pistol, as large and as deadly as a blunderbuss.

"Haven't you got anything smaller?" asked James.

"What smaller! You tell me you don't want to shoot no one, so I figure you just need it to put the frighteners in. For that, you need a gun that looks like a gun. This looks like a gun."

James had to agree it certainly looked like a gun.

"So . . . you want it or you don't want it?"

"I'll take it. How much?"

"Thousand quid," said Solly, without batting an eyelid. They spent the next fifteen minutes arguing about price. James didn't care what it was going to cost, and Solly didn't need the money. But he was an old street trader and he hadn't had so much fun for years, so James played his game. Finally, even Solly started to get bored. "You're insulting me. If I let you have this for less than a thousand quid, I'll be a laughingstock. So take it as a gift from an old friend." He walked James to the door. "Drop in anytime," he said. "It's good to see the old faces."

"Thanks for the gun, Solly," said James.

"Use it in good health, my boy," said Solly.

On his way back to the hotel James went to Harrods again. He was getting to be an old customer. This time he went to the book department where he bought a copy of *The Oxford English Dictionary*. Then to stationery, where he bought wrapping paper and string and, finally, to hardware for a sharp knife and a pair of heavy-duty scissors. As soon as he arrived back in his hotel room he unpacked his purchases. First the gun, which Solly had let him have for free. Then the two clips of ammo, for which he had been charged £250 apiece. Solly might be getting old, but not that old.

He used the knife and the scissors to cut a hollow in the center of the dictionary large enough to take the gun and the two clips.

He wrapped them in paper and wedged them in between the two covers. Then he wrapped the dictionary and addressed it to himself, c/o Jersey Airlines at St. Helier Airport. Across the top he printed TO BE CALLED FOR BY PASSENGER. He walked to the nearest post office and mailed the package, airmail express.

There were no customs regulations between the U.K. and Jersey. The package would go through without any problem. Had he tried to carry the gun through airport security, he would have rung enough warning bells to turn out the entire police force.

All he could do now was wait. It was still four days before Bradley's party could draw the money from the bank in Jersey. So where were they right now? Would they have remained in Caracas? Not likely, after what they'd done to young King. They'd have gotten out of there fast. Right now they'd be holed up in one of the American gateway cities until it was time to take a flight to London and then on to Jersey. Maybe they were out looking for the mysterious James Reed, the name they'd blowtorched out of John King. Jesus Christ, but the body count was rising. Cooper, Fairman and Jane in California, and now John King in Caracas. How do you compensate a family for the loss of a son? The answer was, you don't.

At six P.M. he called Jersey Airlines again. No, there was no reservation for either Mr. Potter or the St. Claires. Yes, they'd be sure to tell him. "Of course, they could board without reservations," said the guy on the other end of the phone.

"Is that usual?"

"We're not very busy this time of the year. It happens."

James thanked him and hung up. Maybe he should go to Jersey and wait for them there. The more he thought about it, the more sensible the idea sounded. He called the airline back. "What's your first flight to Jersey tomorrow?"

The first flight left Heathrow at six thirty A.M. James booked himself a seat. He was about to give them his credit card number when he changed his mind. "I'll pay cash when I pick the ticket up at the gate," he said.

"Certainly Dr. Reed. Have a good flight."

He ordered room service and spent the rest of the evening watching English TV, which was marginally better than American only because there was less of it.

He left the hotel at five thirty A.M. He told the night clerk that he would be out of town, possibly for four or five days, but he would continue to pay for his room. He needed a base in London, even if it was only for messages. He used his own car to drive to the airport. He left it in the long-term parking lot and took the shuttle bus in.

The flight was practically empty so the stewardess was able to give James a lot of attention. She was pretty and, considering it was six thirty in the morning, remarkably cheerful. She told him she'd be making this trip five times today, the last at eight thirty P.M., getting her into St. Helier at nine thirty where she was on layover until the first flight out tomorrow. She didn't know anybody on the island, and it was a real drag there on one's own, not having anyone to talk to over dinner and not able to go out afterward, because a girl on her own . . . you know! James said he knew how she felt and if he knew where he'd be this evening he'd certainly like to have dinner with her, but, for all he knew he could be back in London by then. She smiled at him sweetly and moved away to chat up the only other single male passenger. Maybe he'd made a mistake. What the hell was he going to do with himself while he was waiting? He was about to press the buzzer to recall the stewardess when he saw her take the seat next to the guy she was talking to and buckle herself in for landing, still talking up a storm.

At St. Helier Airport he asked at the airline desk what time the mail arrived. Apparently it was on the flight that he had come in on, but had to go to the sorting office first. It would be delivered around nine.

He rented a car and had it brought around to the front of the terminal building, where he left it parked while he had some breakfast. At nine A.M. he was back at the airline desk waiting for the mail delivery. He collected his package and took it with him to the men's room. There he unwrapped the gun, loaded one of the clips and put the other in his pocket. He unbuttoned his jacket and stuck the pistol in the waistband of his trousers. It weighed a ton. He checked himself in the mirror. With his jacket buttoned over the gun he looked like he had a particularly savage hernia. Buttoning his overcoat just make him look like a guy with a gut. He didn't want to admit it, but what it actually made him look like was a guy with a larger gut than the one he'd got. A week in England and already he was out of shape. No exercise and expense account living; no beach to run on and too much money to spend on food and booze. Better for one's physical well-being to be poor in California than rich in London.

He drove to the bank. He parked the car just off the main street and locked it. He walked back to the bank and took a good look at the buildings on the opposite side of the street. There was a hardware store, a liquor store and a place selling souvenirs. This time of year only the hardware store was doing anything like a reasonable amount of business. Unlike the tourists, residents didn't buy their booze at ten o'clock in the morning and they didn't buy souvenirs at all. James went into the souvenir store. As he came in, the bell affixed to the door jangled loudly. A moment later an attractive woman in her early forties appeared from the rear of the store, wiping her hands on her apron. She looked surprised that anyone would have walked into the store. "Good morning. Can I help you?"

"I wonder," said James. "Do you have a room to rent?"

Everybody in St. Helier had rooms to rent, especially out of season. "What kind of room would you be looking for?" she asked.

"Something facing the street. And I'll need meals in my room."

"I *do* have a room, as a matter of fact. But I don't know about the meals."

"May I speak to you in confidence?" said James.

She was suspicious immediately. "You'd better talk to my husband," she said.

"Fine," said James.

"He's not here right now."

"When will he be back?"

She stared at James hard. Obviously she was involved with some kind of internal debate.

"I'm a private investigator," said James, giving her a helping hand.

It did the trick. "Actually, I don't have a husband," she said. "I just said that because . . . you know . . . a woman living on her own . . . you can't be too careful." James agreed that she couldn't be too careful. "What do you need the room for?"

"You see the house next to the bank? I've got to keep my eye on it for the next few days."

"Mr. Cookham's house!"

"Right. Mr. Cookham's house."

"What's he done?"

"Nothing," said James quickly. "But we've had word."

"About what?"

"I'm sorry, I can't tell you that."

"No . . . of course not." She looked disappointed that Mr. Cookham wasn't in some kind of trouble.

"You'll need meals, you said."

"Just breakfast and lunch," said James.

She was still doubtful. It was one thing having a lodger, it was something else if you had to cook for him twice a day.

"I can pay you thirty-five pounds a day," said James.

"My goodness," she said. "When do you want to move in?"

It was an okay room. It had a double bed, a nightstand, a small dresser and a straight-back chair. It was clean and light, with net curtains over the window that overlooked the street. The bathroom was down the passage next door to Mrs. Chambers's room. When she had shown him the bathroom she had offered to clear off one of the shelves in the medicine cabinet for James's toilet gear. He thanked her and said he didn't want to put her out, he'd keep his stuff in his room. He'd just finished unpacking his overnight bag when she tapped on his door.

She came in carrying a notebook and pencil. "What would you like for lunch?" she asked.

"Whatever you're having," said James.

"How about a nice piece of fish."

"Great."

"Some soup to start with. A green salad. And some ice cream for dessert."

"No dessert," said James. He patted his stomach to emphasize the statement. The gun, which was still tucked in his waistband, became dislodged by the movement and slipped down inside his trousers. He sat down on the bed quickly before it dropped out the bottom of his pants or he shot off his balls. Amazing how quickly he'd gotten used to having it there; he'd forgotten all about it. If Mrs. Chambers noticed anything strange, she didn't remark on it. "Wine?" she asked.

She was taking her catering chores far too seriously. "Let's make a deal, Mrs. Chambers. Forget running the menus by me every day. Surprise me. As for the wine, I'll go next door and buy some."

"Tell them you're staying here, they'll give you a ten-percent discount. Here are your keys." She handed him two keys, both for the front door of the shop. "There is a back door," she said. "But I keep it bolted all the time. Anything else you need?" He told her there was nothing else. "I'll be off to buy your lunch then."

"Who's going to mind the store?"

"I'll close up. I'll only be gone fifteen minutes."

After she left, James was aware she'd trailed the smell of perfume into the room. She hadn't been wearing any when he had arrived. He figured it had to be for his benefit. Either that, or she had the hots for the fishmonger.

The room was ideally located for watching the bank. The window was set into a small bay so he could see up and down the street. Okay, what did he need to make himself comfortable? A radio. A deck of cards. And, unless he was wrong about the perfume, the landlady. He went to the liquor store next door and bought a mixed case of wine and a bottle of Scotch. When he got back, Mrs. Chambers was already back from her marketing. He could hear her out back of the shop. He tapped on the door and stuck his head around the corner. There was a workshop, with a potter's wheel and a small glazing oven. Apparently Mrs. Chambers made a lot of the souvenirs she sold in the shop. James had checked them out. He hoped she was a better cook than she was a potter. "I wonder if I can put the white wine in the fridge?" he asked. She came upstairs with him and showed him where the fridge was.

The upstairs floor consisted of a small living room and kitchen, the two bedrooms and the bathroom. If they were going to be in this close proximity for any length of time, James could foresee problems. He now knew that the perfume had not been for the benefit of the fishmonger. Already she had started to call him James. Now she insisted that he call her Lee. "Silly to be so formal when we're practically living together," she said. She started to tie on an apron. "Lunch in half an hour."

He had his lunch in his room. The people he was waiting for couldn't do business in the bank across the street for at least another couple of days. But he wanted to establish a routine, both for his own benefit and for Lee Chambers. Apart from that, there was an outside chance that they might pitch up a couple of days ahead of time to check things out. Not that he had any intention of making a move until after they'd been to the bank, but if they did turn up and he was able to identify them, it would give him a hell of an edge. In this whole goddamn mess, one thing was certain: he needed all the edges he could get.

Around five P.M. he watched as a couple of female clerks left the bank. Twenty minutes later, Roget came out accompanied by a young man James hadn't seen before. Roget stood by as the young man locked up. For somebody who was about to have half a million dollars on the premises, he was very casual about it. Roget and the young man said their good nights and took off down the street in opposite directions. James could close the store for the day. He wondered what he was going to do with the evening. He shouldn't have been so cavalier with the stewardess. At least he would have had somebody to talk to over dinner. Maybe he should ask Lee Chambers if she would dine with him.

"I'd love to," she said, almost before he could get the words out.

She took him to a little French restaurant, off the tourist beat, where she was welcomed as an old customer. There was a lot of hugging and cheek kissing and gabbling in French between her and the proprietor, who took their order personally and then rushed off to cook it. It was a good meal, accompanied by a bottle of wine recommended by the house. Lee Chambers managed to make it halfway through the main course before she started asking questions. "You're not watching Mr. Cookham, are you?" she said. She continued while James was still thinking of how he was going to answer. "Mr. Cookham hasn't been on the island for more than a month. The house is all locked up."

"You're right," said James. When you were caught in a lie, the best thing was to tell as much of the truth as necessary to wriggle out from under. "I'm watching the bank."

"They're always trying to launder their money over here," said Lee.

"Who are?"

"International drug dealers. I bet you work for Interpol or customs or something like that."

"You must promise not to tell anyone," said James, pouring her another glass of wine.

"I promise."

"Tell me about yourself," he said.

The one way to get a woman off a particular subject was to ask her to talk about herself. In the next twenty minutes James learned that Lee had been married; that her ex-husband was a bastard; that she'd lived in Jersey for five years; that she couldn't stand the place. She didn't have any men friends. If something didn't come along soon to change her life she was going to go stark raving mad.

Acting under the old axiom that attack was the best form of defense, James started to make a pass at her. Maybe if he came on strong enough, she'd back off and leave him alone. Not that she was unattractive or that he couldn't have fancied her in different circumstances, but he needed an emotional entanglement right now like he needed a hole in the head. Lee Chambers was the kind of lady who could only justify climbing into bed with a man if she first convinced herself that she was falling in love with him. It had been quite a time since he had met one of those. They were thin on the ground in California. So he leered a little, touched her hand a couple of times and even managed to play a little footsy under the table. It seemed to work. The more suggestive he was the more distant she became. By the time he paid the bill, she had almost reverted to calling him Mr. Reed.

They walked home in silence. He used his keys to let them into the shop. Upstairs, she disappeared into her bedroom saying he could use the bathroom first. Five minutes later, he was ready for bed. Ten minutes after that, she knocked on his door. She was wearing something diaphanous that smelled very faintly of mothballs. Without actually throwing her out bodily, James could think of no way of getting rid of her. And she did look very sexy in a rangy kind of way, with small breasts and narrow hips. The last woman he'd been to bed with had been Betsy Carmichael. Where Betsy was opulent, Lee was spare. Where Betsy had been aggressive, Lee was almost apologetic. "I've brought you clean towels," she said. Even she didn't expect him to believe her.

What the hell, thought James. But he owed her one last warning. "There's no future in this," he said as he pulled back the bed covers for her to climb in.

"I don't care," she said.

"I mean it."

"I'm sure you do." She grabbed at him fiercely.

There had to be no room for doubt. "Are you listening to what I'm saying?" he persisted.

She was chewing on one of his nipples. She looked up at him. "You're telling me this is nothing more than a one-night stand."

"Exactly. I don't want you to think that there's—"

"Shut up and fuck me," she said.

■ ■ ■

She brought him breakfast in bed. He knew he'd made a terrible mistake the moment she started sorting through the clothes that were strewn around the room. "I'll run these through the washer," she said, gathering up his underpants, socks and shirt. Just before she walked out, she turned back to him. "About last night," she said. James waited. "I understand what you meant when you said there's no future in it."

"I'm glad," said James, allowing her to get away with the lie. She left the room clutching his dirty washing like it was her most precious possession.

After she'd gone, James pushed his breakfast tray aside and got out of bed. He walked to the window and looked across at the bank. It was early. Nobody had come to work yet. He climbed back into bed and contemplated the day ahead of him. It was going to be long and, if he read Lee's signals right, fraught with hazard. But shit, it wasn't his fault. He'd given her every warning. Why hadn't he tried to get a room above the liquor store next door?

He watched the bank being opened by the young man who had locked up last night. The two girls arrived and, twenty minutes later, Roget turned up. James finished getting dressed and went downstairs. He could hear Lee humming to herself happily from the workshop. As he walked out, the bell on the door jangled loudly. She appeared in the door almost as if she'd been waiting. Her smile was warm.

"I'm going out for a few minutes," said James.

"You don't have to account to me for your movements," she said brightly. "Where are you going?"

Now was the time to make a point. Tell her something and then do something different. Make sure she knew he was lying to her. That should help to set her straight.

"To the bank," he said, which was exactly where he was going.

Roget kept him waiting ten minutes before having him shown into his office. He looked as if he hadn't had his suit pressed since James was last here. "What can I do for you, Mr. Reed?"

"Has there been any further word from Mr. Peterson?"

"Not since I spoke to you."

"So you're expecting him to show up any time now."

"Officially, he shouldn't be here for three more days. Unofficially, we have already released his funds."

"Meaning if he walked in right now, he could take the money?"

"He could."

"Does he know that?"

"I have no idea."

"Half a million dollars. Right?"

"Plus interest."

"Which amounts to . . . ?"

"After deductions for early withdrawal, approximately twenty thousand dollars."

James thanked him. He started to get to his feet.

"A word, if you wouldn't mind, Mr. Reed," said Roget. James sat again. "You will admit that I have been frank and open with you from the start?" James admitted it. "Then perhaps you will do me the same courtesy. What is Mr. Langer's interest in John Peterson?"

"You'd better ask him yourself. I just do as I'm told."

Roget looked at him solemnly for a long moment. There were more creases in his face than James remembered from his last visit. He was a worried man. But that was his problem. He'd accepted whatever carrot Langer had dangled in front of him. If there were going to be any consequences, he was going to have to live with them. James stood up again.

"Will I be seeing you again?" asked Roget.

"I doubt it," said James.

"Good," said Roget.

James crossed the street and then, in case somebody in the bank was watching him, he walked past the souvenir shop and round the block to where he had left his car. He unlocked it and turned the engine over. He'd been caught out once before when he was supposed to be tailing somebody and his car hadn't started.

In that particular case he'd done the only thing possible and stolen another vehicle. He didn't need that kind of complication again. He relocked the car and walked back to the shop. The bank may or may not have been watching him, but Lee Chambers certainly was. She appeared from the workroom before the bell had stopped jangling. She still had the warm smile on her face.

"Successful?" she asked.

"More or less?"

"Where did you go?"

"I told you. The bank."

"After the bank." The smile had started to crack a little around the edges.

"I went for a walk," said James.

She looked for a moment as if she might say something else, then she changed her mind and went back into the workroom. James went upstairs. Roget had said they could pitch up anytime. That meant from now on he was going to have to stay by the window during banking hours. With nothing to watch but the street, he was in for an exciting time.

For a bank holding a half million dollars for one customer, there wasn't much activity. No more than half a dozen customers the rest of the morning. He was just wondering whether he could knock off long enough to take a pee, when Lee brought him his lunch. She put it down on the card table she'd set up and joined him at the window.

"What are you waiting for?" she wanted to know.

"If I tell you will you keep watch while I go to the bathroom?"

She loved the idea. Whether it was just plain excitement, or an opportunity to become more involved in his life, James didn't know. Right now, he didn't care either. He was bursting. He told her to look out for a man and a woman, with a third man who would probably stay outside in a car. He had reached the bedroom door when she suddenly called to him. "There they are," she said. James came back to the window fast. A middle-aged couple were just going into the bank. He explained that the couple she was watching for were younger; the man was sick and might need the help of the woman. "If you see anyone like that, come get me straight away."

"Don't be long, your lunch will get cold," she said.

He was back inside three minutes. She was still glued to the window. She didn't even turn around as he came in the door.

"They haven't shown up," she said.

"I'll take over," said James.

"Perhaps I could bring my lunch up here," she said. He could think of no adequate argument against the suggestion. She ran out of the room and reappeared two minutes later with her own tray.

"This is cozy," she said, sitting down opposite him. In fact, it was quite cozy. It was a bright winter's day, with the sunshine streaming into the small bedroom. The lunch was well cooked and the wine suitably chilled. But James didn't want "cozy" right now. "Cozy" could lead to an afternoon of rolling around on the bed. He could hardly do that and watch the bank at the same time. So he deliberately kept the conversation from becoming too personal. It wasn't difficult. Lee was happy to chatter on about practically nothing at all while he ate his lunch and kept watch out of the window. By two thirty P.M. he had counted no more than a dozen people going into and coming out of the bank. The staff, such as it was, had taken their staggered lunch breaks, forty-five minutes each, except for Roget, who took an hour. At two forty-five, Lee had cleared away the lunch trays and rejoined him in his room. James had been right about what "cozy" could lead to. She was having problems keeping her hands off him. He didn't realize how distracting it was until he saw somebody come out of the bank whom he hadn't seen go in.

"The bank closes at three thirty," he said to Lee.

"What about it?"

"It means at three thirty I can give you my undivided attention. Until then, why don't you go make a pot."

"You don't make pots, you throw them." But she liked the idea. "See you at three thirty," she said. She left the room humming happily to herself.

James moved his chair so he could see out of the window without having to shift his bottom, adjusted the drapes so the sun didn't shine straight into his eyes, stuck his feet up on the card table, and promptly dropped off to sleep.

Fortunately, Lee was punctual. At three twenty-seven she came back into the bedroom. She was wearing a housecoat over whatever she was or was not wearing underneath. "It's nearly three thirty," she said.

He woke up with a start and looked at his watch. Shit! He'd been out for fifteen minutes. They could have come and gone by now. He looked down toward the bank. The front door was still open. There was a car parked a few yards up the street. But then there often was. There was nobody behind the wheel. "Come here," he said to Lee. She joined him at the window. "Do you recognize that car? Does it belong to any of your neighbors?"

She told him she'd never seen it before. At that moment, James saw one of the girl tellers appear at the door of the bank. She glanced up and down the street without much interest, then she went back inside and closed the door behind her. Banking hours were over for the day.

"Bank's closed," said Lee happily. "Let's go to bed." She headed for the bed starting to unbutton her housecoat. James was on the point of joining her when he saw a man walk from the liquor store unwrapping a pack of cigarettes. He headed up toward the parked car. He was in his early thirties, neatly dressed, with blond hair and wearing dark glasses. It was the hair that did it, it was too blond to be natural. He didn't look anything like the man in the photograph provided by Langer, but James just knew it was Alain Christophe.

7

Lee let James out of the back door. She hadn't wanted him to go at all. She had decided that what he was doing might be dangerous. It was the sight of him sticking the gun in a plastic shopping bag that set her off. She followed him downstairs pleading with him not to get involved. "It's my job, Lee," he said, trying not to sound like a man going off to war. He started his car, and thirty seconds later he was parked twenty-five yards behind Christophe's. He left the engine running.

Christophe was back behind the wheel. From his viewpoint, James could see the back of his blond head in the driver's seat. He checked his gun, then put it back in the shopping bag on the seat beside him. And there he sat for the next ten minutes. He wondered if Christophe was as edgy as he was. He certainly didn't look it from where James was sitting. James could see Lee Chambers pretending to redress the window of her gift shop. If she kept staring out like that, Christophe would be bound to notice her eventually. Maybe he should just stroll past the window and try to signal her to cool her curiosity before she blew everything. Then he stopped worrying about Lee as he saw Christophe open the door and get out of the car.

Jonathan Bradley and Marianne Langer came out of the bank.

She was carrying a briefcase in one hand. The other she used to support Bradley, who looked barely capable of walking. He'd looked pretty grim when James had seen him in California. Now he appeared just moments away from death's door. He was leaning heavily on Marianne's arm and supporting himself with a walking stick. Christophe took the briefcase from Marianne and put it on the front seat. Then he opened the back door and helped Marianne get Bradley inside the car. She got in the back beside him. Christophe slammed the door, climbed back behind the wheel and the car took off. As James started after it, he managed a quick nod of acknowledgment to Lee Chambers who was waving to him from the window of her shop. She obviously expected to see him again, probably for supper. That was the reason he'd left all his stuff. Where Lee came from, if a man left his clothes lying around, it meant he was coming back.

He followed Christophe's car toward the center part of town, to Royal Square. From there it turned in the direction of the harbor. Wherever they were going, it wasn't the airport. That was in the opposite direction. They had skirted the main harbor and driven for another quarter mile when James had to haul on the brakes suddenly. Christophe's car had signaled a turn and was slowing down. It made the turn, and as James cruised past, he could see Christophe talking to a man who was standing outside a gate hut with a barrier. Beyond the barrier was a parking lot and beyond that James could see a small forest of masts. It was a marina. A moment later, the barrier was lifted and Christophe's car drove through. I'm in deep shit, thought James. They'd come by boat.

He parked his car just off the road and walked quickly back to the entrance to the lot. The guy who'd been talking to Christophe had disappeared back into his hut. A crudely painted sign over the door announced that this was the office of the harbormaster. James leaned in the window. The man he had seen talking to Christophe was lacing a cup of coffee from a bottle of rum. "Anywhere round here a guy can rent a boat?" asked James.

The man looked at him speculatively for a moment. He was

a weatherbeaten old guy who looked as though he'd spent his entire life at sea and was really pissed off he wasn't still out there. "What kind of a boat?" he asked.

"A fast one," said James. At the far side of the lot, he could see Christophe had parked his car. He and Marianne were helping Bradley out.

"What do you need with a fast boat?"

Nothing, if he didn't get it soon. He pulled a twenty-pound note from his pocket. "Let's start all over, from the top. Anywhere round here a guy can rent a boat?"

The money disappeared quickly. "Number three jetty. Slip eighteen. Tell Pierre that Gaston sent you."

The price would go up because Gaston would have to get his cut.

"Is everyone on these islands French?" he asked.

"Just the best of us."

"My buddy's French. He just came through here. Blond guy. Maybe you know him?"

"If you're with the Frenchman, what do you want with a boat of your own?"

"I've got a bet on with him. I'm gonna get there first."

"Won't be hard. I reckon his boat only makes ten, twelve knots. Pierre can get you to Granville probably an hour ahead of him easy."

James hoped that Pierre knew where Granville was. He'd never heard of it. He peeled off another twenty. "Can you make a phone call for me?"

The twenty disappeared into the same pocket. "Providing it's on the island."

James asked him to call Lee Chambers. "She owns a gift shop on Berners Street, opposite the bank. Tell her not to worry, I'll be in touch."

"Who'll be in touch?"

"Tell her James," he said. The last thing he needed right now was for her to start worrying about him and maybe going to the police to report her pistol-packing lodger had gone missing. The harbormaster agreed to do as he asked and told him once more how to find Pierre with the fast boat.

James walked down to jetty number three. He could see Bradley with Marianne and Christophe flanking him. They were walking along jetty five. They stopped alongside a twenty-five-foot cruiser. It was painted white with light blue trim. There was a French flag mounted at the stern. As they started to board, James found slip eighteen. It was occupied by a wicked-looking speedboat whose only practical function could be the towing of water skiers or showing off. A pair of legs protruded from the hatch that gave access to the engines.

James stepped aboard. The motion of the boat alerted the guy, who struggled out of the hatch and, still seated on the deck, turned toward James. He looked like Roger from Malibu, stiff with engine grime and about the same age. "Pierre?"

The boy wasn't going to admit to anything without first knowing what it was about. "Who wants to know?"

"Gaston said you could rent me this boat," said James.

"Where you want to go, mister?"

"Granville."

"Are you legal or hot?"

"I'm legal."

"I'm only asking 'cause it makes a difference which way we go into Granville. Front door or back."

"Let's use the back," said James. He still didn't know where Granville was. If it was off the islands, on the French or English mainland, he didn't want some enthusiastic customs official patting him down and coming up with a loaded gun and a two-week supply of methadone.

"That'll be two fifty quid."

"Deal," said James.

Pierre looked surprised that he wasn't going to get an argument.

"When do you want to leave?"

"About ten minutes ago."

"You've got it, mister." His head disappeared under the engine hatch for a couple of seconds, then he climbed to his feet and slammed the hatch. He moved to the controls and started her up. The engines exploded into life, belching out a huge cloud of black smoke. He throttled them back. "You wanna cast off the bow line," he said to James. James clambered out of the boat and did as he was told. "Give her a shove," shouted Pierre. James did so, then jumped back on board as Pierre throttled down and engaged the reverse gears. The boat started to reverse out of the slip. He looked across toward the French boat. It hadn't moved yet. He was in good shape, decided James.

Pierre threw him a lifejacket and told him to put it on. As soon as he'd done so he joined Pierre at the controls. "How long is it gonna take us?" he asked.

"Three hours. Maybe four. Depends on the weather between here and the mainland." Okay, so now James knew it was France. It was a hundred miles to the southern coast of England. As they turned into the main channel and headed toward the sea wall, they passed the slip containing Christophe's boat. James could see Christophe slipping the moorings. Somebody else was at the controls. It wasn't Bradley or Marianne. They'd disappeared below. Remembering how Bradley had looked when he came out of the bank, James figured it had to be for another fix. He'd seen some pretty heavy junkies during his time in the force, but Bradley had looked like he took the prize. He had to be on a four-hourly fix and climbing the wall if it was ten minutes late. He revised some estimates he'd made. He was going to have to hit Dr. Quigley for a few more prescriptions.

The boat reached the end of the sea wall and moved beyond its protection. Immediately it started to roll heavily and James knew he was going to be sick. As Pierre fed more power to the engines James tapped him on the shoulder. "Where do I throw up?" he shouted above the engine noise.

Pierre grinned. "Anywhere you like so long as it's not in my boat." James moved to the side of the boat and got rid of his lunch and his breakfast.

Twenty minutes later he was feeling better. Not much, but enough to rejoin Pierre at the controls. They were traveling fast, the hull of the boat slamming the surface of the water hard enough to make James wonder whether the bottom was going to survive. It didn't seem to worry Pierre. "Lovely day," he shouted.

"How well do you know Granville?" yelled James.

Pierre pointed to the back of his hand. "Like that," he said.

"Can I rent a boat there?"

"You already rented a boat."

"A cabin cruiser. Something large enough to take me and one other guy to England and drop us off someplace quiet."

"It'll cost you," shouted Pierre.

"She has to be ready to move out a couple of hours after we arrive and whoever takes us has got to have a short memory."

"Short memories come extra," said Pierre.

"Can you help?"

"That'll come extra too."

"Whatever," said James. He wasn't going to argue. Carrying on a conversation at a bellow was exhausting. Added to that, he started to feel sick again. He spent the remainder of the trip with his head over the side of the boat.

They made Granville, on the Normandy coast of France, in exactly two hours. James reckoned it would be two more hours before Bradley and the others could possibly arrive. The ramparts of the old town, high above the harbor, looked as grim as James felt.

Long before they reached the harbor entrance, Pierre changed course and throttled way down. They slid past the harbor and eventually edged into a small marina to the south of the town. Pierre tied up at an empty slip. Nobody appeared to question his arrival. Smuggling from St. Helier to Granville had got to be a breeze, thought James.

Two slips away from where Pierre tied up was a thirty-foot cabin cruiser. Pierre told James to stay with the speedboat while he went to have a word with the skipper. James watched him climb aboard and disappear below. A couple of minutes later he reappeared and beckoned James to come aboard.

The boat was a little grimy, but it looked seaworthy enough. Below, in the main cabin, James was introduced to the captain/

owner, Alistair ffyfe. "Three *f*s, old boy, no capitals," said ffyfe. He was a tall, languid Englishman in his early fifties. He looked as if a stiff breeze might blow him overboard. "Young Pierre tells me you want me to drop you and another bod somewhere in Blighty." James confirmed that this was his requirement. "One thousand pounds," said ffyfe. "Half now, the other half on arrival."

"Deal," said James.

They were sitting on the headland that overlooked both the main harbor and the marina when Christophe's boat chugged into view. During the past ninety minutes James had heard ffyfe's life story three times over.

"Used to be a stockbroker a few years ago. Pinstriped suit, rolled umbrella, house in Virginia Water, all the trappings. Got involved in a spot of inside trading. Nothing to do with me, of course, but my guvnors threw me to the wolves. Thought it best to make a clean break. Bought the old tub and came out here. Make a good living nowadays smuggling God's dumb creatures into Blighty."

"Illegal immigrants?" asked James. He wasn't really interested, but he needed ffyfe on his side and there was no point in offending him. Not yet anyway.

"Animals, old son. Our furred and feathered friends. Six months quarantine if you try to take Fido or Pussikins into England legally. Some old biddies would rather lose their children than their pets. I load the old tub up with a couple of dozen assorted dogs, cats and canaries at a hundred quid a time and run them across the water. Their mummys and daddys pick them up the other side. If I get spotted by a customs launch all I have to do is dump them over the side with weights tied to their flea collars. Good safe business. Which is more than I can say about what you're mixed up in."

"It's not illegal," said James. If truth could be told, the whole operation had become so complicated that he honestly didn't know anymore whether he was breaking any laws.

"So why are you hiring me when you could go a few miles

up the coast and hop the ferry from Cherbourg?" asked ffyfe.

"I'm buying privacy," said James. "It's for my brother's sake."

"A hopeless addict, you said."

"If I don't get him away from those people, the stuff's going to kill him." That part at least was true.

Ffyfe looked at him for a moment from his pale blue, red-rimmed eyes. "Humph!" he said.

James had the feeling that he didn't believe a word he'd been told. But before he could go into it further he spotted Christophe's boat. "There she is."

Ffyfe used his binoculars. "I know her," he said. "She berths a few slips down from me. Belongs to some German chappy. Werner something or other. Don't know what he does for a living, but I'd stake my life it's nothing legal. He's just the kind of a man who'd be mixed up in this business with your brother. Can't stand the fellow, as a matter of fact." Maybe he was only trying to convince himself that he didn't like Werner so that what was to follow would be easier to live with. On the other hand, he may have been telling the truth. Most Englishmen of ffyfe's age didn't like the Germans.

James got to his feet. "Shouldn't we be going?"

"Plenty of time," said ffyfe. "She won't be berthing for another twenty minutes." But he stood up anyway. Just before they started back toward the marina, ffyfe took James's arm. "Sure you want to go through with this, old man?"

"I've got to. For the sake of the family."

"Understand perfectly," said ffyfe. "You can rely on me."

You'd better believe it, thought James.

In fact it was thirty-five minutes before the boat berthed. By then James was sitting at the end of the jetty with a fishing rod in his hand, wearing an old sailor's cap borrowed from ffyfe, who was doing the same thing twenty-five yards further down the jetty. As the boat churned water in the main channel in preparation for reverse docking, the man at the controls, James assumed it was Werner, called down below and Christophe came on deck. Werner needed help tying up. Christophe took the stern line, and as the boat reversed into the slip, he jumped ashore and started to make fast. He wasn't wearing the topcoat that James had seen outside the bank at St. Helier. He had on jeans and a sweater. He looked like solid muscle from the neck down. James had never considered himself a particularly brave man, neither was he foolhardy. The only way he was going to be able to tackle this guy with any hope of coming out in one piece, was from behind. That's what he did.

Christophe had made fast the stern line. Now he moved forward to the end of the slip and grabbed at the bow line. He bent over to tie up. James deserted his fishing tackle. He covered the fifteen feet to Christophe very quickly. There, he planted the sole of his shoe on Christophe's backside and shoved hard. The Frenchman went head-first into the harbor. "Man overboard," yelled James. Werner killed the engines and, deserting his post at the wheel, came running forward. Christophe had just surfaced and was splashing around in the water trying to make some sense out of what had just happened. Werner unhooked a life preserver and leaned over the deck rail to throw it to Christophe. James reached up, grabbed at his wrists and pulled hard. Werner flipped over the rail and landed in the water practically on top of Christophe.

James swung himself aboard. Ffyfe had already cast off the stern line and was at the controls. He had pulled on a ski mask. He was going to have to live around these parts for a long time to come and he didn't want any of the neighbors to recognize him. Werner had left the engines idling. All ffyfe had to do was engage the gears and advance the throttles. The boat crept out of the slip just fast enough to swamp Werner and Christophe, who were still thrashing around in the water. But James didn't even wait to wave them au revoir. He pulled his gun and opened the door leading down to the main cabin. There, he came face to face with Marianne Langer for the first time.

On reflection, he had to admit it was no big deal. She didn't look much different than she had in the photograph Langer had shown him. But right now, he wasn't paying as much attention to how she looked as to what she might try to do. Bradley was stretched out on one of the berths dead to the world. Marianne had started out of the cabin when she heard the ruckus outside. As she saw James, she stopped. She didn't look particularly surprised, or even upset. "Go sit down, Mrs. Langer," said James.

She looked at his gun, then back to his face. Without change of expression she did as he asked, sitting on the berth opposite Bradley. James checked out the unconscious man by poking at him with his gun. There was no reaction. He turned back to Marianne. She was watching him carefully. She was wearing jeans, a cotton shirt knotted at the waist, and sneakers. He noticed for the first time that she had the bluest eyes he'd ever seen . . . no, they weren't blue, they were violet. She had a small, straight nose, a mouth which seemed about average, a well-shaped face, and her hair was tied back in a short ponytail. She looked about sixteen years old. Attractive enough to make a guy turn for a second look, but hardly a face to launch a thousand ships.

"How long is he going to stay like that?" asked James, indicating Bradley. She didn't answer. In fact she didn't move a muscle. It was as if he hadn't said a word. "Don't give me a hard time, Mrs. Langer. It's been a tough day and it's about to get tougher." Still there was no reaction from Marianne. James heard the engine noise change. He glanced out of the porthole. The boat had moved to the center of the main channel and ffyfe was shifting the engines into full ahead. He had a momentary glimpse of Werner and Christophe, still thrashing around in the water, then he returned his attention to Marianne. She was still watching him carefully. They really were the most remarkable eyes; and maybe the mouth was a little better than average. "I'm going to tie your hands, Mrs. Langer," he said.

"Why, Mr. Reed? I assume you're James Reed." Her voice was husky. Maybe she had a cold. Or maybe she sounded like she had a mouthful of honey all the time.

"Because I'm going to have my hands full in a couple of minutes and I won't be able to keep an eye on you. Stand up, please." She stood up and put her hands behind her back. "In front," said James. He stuck the gun in the waist at the back of his pants and tied her wrists with a short length of cord. She had small hands, with neatly trimmed unpolished nails. In fact, everything about her was small. She couldn't have stood more than five feet and a bit. Her face was level with James's chest, and while he was tying her she tilted her head and didn't take her eyes off his for a second. She was wearing no makeup. Her skin was flawless with the exception of a tiny mole high on her right cheekbone. She smelled . . . exotic, was the only way James could describe it. He had a feeling it was her own body smell and had nothing to do with perfume. "Go sit down again," he said, when he had finished tying her.

He transferred his gun from the back of his pants to the front and turned his attention to Bradley. As he did so, ffyfe called down from the deck. "Three minutes, old man."

James levered Bradley into a sitting position, propping his back against the bulkhead. He was skin and bone. He probably didn't weigh more than a hundred pounds. Just as well, thought James, who was going to have to carry him. Now he turned back to Marianne, who was still watching him. "Where's the money?" he asked. She did him the compliment of not asking "What money?" She nodded toward the drawer beneath Bradley's berth. He opened it and took out the briefcase he had seen her carrying from the bank. "Is the Nassau money here too?"

He'd have liked to think he'd got a small reaction here, but he couldn't be sure. She continued to stare at him flatly. Jesus Christ, but she had sensational eyes. "The two fifty grand from Nassau," he said. "Minus the early withdrawal penalty, plus the interest, I figure it should be about two hundred and twenty grand. Then there's the five hundred twenty thousand from Jersey . . . close on three quarters of a million. Right?"

Why the hell was he trying to impress her with how clever he was? He flipped open the briefcase. There was a large number of neatly taped bundles of one-hundred-dollar bills, one hundred bills in each stack. That came to ten thousand dollars per stack. There were more than seventy-five stacks. James counted them quickly. A hundred stacks in all. One million dollars cash. "Now we know why you went to Caracas," he said.

If she was impressed by his deduction, she didn't show it. He shut the briefcase and threw it up onto the deck. "Take care of this," he called to ffyfe. Then he turned back to Marianne. "On deck," he said.

She stood up and walked to the companionway without a word.

"One other thing," said James. He nodded toward Bradley. "Where's his stuff?"

She didn't even ask what he was referring to. She nodded toward a cupboard set above one of the berths. James opened it. There was a small case holding half a dozen unwrapped syringes and enough heroin to knock out a herd of elephants. Obviously they had intended keeping Bradley in a comatose state for quite a time to come. James left the heroin where it was, and followed Marianne up on deck.

If ffyfe was surprised to see a woman with her hands tied, he masked it well. "Everything tickety-boo, old man?"

James confirmed everything was okay. He looked back toward the harbor, a few hundred yards off the stern. Nothing seemed to be happening from that direction yet. "Can you handle the next bit on your own?" he asked ffyfe.

"Providing the young lady gives me no trouble."

"If she does, push her overboard," said James.

Already they were drawing alongside ffyfe's boat, which they had tied up to a mooring buoy an hour ago. Now, as ffyfe maneuvered Werner's boat alongside, James went back below. He heaved the unconscious Bradley across his shoulder and staggered back on deck. As he did so he caught Bradley's head a blow on the top of the hatchway. It could have decapitated him for all Bradley cared.

As James came up, ffyfe had put the engines in neutral. The two boats were side by side now, bumping gently against each other. "Over you go, young lady," said ffyfe to Marianne. She did as she was told. "You next, old man."

James managed to step from one boat to the other without dropping either himself or Bradley into the water. He lowered Bradley onto the deck, propping him against the wheelhouse bulkhead. He started to slide sideways. James moved to prevent his head from hitting the deck, but was too late. The hell with it, he thought. He moved quickly to untie the mooring rope.

Meanwhile, ffyfe had returned to the controls of Werner's boat. Now he advanced the throttles and put her in forward gear. She started to edge away from his own boat. He checked the compass reading, then he looped a cord over the wheel. Now he opened the throttles wide and ran for the rail.

"The briefcase, for Christ's sake," yelled James.

Ffyfe scooped up the briefcase and just made it to his own boat before the widening gap between them made it impossible. He went straight to the controls, started her up, and a moment later they were pulling away from Werner's boat, which had now built up a good speed and was heading vaguely southwest. In about an hour it would hit the French coastline around Cancale. That's if it wasn't boarded before then.

James told Marianne to go below. She did so without a word. He hefted Bradley onto his shoulder again and followed her down. She was sitting at the galley table. She watched him with complete detachment as he dumped Bradley on the port berth. James checked his pulse. It was weak, but steady. "What time will he need his next fix?" he said to Marianne.

"Two hours from now." She still had honey in her voice.

James didn't fool himself into thinking it was for his benefit. He called up to ffyfe. "Any firearms down here?"

"Good heavens, no," answered ffyfe.

"I'm locking you in," said James, to Marianne. "Make yourself comfortable. We've got a long trip ahead of us."

He went up on deck and locked the cabin door. He had just joined ffyfe at the wheel when the skinny Englishman pointed off, handing him the binoculars. James focused them on the entrance to the marina, now nearly three quarters of a mile away. An outboard motorboat was coming out fast. James could see it carried two men. As it emerged from behind the sea wall, one of the men pointed toward the southwest. The boat turned in that direction. James moved his binoculars ahead of it.

Werner's boat was making good speed by now. It would take

the speedboat at least twenty minutes to catch up, then another ten minutes for the men to circle around yelling threats. Finally they'd realize the boat was doing a *Marie Celeste* and they'd board her. By then James and ffyfe would be long gone in the opposite direction.

"Nice timing," said James. He picked up the briefcase.

"What's in the briefcase, old man?" asked ffyfe.

"One million dollars cash," said James.

"Very droll," said ffyfe.

James stayed on deck with ffyfe for an hour before going below once more. Ffyfe showed him how to use the ship-to-shore radio. He made an open call to the French maritime authorities, not identifying himself. It was picked up in St. Malo. Fortunately the operator at the other end spoke some English so he was able to get his message across.

Not once did ffyfe ask any questions. What he did talk about was bettering his deal. "When old Werner von Kraut gets back to the marina and finds my boat gone he might start asking questions."

"So?"

"You never know with the Germans. They're pretty dim most of the time, but he might put two and two together and come up with four. What if someone recognized me making off with his boat."

"Your own mother wouldn't have recognized you in that ski mask."

"Still, it's a thought. Bears consideration."

"What kind of consideration?"

"To tell the truth, I don't much fancy going back there. Not for a time, anyway."

"How much is it going to cost me?" asked James.

"See, I didn't know about the young lady. One bod, you told me."

"I wasn't sure she'd agree to come along."

"But she did, old boy. Soon as you showed her that shooter

of yours. Which is something else you didn't bother to mention. I don't care for shooters. Don't much care for the individuals who carry them either."

"We'll talk about it later," said James.

"Not too much later, if it's all the same to you." James thought he could detect an edge in the voice, one he hadn't heard before. "After all, it's a big ocean. I could lose my way, then where would we all be? Wandering around the English Channel like the Flying Dutchman, until some nosy coast guard launch came alongside to see what's what."

"Are you trying to threaten me?" asked James, knowing full well the answer.

"Heavens, no. You're the one with the gun," said ffyfe. "Providing you can navigate and read charts, I haven't got a leg to stand on."

"How does five thousand sound?"

"Pounds?"

"Dollars."

"For five thousand dollars you're going to have to give me some answers. See, I'll have to weigh the pros and cons. On the other hand, for seventy-five hundred, no questions and I'll help you throw them overboard if that's what you want."

"It's not what I want," said James. "But you've got a deal."

James opened the briefcase and took out one of the stacks of hundred-dollar bills. He peeled off twenty-five of them and stuck them in his pocket. The balance he held out toward ffyfe. "Seventy-five hundred dollars," he said.

Ffyfe was staring at the briefcase. "Jesus Christ," he said.

James snapped it shut again. Ffyfe looked like a man who'd just had the TV go out in the middle of his favorite show. "Well!" said James. "Do you want it or not?"

Ffyfe took the money. "You've got a friend for life," he said.

"I've also got a gun," said James. He went below, taking the briefcase with him.

Bradley was still out cold. Marianne was sitting where she had been when James went on deck. Her roped hands were folded neatly in her lap. Now she held them toward James. "Untie me, please."

"I don't think so," said James. He wondered if she'd been the one to use the blowtorch on young King. Or had she left it to Christophe and just watched?

"Then you'll have to take me to the bathroom yourself," she said.

He was sorely tempted. He went through to the head and checked there was nothing there she could use as a weapon. Only then did he untie her hands and let her go. When she returned, she held her hands out toward him, wrists together. "Forget it," said James.

If he was expecting thanks, he was unlucky. She returned to her seat without a word. He checked on Bradley again. Then he moved to the table and sat across from Marianne. "Where were you planning on going next?" he asked. She just continued to look at him. "Let me guess. How about Monaco? Another two hundred and fifty grand to swell the coffers." Maybe there was the faintest hint of surprised curiosity in those startlingly violet eyes. It was enough encouragement for James to push on. "Your husband spreads a wide net, Mrs. Langer. Knowing him like you must, I'm surprised you thought you could get away with it." Still nothing from Marianne. Man, this was hard work. "What was your target? Five million? Ten? How long were you going to lug that poor slob around, pumping him full of shit so's he'd loot his own bank accounts. And what did you plan for him when you and lover boy decided you'd got enough? Another Venezuelan blowtorch job or something cleaner, a bullet like in California?" Definite reaction this time. Nothing spectacular. A millimeter raising of one eyebrow. But it was encouraging. Maybe he was beginning to impress her at last. All things to all men, Langer had said. Well, as far as he was concerned, she was just another dame . . . violet eyes perhaps, and a hell of a cute mouth, with a figure to match . . . but he was immune to ladies who killed people. As long as he kept telling himself that, he'd be okay. "Anyway, it's all hypothetical now, isn't it? Bradley's back from the dead, and you're going back to your husband."

A definite reaction this time. "I'll kill myself first." She didn't overdramatize the remark. It was a plain statement of fact.

"That would be a hell of a waste after all the trouble he's gone to," said James. She shrugged her indifference. "On the other hand, it's no skin off my nose," said James. "I was paid to find the two of you. Okay, so I've found you. What happens next is strictly between you and him."

"You're not going to deliver me to him bound hand and foot!" He could be wrong, but the honey in her voice seemed to have thickened.

"I'm just going to tell him where he can pick you up."

"Surely that amounts to the same thing."

"You're a grown-up lady, Mrs. Langer. If you don't want to stay around, you just have to walk."

"People don't walk away from Karl Langer."

"You already did. He's got the scars to prove it." He nodded toward Bradley. "So has he. What beats me is why either of them would want you within a mile of them."

"Jonathan loves me," she said. She glanced across at the unconscious Bradley. "Poor Jonathan."

"And Langer?"

"He hates me."

"But he wants you back."

"So he can keep an eye on me. As long as I was with Jonathan, he felt safe. He knew where I was, what I was doing. He knew I would do him no harm."

"Like pushing him down the stairs and carving him up with scissors?"

"Is that what he told you?"

"It's true, isn't it?"

"I was angry. But that's not what he's worried about."

"What is?"

She looked at him for a moment as if trying to make up her mind about something. "It doesn't matter," she said.

"Why did you leave him?"

"I met Jonathan. It happens, Mr. Reed. Karl was old, Jonathan was young. Karl was ugly, Jonathan was beautiful. He really was in those days. That was before he started killing himself with drink and drugs. It took eighteen months for him to become what you see there. In the end, I couldn't stand it any longer. I left him."

"With Christophe."

"Alain just happened to be there when I needed somebody. I knew once Karl heard I'd left Jonathan, he'd come looking for me. So I disappeared."

"Until the money ran out."

She nodded toward Bradley, who'd started to move slightly in his stupor. "Look at him. What does he need with the money he's got put away all over the world. He'll be dead in three months, perhaps sooner. I don't mean to sound callous, Mr. Reed, I'm just making a statement of fact. And if Jonathan's money is going to keep me insulated from Karl, that's all that concerns me right now. It's the difference between life and death."

"You're an expert on death, aren't you, Mrs. Langer. Four up to now. Or are there some I don't know about?"

At that moment, ffyfe called down from above. "How about some nourishment, old man?"

James got to his feet and started opening the cupboards in the galley, looking for something to eat.

"I'll do it," said Marianne.

James was happy to let her get on with it. "Just stay away from the kitchen knives," he said.

He sat watching her as she started to prepare the food. She had trouble reaching into one of the top cupboards so he went to help her. As he reached across, his body came into contact with hers. She turned those huge violet eyes on him for a moment. Her expression was unreadable. He handed her what she had been reaching for and sat down again. Then Bradley started to make noises. She glanced toward him, then continued what she was doing. James moved over to Bradley and dragged him into a sitting position, stuffing a couple of pillows behind his back.

"He's going to give you lots of trouble," she said casually.

"I'll handle it," said James.

"You left his stash behind."

"I know," said James. "Soon as your boyfriend docks, he's going to know it too."

"You told the authorities."

"Don't worry. If he's lucky he won't get more than a couple of months. Unless they check his record."

She stared at him for a long moment, then went back to preparing the food.

Bradley finally cracked open his eyes. For a full minute they remained completely blank. He was like a computer having information fed in by a very slow one-fingered typist. Gradually things began to click into place. He shifted himself to a more comfortable sitting position. His glance slid across James incuriously and finally settled on Marianne. "I'm hungry," he said.

"Fifteen minutes," said Marianne.

Now his gaze came back to James. "Don't I know you?"

"James Reed. California."

"Right. The man with the house. What are we doing in California?"

"We're not."

"Where are my sunglasses?"

"They're in his top pocket," said Marianne. James pulled out the sunglasses and handed them to Bradley. He nearly poked out his eye trying to get them on. Finally James took them from him and stuck them on the end of his nose.

"Thank you, James Reed," said Bradley. He looked toward Marianne again. "I feel pretty shitty," he said.

"You'll have to talk to Mr. Reed. He's in charge now."

"Does he know what he's in charge of . . . of what he's in charge? Do you know what of you're in charge, James Reed?"

James took a bottle from his pocket and shook out a couple of methadone tablets. "Take these," he said.

"What for?"

"You heard the lady. I'm in charge."

"Right. Mr. Reed's in charge." He took the two tablets, tried to swallow them and nearly choked. James fetched him a glass of water. Finally he got the tablets down. "Now can I have my fix?"

"You've just had it," said James.

By the time Bradley had worked out what this meant, he'd dropped off to sleep again. "It's not going to work," said Marianne.

"Did you ever try?"

"I tried. Perhaps you don't believe me, but I tried very hard."

Maybe she had. But it sure hadn't worked. James looked across toward Bradley. The methadone wasn't going to save him either.

Marianne offered to take ffyfe's food up on deck. James told her he'd do it. He didn't want to risk her flashing her baby violets at ffyfe and convincing him she was the victim of some ghastly plot concocted by James.

"Pretty little thing, the memsahib," said ffyfe. "But the chap's in a bit of a state." James grunted something unintelligible. Ffyfe got the message and shut up. At least, he shut up about the passengers. Other things had to be discussed. "About where would you consider a suitable landfall, old man?" he asked.

"Somewhere east of Portsmouth," said James.

"I know just the spot," said ffyfe. "Drowned many a puppy dog off Selsea Bill in my time." He pulled a chart from the locker in front of him and started to make some calculations.

"How long?" asked James.

"Five or six hours if the weather holds."

"I need to make a phone call to Switzerland," said James.

Ffyfe thought about it for a moment. "Do it through the U.K.," he said. "But you'll have to wait a while. Radio's not all that powerful. We're too far out. Say a couple of hours offshore."

"I'll need you to run an errand for me tomorrow morning," said James.

"Nothing dodgy, I hope. It's not that I mind personally, but I don't want to risk some country bobby stopping me and asking for my ID. I'm persona non grata in Blighty right now."

"I need you to rent a car for me."

"Be easier if you did it yourself."

It would be easier. It would also mean leaving ffyfe alone with Marianne and Bradley. "I'd prefer you do it," said James. Then he answered ffyfe's question before he could ask it. "I'll pay for your time."

"Whatever you say, old man."

James stayed on deck with him until he'd finished his meal. A fairly stiff breeze had sprung up. James hoped he wasn't going to be sick again.

When he went below, Bradley was awake and sulking. He'd decided he didn't want any food after all. What he did want, Marianne had told him she couldn't provide. He glared at James as he came down into the cabin. "Marianne says you're cutting me off," he said.

"Marianne's right."

"Where the hell do you get off telling me what to do."

"I'm your minder. Remember? You paid me."

Bradley groped around in the fog of his memory. "Right! My Californian minder. Where's Bruce? He's my minder too."

James glanced at Marianne, who was washing the dishes. She refused to meet his gaze. "He quit," said James.

Bradley shuddered suddenly as though a draft of cold air had swept through the cabin. "Christ," he said. "Give me a fix."

"You already had it," said James. "Shut up and I'll give you another in a couple of hours."

"That shit's no good. Tell him, honey."

"I already did," said Marianne. She moved over to him and pulled a blanket up around his shoulders. Now he started to shiver in earnest. As she came back into the galley she looked at James.

"I wish you luck, Mr. Reed."

"I'm calling your husband in a few hours. You want to talk to him?" said James. He needed to get under this girl's armor.

"No."

"He'll come for you. You know that."

"Yes."

"Unless you can give me good cause not to tell him about you."

"You've made up your mind already."

"So change it. Tell me the real reason he wants you back. Everyone tells me you're great in the sack, but it can't be just that."

She looked at him steadily. "I'm not 'great in the sack' as you put it, Mr. Reed. I'm amenable and inventive, and when it's all over, I'm suitably grateful. That's all it takes. But you're right, that's not the reason Karl wants me back."

"So tell me."

She looked past him toward Bradley, who was hugging the blanket around him and shaking like a leaf. "Give him another methadone," she said.

"It's too soon."

"Give it to him." There was a hard, flat edge to her voice. No honey this time. James fed Bradley another methadone tablet. It wasn't heroin, but it gave an addict the kind of high that helped him to cope with the pain of not having the real thing. Eventually he'd become addicted to that too, but the side effects weren't going to kill him. At least, that's what the experts said. It got to Bradley. He stopped shaking and tried to join in the conversation. "What are you two being so fucking secretive about?" he asked. Neither of them replied. "We get the money?" he said to Marianne.

"We got it," she answered.

"Where? Sorry, I forgot."

"The Channel Islands. Jersey."

"Right. I remember now. Luxembourg next stop." He looked around the cabin. "Where's the Frenchman?"

"He's not with us any longer," said Marianne.

"What did you do? Fire him?"

"Something like that," said Marianne.

So that was how they'd managed to trail Bradley around with the two of them. By telling him Christophe was just an employee. Bradley thought Marianne and he were together again for real.

James wondered if Christophe took a back seat while Bradley made love to Marianne. It would be no big deal. Men in Bradley's condition had little inclination for sex and practically no ability. Added to that, Christophe was an ex-pimp, he was accustomed to other men fucking his women.

"Perhaps I will have something to eat," said Bradley.

Marianne fetched him some food and sat across from him while he ate it. They talked quietly to each other, too softly for James to overhear. She laughed once at something. They looked like a happily married couple. Except she was married to somebody else, and, for reasons James didn't yet know, her husband wanted her back. He'd thought he'd got her all figured out. Now that he'd met her, he wasn't so sure anymore. Bradley hadn't been kidnapped, he'd gone with her of his own free will. Not that there was much free will left under all that heroin and booze. He hadn't known about the killings in California. Maybe Christophe was the villain and Marianne just another victim. In which case, what the hell was he going to do with the two of them? And what was he going to do about Langer?

James relieved ffyfe at the wheel. Ffyfe told him to keep the compass bearing on 045 degrees, and if he saw any lights to fetch him from below. He went down to the cabin, and almost immediately Marianne came up on deck. She'd found an old duffel coat from somewhere. James was still wearing his Harrods overcoat. It might have been adequate for keeping out the cold of the London streets, but in the middle of the English Channel, it wasn't worth shit. "How is he?" he asked.

"He's sleeping again."

"He does a lot of that."

"You do realize he's dying, I suppose," said Marianne.

"He'll be okay when he gets straightened out."

She didn't believe it any more than he did. But she didn't give him an argument. Instead, she changed the subject completely. "What's in this for you?" she asked.

"Job satisfaction."

"I'm serious, Mr. Reed."

"So am I. I was paid to mind Bradley. I messed up. Now I'm trying to put it right."

"Right for who? Jonathan or Karl?"

"Your husband doesn't come into it."

"Come on, Mr. Reed. You're working for him."

"He's picking up the tab. It's not the same thing."

"I'm not going back to him, you know."

"That's up to you. Soon as I make my telephone call, you're on your own."

"Without Jonathan, without Alain and without any money. What are you going to do with the money, incidentally?"

"Turn it over to someone who can be trusted to take care of it on Bradley's behalf. Not Simon Wilson, just in case you're getting any ideas."

"Poor Simon," said Marianne.

"You use that epithet for most men you're involved with. Poor Jonathan, poor Simon, poor Alain. How about poor Karl?"

"Karl's different."

"Older maybe, richer, but just another of your men, Mrs. Langer." She moved over to the deck rail and looked out at the night. Apart from the phosphorescent highlights on the water, there was nothing to see. The sky and the sea blended into the same darkness. There was a strong current running. James made a slight adjustment on the wheel, bringing the boat back on course. "Why didn't you divorce him when you ran off with Bradley?" he asked.

For a moment he thought she hadn't heard him. He was about to repeat the question when she turned from the rail and rejoined him at the wheel. "Karl didn't want a divorce," she said.

"It doesn't need two to get a divorce these days," said James.

"It does if one of them is Karl Langer. We were in touch while I was with Jonathan. At least, he always knew where we were. I asked him a dozen times."

"You left him for another man. You broke his leg and tried to blind him with a pair of scissors. You told him you'd never go back to him and he still wouldn't divorce you. I find that hard to understand."

"It's the truth."

"Lady, I don't think you'd tell the truth if your life depended on it," said James.

"But it does. I told you I'd kill myself before I'd go back to Karl. That's because I'd prefer to do it myself than have him do it."

"He wants you back so he can kill you, is that what you're saying?"

"I guarantee that if I went back to Karl, within a month I'd have an accident, a fatal accident."

James looked sideways at her. She was staring ahead into the darkness, her chin on her arms, which were folded across the top of the hatchway. She sensed him watching her and turned toward him. "I know you don't believe me. I'm not sure I even care anymore."

"Sure you care, Mrs. Langer, or you'd not be trying to soften me up," said James.

She straightened up, still looking at him. It was almost totally dark, but James could imagine those violet eyes staring into his. "You're an intelligent man, Mr. Reed. Work it out for yourself. If Alain and I didn't murder the people at your house, who did?"

"That's like asking 'If red isn't red, what color is it?' "

"We arrived at the house. I spoke to Jonathan. He agreed to come with me. We left."

"If you'll pardon the cynicism, bullshit!" said James.

"Why is it so hard to believe?"

"You creep in via the beach. You leave the same way. Where I come from, visitors don't behave like that. They ring the front doorbell and wait to be invited in."

"They do if they don't want to be seen."

"By who?"

"The people watching the house."

"Nobody was watching the house, Mrs. Langer."

"Ask your neighbor. The red house two doors down."

James knew the house she was talking about. "It's been empty since the summer."

She didn't seem to care all that much whether he believed her or not. "Your house was being watched from the moment Jonathan arrived," she said.

"Okay. Let's say for a moment that I believe you. You and/or Christophe didn't murder those people. How about Caracas. Did King blowtorch himself to death?"

"He was obviously killed by the same person," said Marianne.

"How did this killer know about Caracas?"

"You knew."

"Just me. And the poor guy I sent there."

"Who told you?"

"He asked questions in Nassau. It wasn't hard."

"It was nothing to do with me," she said flatly.

"And we know the killer couldn't possibly be Christophe because he's a fine upstanding young man who just happens to have a rap sheet like Al Capone before he made the big time."

"Alain doesn't have a criminal record."

"I've got news for you, Mrs. Langer."

"Check with the French authorities. Then think about it. Think about how somebody who wanted to get rid of me might try to frame me with a murder. Think about it after I'm dead."

"There's one thing you haven't told me," said James. "Why?"

"Karl thinks I know something about his past that he doesn't want to come out."

"Do you?"

"Yes, I do. He also thinks I have documents hidden somewhere that will support my beliefs."

"Which you don't."

"How do you know?"

"You'd have used them if you had. You want to tell me the secret of your husband's murky past?"

"No," she said. Light spilled from the hatch, as she opened it and went below. She closed it behind her, leaving James in darkness again. Only this time, it was a lot darker than it had been before.

8

Ffyfe came on deck around midnight. "Want to try your phone call now, old man?" James gave him Langer's contact number in Switzerland. Ffyfe used the ship-to-shore radio and patched through to an international telephone operator who dialed the number. "It's ringing," said ffyfe, handing James the radio mike.

It was a bad connection, but James was able to recognize Langer's voice when he came on the phone.

"I've found them," said James.

Maybe it was the line, but Langer sounded unimpressed. "Where?"

"They're with me right now. At least Bradley and your wife are. Christophe's likely in jail somewhere in France."

"Where exactly are you, Mr. Reed?"

"En route for England. By boat."

"Where and when will you arrive?"

"I'll meet you in London day after tomorrow," said James.

"Where?"

"I'll call you at Struther's and let you know."

There was a long pause. The static on the line was pretty bad. "All right, Mr. Reed. I'll be waiting for your call. I assume Mrs. Langer will be with you."

"I haven't made up my mind yet," said James. He switched off the radio without saying good-bye.

"Tickety-boo, old man?" said ffyfe.

"If I told you I hadn't the faintest idea, would you believe me?" said James.

"As long as you keep paying me, I'll believe anything."

"What's happening below?" asked James.

"Both sleeping like babies. What it must be to have a clear conscience."

"I wouldn't know," said James.

At a quarter past two, ffyfe cut the engines and announced that they had arrived. For the past twenty minutes they'd been traveling slowly up an inlet that had been getting narrower all the time. He'd refrained from using any lights, so James had been unable to see what was ashore. Now, as the engines died and complete silence took over, ffyfe switched on a spotlight mounted just above the wheel. The boat was bow in to a grass-covered bank encircled by a small grove of trees. "Hop ashore and tie her up, there's a good fellow," said ffyfe.

James did as he was asked, tying the bow line to a tree trunk. He came back aboard. "Where exactly are we?" he asked.

"A couple of miles from Chichester."

At that moment Marianne came up from below. Ffyfe had switched off the spotlight, but the light from the open hatchway spilled out across the trees. She asked the same question. "Where are we?"

"Just south of Calais," said James quickly. "Right, ffyfe?"

"Bang on," said ffyfe.

"Did you speak to Karl yet?"

"I did," said James.

"And?"

"I haven't made up my mind yet. How's Bradley?"

"Still sleeping. What happens now?"

"You'll be the first to know," said James.

■ ■ ■

James, Marianne and Bradley spent the rest of the night in the main cabin. Ffyfe disappeared to a small cabin forward where there was a single berth. Marianne slept on one of the bunks, Bradley on the other. James spent the night dozing at the galley table, waking every now and then just to make sure he wasn't alone. Bradley woke up yelling at three A.M. James gave him another dose of methadone, and he went back to sleep, cursing James to hell and beyond. At seven thirty A.M. ffyfe reappeared looking spruce and well rested. "Thought I'd go rent you the car you asked for, old man," he said. "How do you want me to pay for it?"

"Cash," said James. Marianne was watching them both from her bunk.

"You want to step up on deck for a moment," said ffyfe. James creaked his way upright. His bones cracked like somebody stepping on dry kindling. He followed ffyfe up on deck. It was a gray, cold day. It was going to rain later. Maybe it was cold enough to snow. "How long before I can be on my way?" asked ffyfe. "I mean, I don't want to rush you, but I get edgy hanging around the old U.K. for too long."

"You can leave as soon as you get back with the car."

"About the extra you promised . . ."

"When you get back," said James.

"See you in a couple of hours," said ffyfe. He went ashore and disappeared into the trees. James went back below. Marianne was in the galley making some coffee. For somebody who had spent the night sleeping in her clothes, she looked remarkably fresh. James knew he resembled a badly packed duffel bag. He wanted a shower and a change of clothes, neither of which he was going to get.

Bradley woke up. He looked particularly bad this morning. He was sweating profusely and couldn't stop shivering. He didn't even complain when James fed him a methadone instead of the heroin fix he was accustomed to. Marianne tried to make him drink some coffee. When he refused it, she wrapped him in an extra blanket and sat on the opposite bunk, holding his hand until he drifted off into an uneasy sleep once more. "I'll be moving him out in a couple of hours," said James.

"And me?"

"I haven't made up my mind about that," said James. In fact, he had. But he wanted to check out a couple of things before he committed himself fully. He wasn't able to do that until he could get to a telephone.

Ffyfe returned just after nine A.M. James heard somebody crashing through the trees and went up on deck, pretending to wipe down the handrail with one hand while he kept the other firmly wrapped around the gun, which he had slipped into his coat pocket.

"Only me, old man," said ffyfe, as he climbed aboard. He handed James a set of car keys and started to tell him where it was parked.

"You can show me," said James. "I'll need help. We've got a sick man on our hands this morning."

"We had a sick man on our hands yesterday," said ffyfe. "Word of advice, old man. Get rid of him soon. He's not long for this world, if you ask me."

"Maybe you'd like to tie a weight around his flea collar and do it for me," said James.

"For the right sum."

"I was joking," said James.

"I wasn't," said ffyfe.

Together, the two men half-carried and half-supported Bradley to where ffyfe had left the car parked. It was a mid-size coupe, in need of a coat of paint. Ffyfe assured him that the engine was reliable. He'd left it parked amid some trees just off a small country road. Across from the trees, bleak fields stretched away as far as a small group of farm buildings. A couple of miles beyond the farm James could see the spires and towers of Chichester Cathedral. He hadn't been sure what he was going to do with Marianne while he and ffyfe were moving Bradley. She had solved it for him by gathering James's things together with the briefcase and accompanying them. She was still wearing the same clothes from yesterday: jeans, a shirt and sneakers. Ffyfe insisted that she take along the duffel coat she'd borrowed last night. James told her to get into the driver's seat, while he and ffyfe put Bradley in the back, where he promptly fell asleep again.

"How much do I owe you for the car?" he asked ffyfe.

"Five hundred quid," said ffyfe. "I told them you'd be keeping it for a fortnight."

James felt like saying he could have bought it for that much. But he didn't argue. He gave ffyfe a thousand dollars, which he took from the briefcase. "Seven fifty for the car, the balance for collecting it. Okay?"

"I suppose you couldn't manage another hundred or two? After all, the old briefcase is bulging at the seams."

"It's not my money," said James.

Ffyfe shrugged. "No harm in asking. Been a real pleasure. Bon voyage." He looked toward Marianne, who was sitting behind the wheel. "You too, my dear." A moment later he had disappeared into the trees on his way back to his boat. James climbed into the back of the car alongside Bradley. "Let's go," he said to Marianne.

"Where to?"

"Just drive. I'll tell you on the way."

She started the car and pulled out onto the road, on the right side.

"You're driving on the wrong side of the road," said James.

"You told me we were in France," she said, pulling over to the left.

"I was lying," said James.

James wouldn't have put it past ffyfe to have stolen the car, so he made Marianne stick to back roads. It was just over two hours later when they pulled up outside the Queen's Arms in Little Wycherly. He told Marianne to wait in the car with Bradley. Just to be on the safe side, he took the car keys with him. Fred Carter was behind the bar checking his stock. "Jim, boy! Where the fuck have you been?"

"Couple of things I had to take care of," said James.

"Where's the bloke I'm supposed to mind?"

"In the car. There's a girl too."

"You didn't tell me about no fucking girl."

"She won't be any problem," said James, hopefully.

"Bet your arse, 'cause she's not staying here."

"Come on, Fred. She'll do the nursemaiding."

"You mean he's sick."

"He's not A-one."

"I don' know about this, Jim boy. A nice safe house you asked for. Now it's turning into a cross between a hospital and a holiday camp."

"How much, Fred?" said James.

"Cost you a hundred quid a day."

Ffyfe should have been so cheap. "You've got it," said James. He went back out to the car. He and Marianne dragged Bradley out of the back. He was awake again, with absolutely no idea where he was or what was happening. As they brought him through the bar, he saw Fred. "More wine, innkeeper!" he shouted.

"Jesus H. Christ," said Fred. "He's fucking crazy." Then he saw Marianne. "Sorry, ma'am . . . miss." He tried not to use bad language in front of a lady. " 'Ere, let me give you a hand." He took over from Marianne, and together he and James took Bradley behind the bar, through the door at the back and up the stairs. At the far end of the upstairs passage were more stairs leading to the attic room. It was large, with the roof angling down to the floor. In the slope of the roof, around eye level, was a skylight. It was dirty on the outside, but still allowed for plenty of daylight and a view across the fields at the back of the pub. Normally the attic was used for storing unwanted furniture. It still was, but Fred had moved it all to one side and covered it with dust sheets. He'd set up a camp bed, a table and chair and a small bureau.

"I'll find another bed," he said to James as they brought Bradley in. They supported him to the bed and lowered him to a sitting position. He looked around him. "Be it ever so humble," he said to nobody in particular. Then he started to shake.

"On the 'ard stuff I see," said Fred.

"Off the hard stuff," said James. "That's his problem."

Marianne had followed them upstairs. Now she pushed between them and sat on the bed beside Bradley. "You want something to eat, miss?" asked Fred.

"That would be very nice. Thank you." She smiled at Fred. Any doubts that he was still entertaining about allowing her to stay disappeared under the warmth of her smile.

"I'm going to lock you in," said James.

She looked toward him, the smile gone. "Of course you are, Mr. Reed."

He and Fred went downstairs again. Fred opened the pub for business. Nobody came in. Using the phone in Fred's parlor, James called the bank in Jersey and asked to speak to Mr. Roget. "Remember you told me that you had a cable from Caracas?" he said. "Did you tell anybody else?"

"Only Mr. Langer."

"Thank you," said James. He was about to hang up when Roget spoke again. "Somebody has been asking about you, Mr. Reed."

"Who?"

"The woman who owns the gift shop across the road."

"What did you tell her?"

"What would I tell her? I don't know anything."

Poor Lee. Maybe when this was over, he'd go back to St. Helier, to apologize and set things straight. Then again, maybe he wouldn't.

He called Solly Seligmann in London. "You said I could borrow your two lads if I needed them."

"For all I care, my boy, you can adopt them."

James told Solly where and when he wanted Mike and Henry Seligmann. "Nice day in the country. They'll like that," said Solly.

"Tell them to bring their twelve-bores. It's a shooting party."

"What'll they be shooting at, my son?"

"Hopefully nothing. Have them pick up a sex doll for me. One of those plastic things you blow up and use to get your jollies."

"You should never have divorced that movie star, my son," said Solly.

■ ■ ■

James offered to take the lunch that Fred had thrown together up to Bradley and Marianne. "I'll do it," said Fred. "You mind the bar."

There was nobody in the place and it looked like it might stay that way, so James came with him. Halfway upstairs, Fred stopped and turned back to James. "Are they hot?" he asked.

"Not with the law," said James.

"Any objections if I asked her to help behind the bar?"

With Marianne behind the bar, Fred's business would quadruple in ten minutes. "Providing you keep an eye on her, you can do what you like," he said. "But if she scarpers, I'm going to be really pissed off."

"She doesn't look to me like she's wanting to go anywhere."

He was right. Although James had been keeping a pretty sharp eye on her, if she'd really wanted, she could have run off half a dozen times already. But he still needed to make one more call before he committed himself completely. "Still got friends in high places, Fred?" he asked.

"Billy Whiteman owes me a favor or two. He's a chief inspector."

"Billy's a CI!" He'd been a sergeant when James had known him.

"Eat enough shit, pay enough dues, and the sky's the limit, Jim boy."

"Could he get me some info from France? I mean, like today."

"If he doesn't, I'll remind him of the file I lost on his kid while I was still in the force."

"What was the kid doing?"

"You don't want to know, Jim boy. Very nasty. Let me take this food up, and I'll be with you." James stood at the door while Fred instructed Marianne in the intricacies of a plowman's lunch. Bradley was flat out again. He looked terrible. Marianne smiled her thanks to Fred. She didn't even look at James.

"That one should see a doctor," said Fred as they came downstairs again.

"I know," said James.

"So what are you going to do about it?"

"I'll have your friend Quigley come down and take a look."

"Make it soon, or he'll have a wasted trip."

There was still nobody in the bar. They went through to the parlor where Fred called Chief Inspector Whiteman at New Scotland Yard. "Hey, Billy. How's everything with you?" He listened for a moment. "Glad to fucking hear it," he said. "How's the boy? A schoolteacher. That's nice. Not a boys' school I hope. Listen Billy, there's an old mucker needs a favor. You know him . . . Jim Reed . . . the one who married the movie star. Do your best for him, there's a pal. Say hello to your boy the schoolteacher." He cupped the phone and handed it to James. "A fucking schoolteacher. That's like turning an alcoholic loose in a distillery."

James took the phone and told Whiteman what he needed. The chief inspector said he would do his best. He'd get back to James in a couple of days.

"It's important I know today," said James.

"Sorry, Reed. That's out of the question," said the chief inspector. He talked as if his mouth was stuffed with gravel.

James cupped the phone. "Have a word with him, Fred," he said.

Fred took the phone. "Billy. Fred here. Do what Jim asks, my old mucker. He's a real nasty bastard when he don't get what he wants. If you was dealing with me, it'd be different. But he's got a mouth on him like the Blackwall Tunnel and he knows all about that boy of yours." There was a pause. James could hear the garbled voice of Whiteman through the phone. " 'Cause I told him, you stupid old fart," said Fred. He listened a moment longer, then he hung up. "He'll call you back in an hour," he said.

James turned over the methadone tablets to Fred. "Give him a couple in about an hour if he wants them. Then no more until this evening. I didn't get any sleep last night. I'm going to get my head down."

Fred took the tablets. "This ain't going to do it, Jim boy. He's too far gone. Is he a drinking man?"

"He likes a glass or two."

"Then you can bet his liver's about as useful as a rock by now. You can see it by looking at him. He's as yellow as a fucking daffodil. The shit and the booze together does it to them every time."

"I'm still going to get my head down," said James.

Fred woke him ninety minutes later. "Billy boy's on the phone," he said. James staggered downstairs to speak to Chief Inspector Whiteman. "Your man Christophe. He's clean," said Whiteman. "At least, he is in France. Whoever told you he had a record was putting you on."

"Thank you, Chief Inspector," said James. He hung up.

"What you expected?" asked Fred, who was polishing glasses while he pretended not to listen.

"More or less," said James. It was all confirmed as far as he was concerned. Marianne was telling the truth. Langer was lying.

He went upstairs to the attic. Fred had forgotten to lock the door when he collected the lunch tray. James knocked and walked in. Bradley was still sleeping. Marianne was standing by the skylight, looking out across the countryside. "Get your coat," said James. "We're going for a walk."

"I don't think I should leave him," she said.

James crossed the room and looked down at Bradley. He was breathing shallowly. Fred was right. His skin had a yellow pigment.

"We'll get a doctor to him tomorrow," he said. "We'll only be gone fifteen minutes at most."

She collected her duffel coat and they went for a walk.

"I've done some checking," he said. They were about half a mile from Fred's pub, walking the footpath that skirted the fields behind the Queen's Arms. They were the first words that had been spoken since they'd left.

"I expected you would," she said.

"Christophe doesn't have a rap sheet in France. At least, none that shows up right away. And your husband knew about Caracas and could have had people there."

"My husband has people everywhere," she said.

"Accepting those two facts, I can't see any particular reason to doubt the rest of your story."

"Bravo," she said. She didn't sound overjoyed. "So what happens next?"

"You tell me what it is that makes you a danger to your husband."

"That'll put you at risk too."

"I'm the fall guy as far as Langer is concerned. Whatever he plans, he's going to lay it on my doorstep. Maybe if I know what his deep dark secret is, it'll give me an edge."

"Karl was in Poland during the war. I think he must have been working for the Germans."

"Doing what?"

"I have no idea. I found out by accident. Somebody came to see him once, when we were married. He came to our home. He said it was business, but Karl never saw any business people at home. He told Karl he had papers and photographs. I heard this from the hall. They were in Karl's study. Then Karl said something to the man that I didn't hear. The man came out and saw me on the stairs. 'Your husband is a murderer, Frau,' he said. 'My wife was your age when he led her to the gas chamber.' Then he left. I never saw him again. I asked Karl what the man had meant. He told me he was some crazy ex-employee trying to make trouble. Two days later there was a photograph of the man in the papers. They said he'd hanged himself."

"But no papers or photographs."

"None were found. But I was curious. I asked around about the man. I even hired a private detective. He *had* been in a concentration camp and his wife had been gassed. Then Karl found out what I was doing. He threatened me. I was frightened, we had a fight. I stabbed him with some scissors and ran."

"Where does Bradley fit in to all this?"

"He was the man I ran to. When Karl found out I was with Jonathan he asked to meet with me. He told me he controlled everything that Jonathan and his family had built up and if I ever spoke to anyone about what I'm telling you now, he'd ruin them . . . all of them. I didn't want to send Karl to prison. I certainly didn't want Jonathan or his family hurt. So, that's where it was left. I went off with Jonathan and Karl went back to his wheeling and dealing."

"That's where things stayed until you left Bradley."

"I couldn't go on living with a man who was killing himself and inviting me to go with him. I thought if I left him he might pull himself out of it."

"So you ran off with Christophe."

"I told you. He just happened to be there when I needed somebody."

"And now?"

"He's been very kind."

It was starting to get dark, and it was very cold. "Let's turn back," said James. They started the walk back toward the Queen's Arms.

He called Langer at Struther's at nine o'clock that evening. He was put through to Mr. Barlow. "How nice to hear from you, Mr. Reed. I'm afraid Mr. Langer hasn't arrived yet. Leave me your number and I'll have him return your call as soon as he gets here."

"I'll call back later," said James.

"I've no idea what time he'll be arriving. It would be much simpler if you—"

"I'll call back," said James. He hung up. Poor Barlow. He'd been told to get James's number. From that Langer would have been able to find out where James was calling from and perhaps gain himself an edge.

James was the one who needed the edges. He went back into the bar. Three of the locals were nursing the same beers they'd bought three quarters of an hour ago. Two more were playing a desultory game of darts. Everybody looked miserable. If this was an example of Fred's trade, no wonder the place was always deserted. He sat at the bar and ordered himself a Scotch and told

Fred to have whatever he wanted. Half an hour later he called Struther's again. This time he was put straight through to Langer.

"Tomorrow morning, ten thirty," said James.

"Will my wife be with you?"

"That's what you're paying me for," said James.

"Not here," said Langer.

"Why not?" said James, who had no intention of taking Marianne anywhere near Struther's.

Langer ignored the question. "Where?"

James told him.

If Langer was curious about James's choice of rendezvous, he didn't say anything. He read back the directions James had given him.

"Bring my money," said James. "In cash, please."

"I'm sorry. I've forgotten the amount we agreed."

"Fifty thousand dollars," said James.

"Good-bye, Mr. Reed," said Langer. He hung up.

Men like Langer didn't forget deals. James had been right. Langer had no intention of paying him anything at all. It was a pity he wasn't going to be able to hit the credit cards for another thousand or two before the whole thing ended. But with the money he'd deposited in the bank in London, at least he wasn't going to be out of pocket.

He went upstairs to the attic room. Bradley was awake and high on methadone. This made him look even sicker than he had earlier. He was propped up in bed, talking quietly to himself and making no sense whatever. Marianne had decided to wash the clothes she'd been wearing for the past three days. She was using her duffel coat as a robe. Her wet clothes were hanging over the back of a chair next to the oil heater. There wasn't much. Her jeans, her shirt and her panties. No bra.

"Is there anything you need?" James asked.

"Some clothes," she said.

"Tomorrow. How about him?" He nodded toward Bradley.

"A doctor."

"Also tomorrow. Would you like a drink?"

"No thank you."

"Something to eat?"

She shook her head. "No."

"I'd like to go on deck," said Bradley.

Marianne sat on the bed beside him. "Later, sweetheart, it's too cold right now."

"Later," said Bradley. He started to shake. She covered him with a blanket. It didn't help. She put her arms around him and started to rock him gently. She didn't even look at James as he said good night and walked out of the attic room. He'd started downstairs before he remembered he hadn't locked the door. Why bother, he thought. It had remained unlocked most of the day and nothing had happened. He came back upstairs and locked it anyway.

He spent the rest of the evening in the bar. A couple of the locals left and were replaced by a group of four, two men and two women who had spent the day at Newbury racetrack and were now drinking their way back to London. They arrived full of high spirits and bonhomie. After twenty minutes in Fred's place, they left looking as if they were about to attend the funeral of a very dear friend. At closing time, James helped Fred rinse the glasses and lock the place up. Before he went to bed, he listened outside the door to the attic room. He could hear nothing, and there was no light visible beneath the door. It was just past midnight when he finally got to bed himself. He didn't expect to get much sleep, there was too much on his mind. The moment his head hit the pillow, he was gone.

Solly's two boys arrived at eight thirty the next morning. Both were dressed in tweed suits, rubber boots and shapeless raincoats. They looked exactly what they were, two sharp guys from the Smoke trying to look like your everyday country folk. James had already been up for a couple of hours, pacing out the territory. He told Henry and Mike to park their car around back of the pub and come have some breakfast. When they came into the bar five minutes later they were carrying twelve-bore shotguns with suspiciously short barrels. Mike was also carrying a cardboard box, which he handed to James. While Fred went into the kitchen and started to fry up a mountain of eggs, bacon and sausages, James unwrapped the sex doll the boys had brought him. Pink plastic, with a garishly painted face and three strategically placed orifices designed to cater to whatever it was that turned you on. He was in the middle of inflating it when Fred came back in.

"What the fuck is that?"

James told him.

"You're sick, Jim boy."

James told him what he was going to use it for.

"It'll never work."

"Sure it will," said James optimistically. "I'll leave her behind as a souvenir."

"What do I need with a thing like that?"

"Stick her behind the bar. Your kind of customer won't know the difference." While they were eating, James told Mike and Henry what he wanted from them. Afterward, he took them outside and explained the whole thing again. They were bright young men when it came to villainy. Mike made a suggestion that Henry refined and James accepted. It was nine thirty. James left them and walked back to the pub alone.

As he came in, Fred was coming downstairs. "Your geezer's in a bad way this morning, Jim boy," he said. "Get a quack to him today or get him out of my place. Okay?"

James went upstairs to take a look at Bradley himself. As he came in Marianne was sitting on the bed wiping his face with a damp towel. She looked over her shoulder at James, then turned her attention back to Bradley. It looked like he was in a coma. "Did you give him anything this morning?" James asked Marianne.

"He hasn't woken up yet."

"I'll call the doctor now," said James. He took her duffel coat from her bed and started for the door.

"Why are you taking my coat?" she wanted to know.

"It's masquerade time," said James.

■ ■ ■

While James struggled to get the coat onto the inflated sex doll, Fred called Dr. Quigley. It seemed there was no way Quigley was about to get into a car and drive out to the country. He had a list of patients as long as his arm who'd be filling his waiting room any moment now. James took the phone from Fred.

"How much?" he asked.

"I just told your friend, I can't leave my—"

"Two hundred and fifty pounds," said James.

Quigley took down the directions and promised to be there as soon as possible.

Fred helped James put the doll into the front seat of the car. They strapped it upright with the seat belt. It wouldn't fool anyone closer than ten feet away. But if anyone was closer than ten feet, they'd be able to see the gun James would be pointing in their direction.

"Take care of my new barmaid," said Fred.

James climbed behind the wheel, started the car, and drove the quarter mile to the road junction that he'd picked for the rendezvous with Langer. There he parked on the grass verge. As soon as he had started the car, the sex doll had fallen sideways. He readjusted her to a sitting position. In the field next to where he was parked, Henry Seligmann was trying to look like a farmer patrolling his crops. Mike was nowhere to be seen, which was as it was supposed to be. James checked the time. Ten o'clock. Unless Langer was early, he had half an hour to wait. Plenty of time to review his options. Trouble was, the longer he reviewed them, the more things he thought of that could go wrong.

9

Langer's car arrived at ten twenty-five. It was the same Rolls that had met James at the airport, the same chauffeur behind the wheel. As it stopped James saw another car pull up a hundred yards behind him. As far as he could see in his rearview mirror, it contained two men. Now, the chauffeur got out of the Rolls and opened the rear door. Langer's man Michael got out. He looked larger than James remembered. He peered up and down the road, then started toward James's car. Langer still hadn't put in an appearance. When Michael was still fifteen feet away, James realized he wasn't going to. Michael was the only passenger in the Rolls. He must have been shortsighted because it wasn't until he leaned down to look in the open window on James's side that he realized exactly what it was sitting in the passenger seat. His pumpkin-shaped face registered no expression. "Where's the woman?" he said.

"Where's Langer?" said James.

Michael was obviously the kind of guy who only asked questions.

"Where's the woman?" he said again.

James figured he'd be flogging a dead horse if he repeated his question. Instead, he pulled his gun from where he'd been holding it on his lap and laid it on the top edge of the car door so that it was six inches from Michael's impressive-looking crotch. "I want you to back off a few feet and we'll have a little talk," he said.

Michael straightened up. Amazing how even the biggest were impressed by the threat of a gun, thought James fleetingly. Then he revised his opinion as Michael reached in very fast and clamped one giant fist over James's gun and the hand holding it. He was gripping the gun along the length of the barrel with his forefinger wrapped around the hammer. Arnold Schwarzenegger wouldn't have been able to muster the strength to pull the trigger. Without seeming to use any effort, Michael started to squeeze harder. James remembered the time Michael had squeezed his foot in Malibu. He knew that Michael was going to increase the pressure little by little until he'd crushed his hand like a ripe orange. Fortunately for James, Michael enjoyed this kind work, so he took his time. If he hadn't, James would have lost his hand as effectively as if he'd stuck it in a vise. As it was, Henry Seligmann had time to come over the hedge and shove the twin barrels of his shotgun hard into Michael's kidneys. "Back off, big fella," he said.

Michael did as he was told.

"Stay out of reach," James warned Henry. He shifted his gun from his paralyzed right hand into his left and waved it in the direction of the chauffeur, who was half in and half out of the Rolls, unable to make up his mind whether or not Langer was paying him enough to get involved. "Out!" called James. The chauffeur did as he was told. "Take a walk," said James. He took orders well. He started up the road at a good clip. James took a quick look toward the car parked a hundred yards back. Mike Seligmann had everything under control. He was leaning against the door on the driver's side, apparently passing the time of day with the two occupants. Even from this distance, James could see he had his shotgun resting on top of the open window.

James turned back to Michael, who was standing there like some monolithic idol with its stone eyes gazing sightlessly into the far distance. "Why didn't Langer come?" he asked.

Michael didn't even look at him.

"I guess there's no point in asking whether you brought my money along."

He might as well have been talking to a cliff face. Here was the man who'd almost certainly killed three people at his house in California, and he couldn't even get a civil word out of him.

"Maybe we should try shooting off your kneecaps," said James.

Either he didn't manage to put sufficient conviction into the threat or Michael figured he could do without his kneecaps. He still didn't move a muscle.

"What was supposed to happen next?" asked James.

Nothing from Michael.

"You're wasting your time," said Henry Seligmann. He was still standing five feet behind Michael, his shotgun held in both hands. "I seen guys like this before. You could take a chainsaw to him and he wouldn't say a word."

"Maybe you're right," said James. He knew damn well Henry was right. Still standing well clear of Michael's reach, James moved into his line of sight. "You can go on back to your lord and master and tell him you fucked up," he said. "Also you can tell him I was lying. I didn't find the lady."

If the prospect worried Michael, he didn't show it. Without a word he turned and walked back to the Rolls. Henry moved to the side of the road, still holding his gun at the ready. James did likewise. It wasn't necessary. Michael climbed in behind the wheel and closed the door. A moment later the Rolls started up and reversed down the road. A hundred yards away it stopped to pick up the chauffeur, who'd heard it coming and was waiting for it. They turned around in the middle of the road and drove off.

Henry joined James, who was examining his hand, checking for broken bones. "What now?" he asked.

"Let's go see if Mike's people are more cooperative," said James.

Mike's people were. In fact, they were downright friendly. There aren't all that many successful villains in London. Those that do prosper form a loose-knit alliance whereby they agree to scratch each others' backs providing everybody stays more or less within their own territory. Consequently the same faces are likely to turn up again and again. It seemed that, in his haste, Langer had been forced to pick up local help. The two men he'd hired were known to the Seligmanns. They were efficient-looking heavies who had even worked for Solly on a couple of occasions.

"Jesus Christ," one of them said to James. "If we'd've known you was a friend of Mr. Seligmann, we'd have turned the job down flat and that's the honest-to-God truth. Right, Toby?"

The one named Toby nodded vigorously. "Right, Sal," he said.

"What exactly was the job?" asked James.

"We was to back up the big guy."

"While he did what?"

They flashed a look at each other.

"If you want to stay working, stop fucking around and tell him what he wants to know," said Henry.

"The big guy was going to drive you and a bird someplace and drop you off a cliff. Right, Toby?"

"Right, Sal."

"And in case he didn't drop you far enough he was going to knock you on the head first."

"Hard," said Toby.

"An auto accident," said James.

"Yeah! An accident. But like I said, we didn't know you was friends with Mr. Seligmann."

"You didn't know we'd all have shooters either, did you, Sal?" said Henry.

"Honest to God, Henry—"

"You finished with them?" asked Mike.

James looked at the two men. "You'd better disappear, fellas," he said. "The big guy's gonna be looking for you. Isn't that what he said, Mike?"

"He said he was going to take you apart."

"Limb by limb, wasn't it?" said James.

"With a meat axe," said Mike.

"So help me . . . we didn't know."

"Go on, beat it!" said James.

They climbed back into their car and drove off.

"Are you guys in a hurry?" asked James.

"The old man told us to hang around as long as you needed us," said Henry.

"What he didn't tell us was somebody wants you dead," said Mike.

"I wasn't sure myself," said James.

"Yeah. Well I'm glad it didn't happen," said Mike.

"I didn't know you cared," said James.

"We don't. But the old man would've skinned us alive." They started back toward James's car. "What was it between you and the old man anyway?" asked Henry. "He usually don't do favors for no one."

"I arrested him a few times," said James. "That kind of relationship is special."

On the outside chance that Michael had decided to hang around waiting for another try, they drove back to the Queen's Arms by a roundabout route. Because of his hand, James asked Henry to drive. Only when he was certain they weren't being followed did he tell him to head back to Fred's place.

There was a strange car parked in front of the pub. It wasn't opening time yet, so James told the Seligmanns to wait outside. Fred was behind the bar, watering the Scotch. "Whose car?" asked James.

"The doctor. He's up there now."

James told the Seligmanns it was okay to come in. Maybe he'd ask Quigley to take a look at his hand. It was hurting like hell. It looked like a bunch of overripe bananas. Then Quigley came downstairs and James forgot about his hand entirely.

"If that man's not in a hospital this afternoon, he'll be dead by tomorrow morning," he said to nobody in particular. Then, to Fred, "Give me a large Scotch."

"What's wrong with him?" asked James.

Quigley looked at him. "Don't I know you?" Then he remembered.

"Right . . . the methadone freak. I'll tell you what's wrong with him. He's dehydrated, his liver's gone, he's got hepatitis and, by the sound of his chest, he's got pneumococcal pneumonia."

"Is he going to pull through?" asked James.

"He's going to die," said Quigley. "But at least he'll do it more comfortably in a hospital. Do you want me to arrange it?"

"A private place," said James.

"Naturally," said Quigley. "What's his name?"

For a moment James couldn't remember the name on the passport Bradley was traveling with. "Peterson . . . no, Potter. Andrew Potter."

"Make up your mind," said Quigley sourly. "Give me another Scotch and point me to a phone," he said to Fred.

James went upstairs. "We're taking him to a hospital now," he said to Marianne. He told her what had happened this morning.

"Why did you lie about finding me?" she asked.

"Maybe he'll give up looking now."

"He won't."

"You may be right," said James. "But you managed to disappear once before. You can do it again. This time when you go to ground, don't get greedy. Stay there."

"He planned to kill you too?"

"Only to make the accident look good," said James. "I'm no threat to him. He's not even going to have to pay me."

"You know about the German connection."

"He doesn't know that."

Quigley came back into the room without knocking. "Ambulance will be here in half an hour," he said. "They'll take him to a place in St. John's Wood."

"Can I go with him?" Marianne asked.

"You can do whatever you like," said Quigley. He went back downstairs.

Marianne moved to the bed and did something to make Bradley more comfortable. It was for her own benefit more than his. He was too far out of things to know what was happening.

"I know you've got a soft spot for him," said James. "But don't hang around London too long. Go back to France. Find out what's happened to Christophe, if that's what you want. If he's been picked up he won't get more than a couple of months as a first offender. Then the two of you go bury yourselves."

"That takes money," she said.

"So get a job. People do."

"What are you going to do?"

"I've got a couple of errands in London. Then I shall go home."

"To California?"

"That's where it is," he said.

Back downstairs, James settled up with Fred, who was busy trying to dress the sex doll in one of his old sweaters. He'd christened her Mabel. He was going to try her out behind the bar this evening. "Anybody comes looking for us, you know from nothing," said James.

"I've never known from nothing," said Fred. "I bought this place, didn't I?"

The Seligmanns refused to take any money. They'd enjoyed themselves, they said. James asked if one of them would travel in the ambulance. The other could follow in their car. Neither of them wanted to ride in the back of the ambulance until they saw Marianne. After that, they couldn't stop arguing. Finally they flipped a coin and Henry won.

"Tell your father the gun's still clean," said James. "He can have it back if he wants. Have him call me." He gave Henry the number of his hotel in London. "I'll be there a couple more days."

Quigley had long gone by the time the ambulance arrived. Bradley was carried downstairs and loaded into the back. Marianne climbed in with him, along with Henry. She looked for a moment as if she wanted to say something to James. Then she changed her mind. She didn't even say good-bye.

He watched the ambulance drive away; Mike followed in his own car. He went back inside, where Fred poured him a large

Scotch and one for himself. "Mud in your eye, Jim boy," said Fred.

"Too fucking true," said James.

James drove the forty minutes back to London. He collected his room key. The clerk gave him his messages. He glanced through them in the elevator. They were all from Betsy Carmichael. Upstairs he put the briefcase with the money in the back of his closet. He stripped off the clothes he'd been wearing for the past three days and sent everything to the hotel cleaners. He ordered a bottle of Scotch from room service. He took the bottle and a glass into the bathroom, where he filled the tub and climbed in. Normally he was a shower man. Right now he needed to wallow. He was still wallowing twenty minutes later when the phone rang. There was no extension in the bathroom so he climbed out of the tub and dripped his way next door. It was Henry Seligmann.

"I'm still at the clinic," he said. "They want some money."

"How much?"

"A thousand quid."

"Tell them I'll be there in a couple of hours," said James. "What kind of a place is it?"

"Discreet," said Henry.

"How is he?"

"Not good. When I told them they'd get paid in a couple of days they started to act like they didn't think he'd be around that long."

"Where's the lady?"

"She's gone out to buy herself a dress. I gave her your number, incidentally."

"Why did you do that?"

"Because she asked for it," said Henry.

James took $2,500 from the briefcase. He put the briefcase back in the closet. He was going to have to find somebody to turn it over to. Maybe Betsy's father. He'd know what to do with it. Perhaps he'd set up a Jonathan Bradley Trust to aid drug abusers.

He walked to the bank where he had opened an account and changed the $2,500 into pounds. While he was there, he drew another $2,000 against his credit cards and cashed out everything he had deposited over the past week. This was his money as opposed to Bradley's, so he kept it separate.

His first car had been wheel-clamped. He didn't figure he was going to need it anymore, so he left it. Let Barlow sort it out with the rental company. He threw away the parking ticket his second car had already received and drove to St. John's Wood.

The clinic was in a tree-lined street of substantial old houses, most of which had been converted to apartments. A small plaque on one of the gate posts announced that this was the Malbury Clinic. Inside, James was shown straight into the office of Dr. Malbury himself. The doctor was a large, florid man who looked as if he would be more at home on a grouse moor. James asked him if he would mind being paid in cash.

"Not at all," said Malbury. "It happens all the time. You understand, of course, this is just for the first two days. If Mr. . . . ." He glanced at a slip of paper in front of him. "Mr. Potter is still with us the day after tomorrow, we shall require further payment."

"How is he?" asked James.

"Fading fast, I'm sorry to say. Perhaps if he'd checked in here a week ago, something could have been done." He shook his head. "Frightful self-abuse over a long period," he said. "Liver's gone, kidney's next to useless, lungs awash, heart's got too much to do . . . just can't cope, I'm afraid. Still, we'll do our best to make him comfortable. Would you care to see him?"

"No thank you," said James. "But I'd like to speak with the lady who brought him here."

"She's gone. I told her you were on your way here. She said she couldn't wait."

As James came out of the clinic, a policeman was walking around his car. At the same time he was muttering into his personal radio. Maybe ffyfe *had* stolen it after all. James didn't wait to find out. It took him ten minutes to find a cab and another twenty minutes to get back to his hotel. He asked for his room key at the desk.

"Your wife already has it, Mr. Reed," said the clerk.

"How long ago did she come in?"

"About an hour."

James took another key and went upstairs. She hadn't made much of a mess of his room. There was a lot of paper scattered around. She'd ripped the wrappings from the stacks of hundred-dollar bills before stuffing the money into whatever she'd brought to carry it. Obviously she considered the briefcase too conspicuous because she'd thrown it into the corner of the room. His gun was gone. So too was his passport. A hand towel was missing from the bathroom. She'd need that so as not to smudge his prints on the gun.

He called Struther's and asked to speak to Barlow. Barlow had been told that James no longer had carte blanche at Struther's. He was frigidly polite. "No, sir, I do not know whether Mr. Langer is in the hotel right now."

"Call his suite," said James.

Reluctantly, Barlow told James to hold the line. He was back on in thirty seconds. "There's no reply from Mr. Langer's suite, sir."

"Thank you," said James. He hung up. He packed his bags and called downstairs to say he was checking out. Then he called the travel bureau in the lobby. Could they get him on a flight to Los Angeles tomorrow?

"Certainly, sir. Tomorrow's Christmas Day. Nobody travels on Christmas Day unless it's absolutely vital."

"It's vital," said James.

She was back to him in five minutes, confirming him on a direct flight tomorrow morning, and how would he be paying?

"Cash," said James. "I'll pick up the ticket in ten minutes." He called Solly Seligmann. "Do me a favor, Solly."

"Anything you want, my boy."

James told him what he wanted.

"What are you, meshuga?" said Solly.

"Will you do it?"

"Do I sound like an Irishman!"

"No, but you sound like a Jew."

He paid his bill and picked up his airline ticket. He took his bag around to where his car had been clamped. He left the bag in the trunk and walked to Struther's. He had told Solly to make the call in exactly fifteen minutes. He was right on time.

As he turned into the square, people were already coming out of the hotel. A dozen guests, shepherded by an equal number of staff, including Barlow. They looked both confused and bewildered, glancing back toward the hotel at the same time as they tried to get as far away from it as possible. Bomb threats were treated seriously these days.

James walked down the alley at the side of the hotel and in through a door that had been left wide open by some of the staff who'd left in a hurry. He used the service elevator to get to the fourth floor. The doors to Langer's suite were closed, but not locked.

Langer was in the living room, sitting in his favorite chair. His eyes were open in what looked like mild surprise, maybe at the fact that the right side of his head was missing. She must have stuck the gun close to his left temple before she pulled the trigger.

Michael hadn't been so easy to kill. It looked like it had taken at least three bullets to the body, maybe four. The gun had been dropped on the floor between the living and dining room. James picked it up and put it in his pocket. Then he started to search the rest of the suite. He could hear the sound of approaching police cars before he found what he was looking for. She'd wedged his passport under Michael's body. Blood had stained the front cover. He put it in his pocket with the gun. He went back down in the service elevator and left the hotel the same way he'd come in.

As he came out into the street, the police were already erecting rope barriers to keep the people back. "What's the trouble, officer?" he asked a bored-looking constable.

"Just move along, sir," said the constable.

James moved along.

He collected his bag from the trunk of the car and took the subway to Heathrow. There he checked into one of the anonymous hotels that serve the airport. In his room, he dismantled the gun and wiped every part of it clean of his fingerprints. He bought an evening newspaper and used it to wrap the individual parts of the gun. Just after dark, he went for a walk. Around back of the hotel he dropped the sections of the gun into three different garbage cans.

Later he called the clinic and asked to speak with Doctor Malbury. "He's taken a turn for the worse," said the doctor. "I don't expect him to last through the night. Will you inform the relatives?"

James agreed that he would. He thought about it. What was the point? Jonathan Bradley was already dead and buried. Why shed fresh tears? He called nobody. Instead, he got drunk and went to bed.

Flying on Christmas Day meant an almost empty aircraft. None of the senior personnel wanted to work over the holiday so it also meant the flight attendants were younger and prettier. They wore paper hats and had a problem not getting as drunk as their passengers. There were no morning papers, but James had listened to the news on the radio before he left. It was a hot item on a normally dull day for news. They talked about the bomb scare and the subsequent discovery of the two bodies by the police. While information was scarce at the moment, this reporter understands that a phone call about the bomb was made by a man claiming to represent a group of Jewish extremists. It is believed that this group murdered international banker Karl Langer and a member of his staff. While the motive isn't yet clear, the mysterious caller made reference to something in Mr. Langer's past that may have a bearing on the case.

James asked the stewardess for some writing paper and an envelope. Into the envelope he put the list of numbers he'd copied from the money wrappers Marianne had left strewn around his room; the serial numbers of each bundle of hundred-dollar bills. Then he wrote a note to Interpol in Paris. "This money was paid to the assassins of Karl Langer." He left it unsigned. He put the letter in an envelope along with the list of numbers. Once the money started to appear, Interpol would look for whoever was spending it. Either they'd find Marianne or she'd get to know they were looking for her. James rather hoped it would be the latter. That way she would have to go to ground with nearly a million dollars that she couldn't spend. Maybe she'd take it out of the closet occasionally and look at it. It might be a comfort in her old age.

He asked the stewardess to bring him another glass of champagne. Because it was Christmas Day, she brought him the whole bottle. And because they weren't busy, she sat with him and shared it. She told him her name was Norma, and this was her first flight to the West Coast. "What does a girl do for laughs in L.A.?" she asked.

James said he couldn't promise to make her laugh, but maybe he'd be able to get a smile out of her. The captain came on the PA to announce that the flight would be on time and the weather in Los Angeles was just great. Norma raised her glass. "Merry Christmas," she said.

"And a happy New Year," said James.